Elizabeth Berridge was born in London but lived for many years in Wales. She was married to Reginald Moore, who died in 1990, and has a son and a daughter. She started her working life at the Bank of England before moving on to journalism, broadcasting and editing.

Her crisp and distinctly English style of writing established her as one of the most significant novelists of the post-war years. Her previous novels include *House of Defence*, *Be Clean Be Tidy*, *Upon Several Occasions*, *Rose Under Glass*, *Across the Common* (which won the Yorkshire Post Novel Award in 1964), *People at Play*, and she has also written several collections of short stories.

Elizabeth Berridge is currently a judge for the David Higham Award for a First Novel, a trustee for the Chase Charity and she also reviews fiction for the *Evening Standard* and *The Tablet*. *Touch and Go* marks her return to novel writing, after a gap of some eleven years.

Touch and Go

Elizabeth Berridge

BLACK SWAN

TOUCH AND GO
A BLACK SWAN BOOK : 0 552 99648 3

First publication in Great Britain

PRINTING HISTORY
Black Swan edition published 1995

Set in 11/12pt Melior by
County Typesetters, Margate, Kent

Black Swan Books are published by Transworld Publishers Ltd,
61–63 Uxbridge Road, Ealing, London W5 5SA,
in Australia by Transworld Publishers (Australia) Pty Ltd,
15–25 Helles Avenue, Moorebank, NSW 2170,
and in New Zealand by Transworld Publishers (NZ) Ltd,
3 William Pickering Drive, Albany, Auckland.

Printed and bound in Great Britain by
Cox & Wyman Ltd, Reading, Berks.

For Karen and Lawrence and Liam

Men and women may, after great effort, achieve a creditable lie; but the house, which is their temple, cannot say anything save the truth of those who have lived in it.

They, Rudyard Kipling

Will he come out of the mountain?
It is touch and go.

Stevie Smith

PART 1

It was not until the middle of October, with dusk curtaining the hills, that Emma at last arrived at the house she had so oddly inherited. The heavy gates had been latched back at the entrance to the drive and she braked short of the house. The journey from London had tired her; she had stopped once only, in the Cotswolds, to eat a picnic lunch and feed the small pregnant cat curled up in the basket on the seat by her side.

She had noticed changes in the village, the school gone and a garage in its place; the old chapel they had all run from as children – thought to be haunted – now razed to the ground, which had reclaimed its own space with overgrown laurels and fine burdocks glimpsed briefly as she drove slowly past. She noted other changes that marked her a stranger and mad to come back. What were these new houses doing on the slopes of what she had always called Doctor's Hill? Council-built, with the slate roofs the Welsh went in for, they spread in slanting rows over the meadow below his house. Her house now.

Here it was then, as she remembered. It had stood solid, red and four-square on top of the hill since the turn of the century, hence its name, Domengastell. An attic window under the roof, three windows along the front and one on either side of the front door, like a child's painting. Tall trees, sycamore and chestnut, loomed about it. Smoke from the chimney and the windows lighted. The window on the right, though, almost obscured, tight in the dense green clasp of an overgrown holly bush. That would have to come down for a start. As she edged slowly up to the front door she realized that she was already thinking like a house owner. Taking a deep breath to calm her nerves, she stepped out of the car to silence and the smell of frost.

Almost at once the door opened and a tiny woman in black ran across the porch and down the steps.

'I'd have known you anywhere, with your mother's hair!' she cried, shaking her own head, tight as a nut. Small round spectacles magnified eyes as black as ash buds. 'Emma? Or . . . it's Mrs Rowlands now, isn't it?'

Shake hands or kiss? Emma impulsively took the hard little hand in both hers, looking down. As a child she had looked up shyly, fearfully, for Dr Lewis's housekeeper was connected with illness . . . a visit to the doctor. 'Wait here. He won't keep you long. What a nasty cough! Never mind, the doctor will soon put you right, cariad.'

At the thought that he would never be there to put her right again, and he wouldn't keep anyone waiting, ever, easy tears pricked, and Mrs Elwyn Hughes liked that. She patted Emma's arm, coaxing her. 'Come in, do. You'll be starved out here with the frost dropping. Tired you look, all that driving on your own. You're to sleep at the Lion tonight, isn't it?'

Warmth struck as they stepped into the bare hall. Doors were open on both sides, giving a glimmer of firelight. But the surgery door on the right had always been shut in the past; only the left-hand door, leading to the waiting-room in the old days, had stood ajar, with a hum of conversation coming from it. Now the house was silent and clean as a pin. What had she expected? Dust and damp and the smell of camphorated oil?

'We've been keeping the fires going. Don't want the damp to get a grip, do we? Not in an old house like this, with the rain we've had here in the valley and the old river rising. Come you through into the kitchen, warm it is with the Aga and you'll want a cup of tea after that long journey.'

Faintly Emma said, dropping on to a hard wooden chair, 'The furniture is coming tomorrow. Mrs Hughes, how kind of you – oh, and you've got electric light!'

Thank God for that. She remembered lamplight.

'We've had the electric since the new houses were built on the hill. Never been back, have you? Only your mam, in all that time.' Mrs Hughes always spoke her mind. Even to the doctor. She had never put up with any of his nonsense, big bluff man that he was. Respect she had for him, because of his calling, but as a man he'd had to be kept in some kind of order; watch where he knocked out his pipe or walked in muddy boots. Now, hands round her cup, Emma said, half out of bravado, wanting to establish things as they were, gossip or no gossip, 'I expect you were all as surprised as I was, this house coming to me.'

Pause, while Mrs Hughes took a cigarette from a battered packet, raised an eyebrow in Emma's direction, receiving a shake of the head, took a draw like a man, and said, 'Aye. Seven days' wonder, that's all. Don't you mind what they say at the Lion. The doctor had no kin, up to him what to do with his own property.' She paused, and what she was about to say next came out like a reluctant cork from a bottle. 'Good to me, he was, I'll say that. *I* can't complain,' and shut up as soon as the cork was drawn.

Emma noted the emphasis and wondered with anxiety, who could complain then? She would undoubtedly find out. She was relieved to know that Mrs Hughes had obviously done her picking over before her arrival. And why not? After all, only the house had been left to her, not the contents. So she nodded, looked with pleasure at the old Welsh dresser across from the big scrubbed deal table at which she sat. Lucky for her it must have been too tall and heavy to go into Mrs Hughes's council house.

'Will you be able to give me a hand until I'm settled, Mrs Hughes?'

Affront in the small keen eyes, a tightening of the withered mouth. Then a relenting. Emma realized that the affront had been in the idea that Mrs Hughes would not be asked to give a hand. Giving a hand was what she intended. There was to be no loosening of the grip she had had on this old house for forty years.

'Well, can't get on by yourself – that's so. I'll be in first thing, then—'

'The van'll be here by dinner-time,' said Emma. Dinner-time was country talk and she fell into it easily. Dinner-time was when working people went home in the middle of the day. Like the angelus sounding in France. Then came high tea at six. It wouldn't be so hard to fall back into country ways.

'I'd like to take a peep upstairs,' she said, and followed Mrs Hughes, feeling like a visitor as they trudged up the stairs. The carpet was thin, the pattern faded. Over her shoulder Mrs Hughes said, 'You'll maybe need new, but I left it down. Feet echo so.' They reached a small landing where the stairs curved to the left. A final flight led up to the top floor.

'I've never been up here – at least, I don't think so,' said Emma, as Mrs Hughes snapped on a light and threw open the door to the big front bedroom. 'This must be the doctor's room. I've only seen it from outside. The windows were always open, winter and summer. We used to look up on our way to school. That dreadful winter, d'you remember, when the snow stayed till March?'

'Only time he filled two wine bottles with hot water and put them in his bed. Only time. Fresh-air mad was the doctor. I'd find snow on his eiderdown many a morning.'

They stood together looking at where the big double bed had stood. There were four deep indentations in

12

the green-and-yellow-check lino. Emma imagined a brass bedstead with knobs you could turn. The trellis-patterned wallpaper had one large patch, outlining what? A vanished chest of drawers? A washstand? Surely there was a bathroom? As if reading her mind Mrs Hughes left the room and opened a door opposite with something of a flourish. 'New basin put in just before he died. Insurance paid,' she said with satisfaction. 'Cracked for years was that old basin. Well, what's the Insurance for? I told him. Look at that bath, girl! Loved it, he did. Big man, the doctor.'

The long, deep outsize bath with noble brass taps was encased in mahogany which gave it substance, making it more than a useful piece of household equipment. It invited ceremony. His bath towels would be like those enormous bath sheets you bought in the sales, Emma thought.

'Does the water still run brown? It did at Glammon Lodge when I was a child,' she said now, noting the deep airing cupboards and the lavatory up on its own dais. She strolled over to see what kind of view there was from the long window, kneeling on a wide window-seat to look out into the damp, dark secrecy of the garden beyond the bushes.

'Takes some cleaning, that bath, enamel's wearing thin,' said Mrs Hughes. '*Brown* water? Dear no! On the mains, aren't we, here?' She added with pride, 'Patients' toilet downstairs, fitted into the old broom cupboard. Liked to keep up with the times, did the doctor.' A bitter note crept into her voice. 'People expect more these days. I say it's that box.'

'What box?'

'The telly, that's what. Wicked nonsense, I say. My man only watches the football.'

The last room they looked into had a couple of Lloyd Loom chairs heaped with discoloured cushions. What luck! A pile, too, of pictures, leaning against a wall.

'I'll take them off you if you don't want 'em,' said Mrs Hughes. 'You could put your daughter in here. Sunny, it is.'

She could, but would she stay? Emma wondered. At present her elusive daughter was somewhere in India, filling in time between school and university.

Four bedrooms and a boxroom. Space to live in. They were there even if she didn't use them. At the thought of spreading herself throughout this house Emma felt a tiny sense of happiness displace her apprehension. Space was something she had had little of in Highgate.

'Well, thanks, Mrs Hughes,' she said, closing the last door. 'I think I'd better be getting along to the Lion.'

They went downstairs and out to the car.

She had brought her special bits and pieces with her, some china wrapped in towels; books swept off the shelves at the last moment. A doormat and some favourite geraniums and miniature roses to be over-wintered. And, of course, Miss Matty, the little stray cat who had adopted her. Mrs Hughes gasped as she opened the door.

'Duw, there's a family on the way! Shall I have her overnight?'

'Thanks all the same, Mrs Hughes, but I'll ask the Pughs at the Lion if she can share my bedroom. I want to be on hand if she has her kittens in the night, she's very young.'

'You'd best get along then. Any trouble with them at the Lion you bring her to me. Second house down.' Lights glittered from windows, smoke rose straight up in the crisp night air. 'Beats our old cottage, does that. Well, missis—'

'Emma, please, Mrs Hughes.'

And Mrs Hughes was still Mrs Hughes. Emma had never known her first name and that was as it should be. Village upbringing brought an instinctive knowledge of what was right and what was wrong.

14

An owl called twice; something small and dark fluttered by. It was time to go.

She was able to avoid the bar in the Lion by the lucky chance of meeting Mrs Tom Pugh in the red-carpeted hallway. It was still early, before opening-time. The place was unfamiliar but it occurred to her that her parents would have recognized it. Her father had played in the darts team.

To her surprise she was warmly embraced.

'There's people want to see you, talk about your dad, Emma. Remember him well, some of the older ones.'

'Mrs Pugh, d'you think I could have my cat up with me? I've got a dirt tray – she's kittening, you see.'

'Mrs Pugh, is it? *Mrs Pugh!* You don't remember me, Emma? Myfanwy Jones that was. We sat next to each other in school. Now Mrs Tom Pugh. We took over this old place when Tom's da died.'

Myfanwy Jones that was. She'd had a band round her teeth and a long pigtail. She'd always been a talker. Whispered and giggled behind her hand and in the little asphalt playground, hopping on one foot, queen of hopscotch, champion twirler of skipping ropes:

> Jump, jump, don't lose your rag
> Here comes the lady with the big black bag . . .

Quick and sassy. Face full of freckles and tongue to poke out at the boys . . . now approaching her forties, like Emma. Busty, filled out like a grown tree, dark curly hair, and a full, creamy neck.

'Oh, Myfanwy,' said Emma, giving her a kiss. 'You've cut off your hair.'

'And you've grown yours. Lovely it is. Is that your own colour? Let's fetch your little cat, then. What's her name?'

Emma told her as she talked her way out to the car,

15

picked up the basket, nuzzling the little cat's distended stomach, talking into the battered ears.

'What's this, *Miss* Matty, is it? You should be ashamed – *Mrs* Matty you ought to be with a bellyful like that . . . Emma, you take the dirt box and I'll bring this naughty lady . . . oh duw, what a pretty puss then . . .' The little cat blinked at this effusiveness, bemused, but did not move. Myfanwy talked her way upstairs, leading Emma into a small room with the curtains drawn and the bed turned down. A solid wardrobe that didn't look as if the door would swing creakily open during the night.

'Bring some milk up, shall I? And some newspaper for the floor, just in case. You'll have your supper with us, Emma, good old chat we'll have about the old times. Fancy Dr Lewis . . . well, who'd have thought, that old fox . . .'

Who indeed? thought Emma, sinking, suddenly tired out, on to the bed, bouncing to test it. She didn't attempt to unpack; it made her too permanent. She liked the freedom of being suspended between two lives; two empty houses, a nowhere feeling. Like her furniture, on the move. She'd sleep tonight. No dreams of broken flowerpots, dusty rooms, a loud accusing voice.

She got through the evening somehow; fending off questions, telling them just enough and no more; nudging up memories of the far-off days when Tom Pugh was just a shy, gangling boy washing glasses for his father behind the bar. Older than the little girls he'd been, she scarcely remembered him. Now he was well fleshed, taciturn, nobody fooled with him, king of his own pub. He left the talking to his wife. Two children they had, the boy courting.

'Sorry about your da,' he said suddenly. 'Well liked he was. Put us on the map with his books and all. Threw a nifty dart. We're in the League now. Won the shield last season.'

'He'd be pleased,' said Emma, and so he would.

'Did a lot for this village. I've got photos somewhere, time we won the District Cup when he was captain. Aye,' Tom's face split into a huge grin, ''ad the Chapel lot by the short and curlies, did your da.'

Emma looked mystified.

'You'd be too young to remember. But my da told me the sports meetings were held in this pub and the Secretary, old Bloodstock Griffiths, wanted them in the Chapel. Drink, y'see. Never held with drink, the Chapel lot.'

'I remember some cricket matches on that field by the bakehouse . . .' said Emma. 'Do you remember, Myfanwy? Running away when the bull got out of Mr Jones's field and lumbered across the wicket?'

Memory is a strange bell, Jubilee and knell. Where did these lines come from, jumping into her head?

'I remember the Wentworths up at the Hall keeping angora rabbits,' she said, striking that strange bell once again.

'The old Wentworths!' exclaimed Myfanwy, hand over mouth to stop her laughter. 'Oh, they're in the Lodge now; Debby and Robert have moved into the Hall. But those rabbits—'

'Debby?' The Wentworths' daughter had been her dearest friend. But time and place had divided them, and Emma had not been able to go to the wedding. She had not invited Debby to hers, a hasty register-office affair.

'Married a boy she met at dancing class. You'd know him. Robert Godfrey. The Godfreys of Pontsarn. Big do that was. Now they run posh weekend shoots for foreigners. They've got a herd of Jerseys, but it's a big place to keep up. They need the cash.'

Everyone's business was known, evidently. No secrets could be kept for long here. To avoid gossiping about Debby she turned the talk back to the angora rabbits. She couldn't bring a Robert Godfrey to mind.

'Oh, yes.' Myfanwy took up the tale with enthusiasm. She was easily tickled into laughter, always had been. 'Well, Mr Wentworth wanted to give them more freedom, see, and moved the hutches and the runs, and they got out on to the mountain and mated with the wild ones. So then there were all colours boiling in the hills . . . brown and black and white and piebald, long- and short-haired. That winter all the village children had angora caps and mittens . . . you could smell rabbit stew everywhere. They gave up the angora wool business after that.'

As soon as she could, Emma excused herself as dropping with tiredness and got off upstairs to bed. She dreamt that she was still driving along the motorway and it curled endlessly before her. Something was shining directly in her eyes and she put up a hand to pull down the sun shield, and the action at once woke her. She faced a full moon framed in her window. She never pulled curtains to, hating to sleep in an enclosed box, and now got out of bed and went to the window, pushed it up and leaned out. Blackness and white moonlight bisected the village street, dramatized the far-off hills. Stars stung and pricked the silent sky around the church steeple. There was no sound at all, not even the lonely bark of a fox. The air she breathed was as fresh and calm as the night. Before the chill made her draw back, she felt a great surge of thankfulness. Could she really have come home?

As she eased herself back into bed, something darkish, wettish and soft touched her thigh. Switching on the lamp, she saw that Miss Matty had sprung up with something in her mouth and stayed a moment, purring. Then she was down again, then up. Not a rat, not carrying a rat, surely? But in the basket by the radiator lay two more small damp bundles.

Quietly, alone, with no fuss, while Emma slept, Miss Matty had given birth to four kittens and was now transferring them one by one to a warmer place. There was a problem here. Either they or Emma would have to occupy the bed. She watched her little cat lick them with a strong competent tongue and marvelled at the instinct that made females such natural survivors. She could have cheered, it seemed such a good omen. She went to her suitcase and brought out her painting smock, edged it underneath them – Myfanwy wouldn't really care for her bedclothes to be soiled. Emma took herself off with the pillows to the end of the bed, pulled the duvet up around her and was careful where she put her feet. She slept with the delicate questing movements of the newborn and their mother's triumphant purring to keep company with her dreams, which were good ones; like all good ones, they evaporated with the morning.

The van arrived on time and dominated the front of the house with its bulk, the great doors open. Years ago, in another time, such a van had gone past the schoolhouse where the children were repeating the nine times table. It had cast a brief shadow and Emma had seen the name CARTER PATERSON on its side. Her neighbour beside her changed the singsong 'Nine times nine are eighty-one' to 'Emma's going away, the van's come.'

Now the van had returned, who could have guessed such a thing could happen? In through the front door, directed by Mrs Hughes, went rolls of carpet, tables and chairs and beds, cupboards and Emma's mother's big old sofa.

Emma chose the doctor's bedroom for her double bed as it was south-facing, but positioned it away from the window. It would do for the time being, before she saw what lay under that cracked old lino. She'd soon have the wallpaper off as well, paint the walls white or a tender yellow. As the day went on she felt a painful excitement; an almost uncontrollable pleasure which gave her a headache; a giant fear that all this would be snatched away. At the afternoon's end Mrs Hughes gave the men cups of tea and some of her jam tarts, brown and bubbling from the oven. 'Take your eye off this oven for a minute and your pastry's done for,' she called over her shoulder to Emma. 'I'll show you.'

After making her bed, lighting a fire and putting up the curtains in her bedroom, Emma took herself off for a walk. It was only a short way up the road to the top of the hill, and the lane she remembered turned off to the left. It eventually led to the house they once lived in. Where the lane met the road there had always been a pile of stones and a heap of gravel beside it. A pile of stones was there now, as if witness to the veracity of her mother's story.

On a summer's afternoon long ago Emma had sat with her mother in the pony trap. (So the story ran.) Emma's mother had reined in the fat and petulant pony at the junction of the lane and the road and up had ridden Dr Lewis on his roan mare, returning from a visit to a patient.

'Ha, young lady,' he had said, after some talk above Emma's head. 'Those tonsils of yours – have to come out, y'know. Many a tonsil I've taken out on this heap of stones . . .' gesturing with his riding whip.

'No.' Saucer-eyed. (Her mother's words.) Six or seven she'd been.

'Save all that trouble with the cottage hospital. Easy as pie. Like taking a winkle from its shell. What about it? How brave are you?'

'If I'm brave, what will you give me?'

'Well now, what would you like?'

'I'd like your shell house. With the King and Queen all made out of shells. I'd like that, please. I played with it.'

'Done!' he'd said, leaning down to give her hand a slap to strike the bargain. Had he exchanged a laugh with her mother? It wasn't in her version of the story.

Maybe he'd misheard her, the way adults do, only half-listening to children. Maybe, like any old bachelor, he'd liked little girls with long shining hair. Then he'd said, 'Not today.' He hadn't got his tonsil-clippers with him just now. He'd maybe let her off the pile of stones; that was for really bad cases that couldn't wait. But he'd come to the cottage hospital and see for himself whether she'd been really brave.

He had come. Walking into the children's ward larger than life (so her mother told her) and Emma in bed, croaking with a sore throat. And he'd laid a scroll of thick paper on the white cover. It was embellished with a kind of old-fashioned writing and crackled with red seals and ribbons. (Surely you remember, Emma? You made such a fuss!)

'This is for you,' he'd said. 'I'm told you never gave a squawk or a squeak. There's a copy in my bank and it's all witnessed and legal. What d'you say to that?'

He'd winked at her mother who sat by the bed.

'Oh dear,' Emma's mother had cried out, unrolling the scroll. 'The doctor's left you his house, darling!'

'I don't want his house,' Emma had whispered. 'I want his shell house. But he's put it back in the attic. When can I have it?'

'He's left it to you in his will, darling. You'll get it when he's dead.'

'I want it now,' Emma had wept. 'I don't want him to be dead.'

But in the course of time the family left the village and she forgot him, but never forgot the shell house and the perfidy of joking grown-ups. Dr Rhys Lewis never married and never made another will of any kind. He wasn't that sort of man, thinking he'd go on for ever.

So when, on a particularly black day some thirty years later, Emma, alone with her own daughter in half a house in Highgate, not knowing what to do for loneliness and the bitterness of a divorce, picked up from the mat an official-looking envelope, she thought it was yet another bullying missive from her ex-husband's solicitor.

Sitting in the kitchen with a strong whisky (she'd taken to drinking in the mornings – a bad sign) Emma saw that the postmark was Dyfed. And soon, incredulous, she was on the telephone to her mother, who was just setting off on one of her jaunts. The Norwegian fjords this time. Since her husband's death she couldn't bear to stay in one place for long.

'Yes, I went to Dr Lewis's funeral. Didn't I tell you, darling?' Her mother sounded breathy and hurried, as if a taxi was at the door. 'Prue Wentworth rang me and I stayed with them. Not a word was dropped . . . such a treat to see old friends, such a mercy they're not all dead . . . I wondered why she asked for your address. I don't believe it! His house, you say? But that was just a joke, all that fuss of yours about a shell house . . .' She broke off into a laugh, high and incredulous. 'Wait a minute, though, Rhys never did anything by halves. I'll come over and tell you all about it, if you don't remember. I say, now tongues will wag. What will you do? Fly the coop? Look, I must go. I'll see you in about ten days when I get back.' Highly excited, she had rung off and was on her way to the midnight sun.

Walking back to Domengastell, Emma knew she had to look for the shell house. But when Mrs Hughes was safely out of the way.

The men had gone. Only Mrs Hughes was in the kitchen, puffing away on a mauled Senior Service.

'What was the doctor like at the end of his life?' Emma asked.

'Demanding, I'd say. Like all men. I never minded him, though. Fine and hearty he was, right up to the day he dropped dead there in the drive by the front door. Fatty heart, they said. A doctor with a fatty heart, makes you think. A law unto himself, the doctor.

D'you know, Emma,' she went on, spitting the cigarette into the front of the Aga, 'women in this village daren't give birth to children in the night? He frightened them into holding on till after breakfast . . . You may laugh. But he'd never get that old horse of his out after supper. Liked to listen to his music then. *Night on a Bare Mountain* on the wind-up gramophone. Aye, a character, but a good man. Saved as many as he lost, and you can't say that for all of 'em.'

'Did he ever take children's tonsils out on that old heap of stones by the lane?'

Mrs Hughes choked into laughter.

'Codded you there, did he? He loved to tease. 'Course not, girl.'

'Well,' said Emma, moving out of range of Mrs Hughes's glinting spectacles. 'Do you remember a little house made of shells? I was a child, of course, and it's years ago—'

'Wait a bit,' said Mrs Hughes. 'Wait a bit. Fair old time back, that is. Only just come to work for him – shell house? Ooh, threw it out, I expect; dust collectors, them things.'

All at once, out of the long past, the Welsh name for the little house came back to Emma.

'Ty Cracen,' she said and smiled.

Mrs Hughes was pinning on her cake-like felt hat and drove the pin into her head. She swore softly in Welsh. 'Ty Cracen!' she repeated. 'Now where did you get that from? Ty Cracen! *This* house was Ty Cracen in the doctor's mother's time. Lived here, she did, with her sisters, all her life. Wait a bit, them days there was a grotto on the front drive, that was it – the girls made it – mad about shells, they were, collected 'em from all over, even abroad. Doted on shells, great dirty things, some of 'em. The Shell House they called this house. See?' Mrs Hughes was red and shiny with the past, it came flooding in on her. Emma felt as if she had performed a marvellous trick in bringing it all back.

'Doctor pulled that heap of rocks and rubbish to pieces when they all died, threw it in the back, changed the name of the house. Domengastell, house on the hill, seeing that's where it was.' Pulling her mouth to one side in a sort of sidling giggle, she added, 'Castle on a dungheap, house on a shippon, if you want the old Welsh. Not so posh. Take your choice.'

'Of course,' said Emma. 'Ty Cracen.' She was content. Of course the doctor would never have bothered to change the name legally, just put it about and told the Post Office and had new writing-paper printed. He'd have to have done that, to make out his accounts.

So the Shell House it remained in law, and as the Shell House it had come to her. The joke, after all, had been on him.

When Mrs Hughes had gone she took a torch and went upstairs. Why should she have remembered that the little door along the passage and past the bathroom, up two wooden steps, led to the attic? There was a disquieting sense of familiarity about this house, no room surprised her; it seemed as if each one awaited her coming. And how did she know that the shell house of her childhood would be in the attic and not destroyed like the grotto? She could see the doctor vividly; tall, bearded, full of hard energy, going at his aunts' grotto with a spade – surely a spade? – or maybe a pickaxe, or even bare hands. Or had he kicked at it as country boys did an anthill?

As the darkness and chill flowed out to finger her when she creaked open the door, she was aware of his fury and hatred of that pile of rocks, stuck in front of the house. Down-draughts from the spaces in the roof tiles teased her hair. Moving up the next flight of steps she at last felt the floor firm beneath her feet; firm but gritty. Space was all round her and her torch flickered on far corners. The attic must stretch over the whole house. Were there rats? Mice? Did squirrels or bats cosy it up with their nests?

The torchlight outlined the water tank (well insulated), some cracked leather suitcases and cardboard boxes by the far brick chimney. She nearly fell over a nursery fireguard. That would do to keep the kittens from roaming about the kitchen until they were older. She put it on the landing outside, ready to take down on her return. Surely there was the faintest smell of drying apples? She had walked straight back into her childhood.

Blowing dust and mouse dirt from the lids of cardboard boxes as she made her way into the shadows, she peered down at labels, yellowed and curling. String broke at her touch, her searching fingers felt china plates and dishes under brittle layers of newspapers. She covered them up again; later would do. Then a box rattled against her foot, and as she opened it there was a pointed roof, covered in small overlapping shells, grey with dust.

Carefully, with both hands, she drew it out; a foot-square wooden house with shells stuck all over it: mussel shells, oyster, others she couldn't name, but graded in size. It looked tawdry in the light of the torch. She tilted it and tried to put her hand into the little door. But the hands that had once confidently put the Queen and King on their thrones had been smaller, a child's.

Now, as the loose objects rolled out she failed to recognize them. Once they had shone in their pearly cloaks and tiny shell crowns. But there had been a palace revolution, evidently; they were deposed, so where now was their power and their radiance?

On her knees, cramped on the hard planks of the floor, she bit back a smile: why should they be unchanged when everything else had fallen to pieces? She replaced the little house in the box and made her way stiffly out of the attic, out of the dark and cold into her bedroom where the firelight threw back the rich coppery yellow of the curtains. Kelim rugs on the floor hid the cracked linoleum.

She put the box on the chest of drawers and went downstairs to fetch some newspapers and her paintbrushes. She had forgotten that the front of the shell house was hinged, and a spot of oil eased the stiffness. When it opened out she saw the extent of the damage. The thrones, made of mother-of-pearl shells, looked chipped and dull. The little figures, two large and two small, were plain cardboard cones stuck over with those fragile rosy shells the size of a child's fingernail, a small pebble for a head and a circlet of tiny spirals for a crown. Had there been arms? Matchsticks must have been glued on. They lay about between fragments of pearly stools like furnishings of a despoiled Pharaoh's tomb.

It was really a very simple house. Clumsily made. Which of the aunts – or maybe it was the doctor's mother – had made it? The roof was strong cardboard glued on to a box just too big to hold cigars. Shells obviously too delicate for their grotto outside had been carefully graded into sizes and then stuck on. Emma gently prized the loose ones free, wondering what glue to use to stick them back on. It had such a sorry garish look, like a cheap trophy from an empty fairground in the rain, all the glitter and pounce gone.

'I must love it again. I loved it so much then, it was a kind of passion,' Emma told herself as she gently stood the four little figures up and cleaned each tiny shell with a paintbrush dipped in soapy water. The King's cloak began to shine, his crown sparkled. He had never had a face, being a mere symbol of majesty. Likewise the Queen. Her crown had been crushed, her cloak nibbled. All Emma could do was to clean her up. The two courtiers had suffered less, and one still had his matchstick arms, painted in what had been pink and blue, like sleeves. Emma took a circlet of tiny shells from one of these courtiers and placed it on the Queen's head. She painted delicate strands of hair on the pointed cone, but no pretence at a face.

Tim and Tam came to mind. Tim and Tam the courtiers!

> Whim wham, Tim and Tam
> Both ran home to cry to mam.

She shook the house and blew out the dust. Cleaning it would be her next job. Several shells rolled out; too large for these shores, a conch, for instance, by the King's throne. Something else fell out of it – an inch-long celluloid baby doll. The kind that cracked, you couldn't buy them today. It didn't really belong in a throne room, she could see that, so it must be her own, from long ago. Its minute legs and arms were raised in protest, its blue eyes stared. A dirty piece of cotton wool had been tucked between its legs as a nappy. Emma had no memory of putting the baby there, but she must have done. As a child she had a passion for small things; from acorn cups to miniature china animals. They made the world more manageable.

Emma sat back on her feet in front of the dying fire. Carefully she fed it with the small logs Mrs Hughes had provided. She had forgotten that fires could be built and lighted by hand and felt a sense of achievement. Ever since the family had left Wales gas or electric heating had superseded the fires and oilstoves of her childhood. She cradled the celluloid baby in one hand. The child who had so lovingly wrapped it up and hidden it in the conch shell was outside time, alive in her own emotional island, filling the contours of her subsidiary world. A child's time had its own weather, its own customs and morals. Maybe she could remember so little of that time because childhood reabsorbs its memories.

This baby must have been her gift to the childless

King and Queen. A memory nudged her; a sense of loss, of rage against her parents. Why was she an only one? Little girls from the village school would come up and whisper, 'Come to our house and see the new baby.' She always went, to marvel at the tiny shell-like fingernails, the fragile neck and downy head. She longed for brothers and sisters of her own, and yet she had only managed to produce one daughter herself. Alex had been careful, not she, and she had never managed to trick him. Idiot to have stayed so long in that unsatisfactory relationship, trying to make a go of it for Charlotte's sake; yet it was for Charlotte's sake that she eventually left him. Loud quarrels were not fodder for a child. Was she too old to have one now? She would be thirty-nine next year.

She must get a guard for the fire, the logs were spitting bright sparks on to the rug. The nursery fireguard she had intended for the kittens would do for this evening, and tomorrow she could bring up the smaller one she had noticed in what had been the doctor's waiting-room. That was another problem, what to do with that big room; her furniture was lost in it. As she opened the door to go along the landing to fetch the guard the telephone shrilled through the empty house. For some reason it frightened her, and with heart beating fast she went downstairs two at a time to stop its noise.

A voice from her childhood stilled her.

'Well, *there* you are! Jungle drums tell me that you spent the night at the Lion! How could you, when you might have come straight to us?'

'Debby?'

'Of course it's Debby. Come on over, jump in your car and have supper with us. Robert's made the most delicious jugged hare and we can't eat it alone, it'd be a sin.'

Habit made her first hedge, then comply: Debby had always had this effect on her. She went to the kitchen to check on Miss Matty and her kittens. They were asleep on a cushion in a big cardboard box she had found. Even as they slept their small bodies twitched in milky sensuality. Pink padded paws, with their tiny claws, retracted and relaxed on to their mother's body, and when Emma bent over her she opened her eyes and increased that deep maternal purr.

'Four babies all at once, and all different colours. What a wise little mum,' Emma told her.

Upstairs she placed the fireguard, dusty as it was, in front of her fire. There was a handsome brass rim round the top, and it was sturdy enough to air nappies on. The shell house looked much better now, having recovered its gleam; like her mother's pearls, she thought suddenly. She washed and dried her paint-brushes before changing to drive over to Debby's. Dark, it was dark. Would she remember the way through the lanes?

Her car lights picked out hedges, disturbed a barn owl silently drifting ahead, and she nearly missed the turn in to the drive up to Talycoed. A stand of Spanish chestnuts on either side and beyond them a sense of space, of turf. One track to the left led off to the Lodge, the big house was round the curve ahead. She could hear the murmur of the shallow river, where they had played as children.

They were on the lookout for her. The light from the hallway streamed across the paved forecourt and there was Debby, tall and leggy in jeans, instantly recognizable, with a man beside her whom she didn't know. Out of the car and a hug. Then a handshake. 'This is Robert,' said Debby. 'You won't remember him because he was always away at school.'

As they went into the hall, Debby's arm round her shoulders, Emma noted the changes. It was warmer than she remembered, a huge log fire burned in the stone fireplace and Turkish rugs were spread on

29

the stone flags of the floor. Up the high wall beside the polished stairs she recognized the patterns of the daggers and swords that had hung there for fifty years or more.

'The fire's just to welcome you,' said Debby. 'We're eating in the kitchen, so much easier. The dining-room's kept more or less for the shooting parties.'

Debby had always had the promise of good looks and now, Emma saw, she was a beauty. Her dark straight hair was sculpted about a delicately pointed face which had settled into a lively contentment. Robert, with a fair moustache, blue eyes and unex-pectedly thick curly hair, set her off. They were a handsome pair. But I do remember him, I have seen him before, she thought. As they led the way through to the kitchen they seemed to her to be full of confidence and grace and her own untidy marriage squalid by comparison. The kitchen appeared to stretch across the whole of the rear of the house and had shelves of books and a desk at the far end, with a telephone and a business-like filing cabinet under the window. Orderly and modern, built-in sinks and electric ovens, fridge-freezers and an automatic dish-washer lined the left wall. There was an Aga as well. Down the centre stretched a long scrubbed pine table set with bowls of fruit and bottles of wine and a wooden cheese platter.

'You must have done something here,' said Emma. 'I'm sure it was—'

'We've taken down a wall and made it bigger,' said Robert, handing her a glass of sherry. 'Yes, we had to modernize, there was an awful stone sink and wooden draining-boards – is that how you remember it?'

'Yes, and there was a little room where your mother washed the eggs and did the flowers, d'you remember, Debby?'

'Well, we've done away with all that.' Debby went across to the Aga and took the lid off a heavy Le Creuset casserole, releasing the delicious gamey smell of stew. 'We more or less live in this room, it's so comfortable and sunny. Robert planned it. And if you want any alterations done to that dreary old house of Dr Rhys's, he's your man.'

Emma laughed, but didn't take her up on the offer. It was an extraordinary meal. She hadn't eaten one like it for years; she had been living on bits and pieces out of the microwave in the Highgate flat, in between furious arguments and banging doors, for so long that to eat in a civilized manner, with conversation, was almost unnerving. There were jacket potatoes piled up on a dish, and broccoli. Wine to drink.

'You're a marvellous cook,' she said. 'Tell me—'

'No,' said Debby, 'you tell us,' and she sent a smile across to her husband. 'You've set everybody by the ears. Are you really coming back? Will you be able to live in that weird house? It's so dark with all those trees round it . . . it'll need everything done to it. And how are you getting on with that old dragon, Mrs Hughes?'

'Let her eat, for God's sake, darling, and don't be so pushy. Here, Emma, have some redcurrant with that. How is it? I shot the chap a couple of days ago. It's Deb's pet recipe for jugged hare.'

'We're trying it out on you,' said Debby, not at all put out by her husband's reprimand. 'If you like it we can go ahead for next weekend.'

'It's delicious. Do you remember that once I turned vegetarian because of that pig we saw slaughtered?'

Away they went, chipping at the past. It was in trivia that one came close to old friends. Old nonsenses and shared fears made unbreakable bonds and Emma was grateful. After a spate of reminiscence Robert said, refilling their glasses, 'You've both forgotten, but I haven't. Emma, your father coached me for Common Entrance. I'd never have got into Upton but for him. I used to come over to Glammon Lodge for extra Maths. Made it interesting. And Latin too. I still remember some Virgil—'

'It's your hair,' exclaimed Emma. 'Of course, I used to envy your curly hair! I thought there was something . . .' So many boys had come to the Lodge, to be taken into her father's study, so many needing help and encouragement. 'You were the one with the racing cars, weren't you?'

'And the acne,' said Robert. 'I thought I'd never get rid of it. I tried to hide my face whenever you came to the door. You know, I'd rather have gone to the grammar school at Llandryssil and been taught by him. I hated boarding-school.'

'You know how things were in those days, Robert,' said Debby, displeased. 'You couldn't possibly have gone to a local grammar school! I was sent away as well. People just did it then. We've survived.'

Was there a hint of the hostess in her manner? Keep things light, do not mention death at dinner. Robert caught her tone, laughed, said, 'I've still got all my Dinky cars. Never let my sons play with them unless I was there. We played the same game your father taught me. We'd make out a track, with the miles pencilled in, in grids, then we'd race them on it, add up the miles per minute, give them handicaps. Wonderful for mental arithmetic. I'm glad you remember.'

'Are your sons away at school? Heavens, I don't know how old they are. My daughter's eighteen. She's in India at the moment.'

'Well, yes, they are.' It was Debby who answered, and Debby who had decided, Emma could tell. No grammar school in the next small town for her children. 'Robbie's coming up for A levels next year and Davie's sitting his GCSEs or whatever they call it now. He's fifteen.'

'Davie's the one who will run the farm. He's practical, not academic.' Robert's tone was matter-of-fact. 'It doesn't matter that he's the younger of the two.'

In the pause that followed, Emma became aware that in this household power was equally divided. If Debby set the pace Robert orchestrated it. In a moment they would ask about Alex – or had her mother told them? If so they would carefully avoid mentioning him. Why did she find it so difficult to tell the truth? Why not come out with it in a forthright voice if they *did* ask? 'My husband and I are divorced. Our daughter ran off to India to get away from our bickering and fights. As a family we were a mess.' Because it was no-one else's damned business, that's why. And because it would embarrass her old friend, spoil the jugged hare, and demand a response these two were not prepared to make. She felt all at once very much alone, with strangers whose lifestyle was so different from her own.

'Your mother was here for the doctor's funeral,' Robert said. 'We were so glad to see her, she seemed quite chipper, full of plans for travel.'

'Yes,' Emma could not help replying, 'my mother never stops travelling, because she can't seem to settle down anywhere without my father.' Debby was taking the plates away, Robert refuelling her glass, as if to cover a breach of good manners, so she went on hastily, 'Did she ever tell you that extraordinary story about the doctor, how it was I inherited his house?' She had recovered her composure, and over the fruit and cheese put herself out to tell the story of the heap of stones, Dr Lewis's promise and the mistaken identity of the house. It came out as an amusing piece of news, a truthful oddity, and Debby and Robert relaxed again, evidently appeased.

'He was an eccentric, even for this village – and the valley's full of off-beat characters,' said Debby. 'There was an old Miss Pemberton up at the Hall above Bwylchyddar who bathed naked in her lake at dawn and ate nettle soup. But the doctor looked like Abraham with that full white beard yellow with nicotine. He used to come to church in breeches and a poacher's jacket and read the lesson. He'd take a

33

candle out of his pocket and light it to see by. Then he'd – oh, it was so disgusting—'

'He did it to wake us all up,' Robert interrupted.

'What did he do?'

'Took out his false teeth with a red handkerchief in the middle of a passage he was reading – mind you, he had a splendid voice to thunder out the Old Testament bits – then slipped them back in as he finished the lesson.'

'He rolled his cigarettes in San Izal lav paper. The shiny stuff,' said Robert. His laugh was unexpectedly loud and entirely mirthful.

'How d'you know?' asked Emma. 'I remember him smoking a pipe.'

'He'd smoke anything he could get hold of. Liked Archie's cigars, didn't he, Deb?'

Archie was Debby's father, and Emma felt a pang of remorse at not having asked about her parents.

'Myfanwy told me they were living in the Lodge now. She couldn't resist dragging up that story of the angoras which escaped.'

'He'll never live that down, neither will we. He enjoys setting the village by the ears. Ma restrains him as much as she can, but they're both very independent.'

'They've been very good to us,' said Robert. 'I reckon I'm lucky to have married into a family with people and land in good heart.'

The two women looked at him in some surprise. A neat turn of phrase, warmly meant. Debby leaned over and took his hand.

'Thank you, darling,' she said. Emma was glad she resisted remarking that it was the wine talking.

'Coffee,' said Robert. 'And while I'm making it get Emma to tell us about her painting. Your mother said you'd had an exhibition somewhere. You're a bit of a dark horse, aren't you?'

'First of all,' said Debby, 'that story of yours – have you found the shell house? I think it's madly romantic

34

and queer. People have been saying that the doc was sweet on your mother and that's why he left Domen to you.'

'What? Well, I don't know about that . . . Yes, I was working on the shell house when you telephoned. I found it in the attic. It's a miracle that Mrs Hughes hadn't thrown it out.'

'You didn't waste any time, did you? What d'you mean, working on it? I can't wait to see it. Where did he keep it? I don't remember seeing it in the waiting-room when I was little.'

To which Emma answered only the second question. If Debby needed proof of her story she would give it to her.

'It was pretty battered,' she said carefully. 'I'm cleaning it up. You must come over and see it . . .' But she knew that Debby would see it only with the sophisticated eyes of a grown woman, and protectively, defensively, she added, 'I just thought it beautiful when I was six or seven. It won't mean a thing to you, Debby.'

'Well, we'll come over anyway. I haven't been in that house since the doc retired.'

'Never mind about that,' Robert returned with the coffee. 'You'll only want to interfere and make suggestions—'

'Oh, I'll be glad of a few ideas, actually—'

'What we want to hear about is your painting. What sort of things do you paint? Is it a hobby, or—'

'No,' said Emma strongly, flushed out of her defensiveness. 'No, painting isn't a hobby. It's my work. Hobbies are for people who have too little to do apart from living.'

'Oh dear!' Debby gave a little whoop of laughter. 'Do you make a living out of it, then? Clever old thing. Have a grape.'

Cornered, Emma had to admit that she didn't.

'I used to teach in between times, but the exhibition

went quite well. I sold half a dozen pictures and was commissioned to illustrate a book of poems.'

'Well, if you need any cash and can spare the time, just trot over here at weekends and help us with the potentates and fat cats who come to shoot and live the life of Riley for three days. We lay it on thick and they lap it up, especially the Americans and Germans.'

Robert frowned. 'Come on, Deb! Some of them are decent sorts, good shots too. They enjoy potting the birds and it keeps us solvent.'

'Oh, it's quite good fun really,' said Debby, 'but exhausting. Even if you *are* learning to cook, Robert.'

'She's wonderful,' Robert said to Emma. 'It's a huge help with farming as it is today, and the EEC putting its filthy oar in.'

Which tribute Debby accepted as her due.

A day or two later, when Emma was walking from room to room downstairs trying to decide what to do about them, she heard the sound of horse's hooves, coming at a pace up the drive. It was Debby. She flung the reins over a jutting branch of a beech tree and was up the steps before Emma could open the door.

'Couldn't resist coming over,' she said, giving Emma a swift kiss. 'Shall I leave Brandy here or put him round the back in the stable?'

'Heavens, I haven't even *looked* round the back yet! Come on, let's see what we've got there.'

Together they walked past the car, which Emma had left beside the house on the beginning of the paved courtyard near the kitchen door. A high draggled hedge bounded the property, and hard up against it was a low wooden building. The door was shut and a large iron key hung by the side. Feeling like an intruder, Emma took it and turned it in the lock. The door creaked open. It was in two halves and the top half swung back to reveal a dim hay-smelling interior with two stalls. On one wall hung an old leather saddle, dusty, but not cracked, and an assortment of tackle. Dented buckets lay about on the unswept concrete floor. At the far end piles of straw, bottles of liniment, a broken stool.

'What happened to his horse?' she asked.

'My parents have him up at the farm. It seemed the best thing. He's in retirement, out to grass, poor old boy. We couldn't send him to the knacker's. Oh my God, Emma, it's so strange.' Debby put her hand on the saddle. 'Kept it oiled, how like the doc.'

'Take it, do,' said Emma. 'I'll have no use for it. And all this tackle. I'll have to make this stable into a garage, if it's big enough.'

It was the best way to lay ghosts.

'Let's leave it here for the moment – but thanks,' said Debby. 'Your car's pretty small. It might just do. Come on, let's see what else there is.'

Beyond the stable was another outhouse, piled inside with stacked logs and coal. Beyond that a tangle of bushes and old apple and plum trees and the sound of quiet running water. A stream ran along the far boundary and they forced their way through brambles and seeding nettles to its banks. Over the drystone wall on the farther side the mountains rose silkily in the still autumn light, across fields of winter beet.

'There should be a kitchen garden somewhere,' said Debby. 'Look, beyond that oak tree, there's an archway and a wall. You'll need some help here. This was once some sort of lawn.'

'Look at the roses!'

They badly needed pruning. Long trailers of hard prickly branches waved in the wind, with dried dead heads and the beginnings of hips. Some last deep red roses were still blooming and Emma reached up to pull them down. They were the fragrant old-fashioned kind and the velvety petals fell into her hand as she cupped them.

But Debby was through the archway and inside a

large area bounded by old brick walls. Knee-high grass and docks and nettles covered half of it, but there were also orderly rows of potatoes and beans and a huddle of rhubarb and spinach.

'Onions!'

'Mint!'

They ran about, bending down, pulling at herbs, smelling them, laughing like children.

'There's a sort of greenhouse over there. What luck!'

But it was dropping with rotten wood and the door was off its hinges.

'Never mind,' said Debby. 'It's wonderful! You'll have loads to do.'

They made their way out of the walled garden and discovered a cleared path which led to the back of the house. A door opened into a small stone-floored room next to the kitchen, with a deep sink.

Mrs Hughes appeared in the doorway, hat skewered firmly to her head. 'I'm just off,' she called. 'Oh, Miss Debby, you're here. Taking a look round, are you?'

'Who put in the potatoes and things, Mrs Hughes? Did you?'

Emma was flushed with exploration, dizzy with ownership. Her small back garden in Highgate had not prepared her for this. Nearly an acre, all told, with the garden in front of the house. It was riches. It was a kingdom.

'My man Elwyn always grew vegetables for the doctor,' she said. 'But his back's gone. You'll have to do the best you can, Emma. Mind, it's hard work. The doctor only liked his roses and a walk round to look at Mount Joseph. Have you found his seat? Near the lavender, that is.' She took a deep breath. 'Well,' she went on, with a hard look at Debby, 'I'll be off. See you tomorrow. The coal's in and I've made up the Aga.'

'She doesn't approve of me,' said Debby. 'Now why on earth not, I wonder?'

'Maybe she thinks you'll be giving me ideas—'

'Well, you need some, coping with this lot on your own. Tell you what, I'll send young Ivor down. He's back from Aber and out of a job. His father's our cowman.'

So the old feudal attitudes still lingered, Emma thought with some amusement. Could she afford what was dangerously becoming the employment of 'staff'? Her parents had had girls from the village to help out in the house, but she could barely afford to employ Mrs Hughes three times a week. She wouldn't need her when she got straight, but she didn't look forward to telling her so. She would have to earn some money, and fast. The flat at Highgate was still not sold, and with Alex in South Africa on a wine-buying trip nothing could be done until he returned. Then there was Charlotte going to university – surely he would cough up for his daughter's education. She would have to write to him. He knew nothing about this house, and she didn't relish telling him.

'That'll be fine,' she said now to Debby. 'Let's go in and have some tea and I'll show you round.'

Debby was openly nosy. She went from room to room, exclaiming over each one. The doctor's waiting-room, where Emma had put all her dining-room furniture, looked gloomy now that the late afternoon sun had moved round the house. They walked together over floorboards pricked with nails where the carpet had been lifted, and Debby stopped by the fireplace and looked up at a faded rectangle on the wall.

'There used to be a picture here,' she said. 'I loved to look at it when I was little. Make up stories about it. It was a woman sitting at a table talking to someone across from her, a man, you only saw a bit of him . . . I wonder where it is?'

'There're some pictures up in the boxroom. But come into the surgery, Debby. I've got to cut down that holly outside, it makes it so dark.'

The surgery was smaller, with shabby green lino

and shelves along the far wall. All Emma's painting gear, her easel, paints, canvases, were stacked under the window. A door in the left-hand wall led into another, even smaller room.

'Mrs Hughes said this was his snuggery. I hadn't heard that word for years. He used to play his records and smoke his pipe and read in here. I rather like it, don't you? Look, there's a French window into the garden.'

'It feels right,' said Debby. 'You ought to have this for yourself; it's a super sitting-room, and it gets the evening sun. You'll have to paint it white, don't you think? Oh, his books are still here . . .'

Emma hadn't really looked at the shelves, set in by the fireplace. Now she glanced at the dingy leatherbound books. Mostly medical volumes with indecipherable titles, close print and anatomical illustrations. Two large volumes of a *Topographical Dictionary of Wales*. 1850. By Samuel Lewis. Beautifully bound, these two, in tooled leather. A bookplate with a crown hovering over a winged bird like a gryphon and the words 'Sans Changer' on a curlicue of a ribbon underneath. The sort of books her father loved. Maybe he had leafed through them for information in this very room.

'D'you think they were friends, the doctor and my father?'

'I expect so. I think all our parents socialized. Here's one of your father's books. One about Sarn Helen. He signed it, look! "You on your horse, me on my bicycle, why didn't we go the length of it?" It's a Roman road, isn't it?'

The sight of her father's scholarly hand moved Emma unbearably.

'That was his first, wasn't it?' Debby was routing through the shelves. 'Da has all your father's books, of course.' She pulled out *Jorrocks*. Richard Gordon's novels. A badly foxed edition of Darwin's *Origin of Species*. Then gave a yelp of surprise.

'Oh, do look, Emma. Do you think he was turning to homoeopathy?'

Debby held up a small blue book. '*The Stepping Stones to Homoeopathy and Health* by a Dr Ruddock. It looks about a hundred years old. He's marked a passage about beards and moustaches preventing bronchitis. They act as a kind of natural respirator. "Can we doubt the wisdom of the Creator in giving this ornament to *man* who is so frequently exposed to atmospheric vicissitudes, and witholding it from *woman* who as keeper of the home, requires no such appendage?" That's rich. So that's why the doc kept his beard!'

'Take it if you want. It'll make Robert laugh.'

Emma was thinking that her father had been too busy schoolmastering to write much after the move to London. He had never finished an anthology of poetry and prose about Wales, although there had been some suggestion that Emma should illustrate it. The waste made her sad.

'Come on, Debby, let's have a cup of tea. Mrs Hughes made some bara brith this morning. I'll chuck all this lot out tomorrow.'

Debby approved of the kitchen, especially the out-size Welsh dresser. Beside the Aga the kittens stretched out feeble paws and opened their eyes. They were safe behind the fireguard Emma had brought down. Yes, said Debby, oh, they're sweet, could she have one, the little brindled one? She reached over and turned it up to see its sex. A tom. Well, they made better mousers.

'You shall have it when it's weaned,' Emma promised, stroking Miss Matty's head in commiseration.

'You could really live in here, it's big enough,' said Debby. 'Like we do in ours. You'd need to do a bit of shifting around. You could move the fridge into that room we saw from the garden. Take out the door . . . where's your washing-machine? That should be in the laundry-cum-muck-room with all your wellies and so on.'

'Mrs Hughes does the washing by hand in the sink in there. She calls it the scullery.'

'Antediluvian! Robert could fix up everything for you in a couple of days. You'd have more space. You could put your telly on that table, or a radio. Move in another armchair. Maybe a lamp to cosy it up, and—'

'Hold on, Debby. I haven't got a television. I don't want one. I won't have time to watch the beastly thing. And what would Mrs Hughes say?'

'Nuts to Mrs Hughes. It's your house. Now for upstairs. This *is* fun.'

'Don't you want any tea?'

'When we come down. I can't wait to see what's hiding from us upstairs.'

In Emma's bedroom she spotted the shell house on the chest of drawers. 'Oh, Emma, *there* it is! Your magical little house. It's pretty, it shines with good living. You're going to be happy here.' She suddenly hugged Emma. 'I'm so glad you've come back. I need a friend.'

'Who doesn't?' said Emma, giving her a kiss. 'You'll love the bathroom,' she went on, disengaging herself in sudden shyness. 'Two people could take a bath in delicious and luxurious depravity, smothered in bubbles.'

In the boxroom they unstacked the leaning pile of pictures, blowing off the dust, squatting on the floor to take a better peek.

'There she is,' Debby breathed. 'Oh, there she is. You must remember her, *Lady with a Tattered Glove*. Look.'

'It's only a print and it's stained with damp.' Emma was terribly reluctant to have anything to do with the picture. 'Oh, do let's put it up again, just for old times' sake. Oh my chickenpox and my measles long ago,' chanted Debby, clattering down the thinly carpeted stairs.

When Emma walked into the waiting-room, slowly, taking her time, the picture was up on the mantelshelf over the fire. It leaned against the wall beneath its old place, which showed a faded patch. There was that remembered muteness about the face, a pure oval the Victorians loved to paint and which hinted at ground-down womanhood, the graceful resignation of a generation of half-submerged women, sombrely dressed. Some years ago the original had greeted her like a forgotten friend in the Fitzwilliam. She had stopped dead in front of it, ignoring the calls of her friends to come and look at the marvellous Impressionists in the further room.

It had given her a sense of unease, a sort of deadly undertow. It showed a woman caught in a moment of crisis; her worn, unmended glove lay on the table or desk by her side and she faced out of the picture, yet looking at a man whose solid back cut across half of it. It was a clever study, a narrative painting quite out of fashion and sneered at nowadays; for painters should not try to be novelists. Yet William Nicholson had caught so well a sense of before and after, which made the viewer turn to look again. Like Sickert's *Ennui*, there was a whole life there.

'I think the poor thing is asking for money,' said Debby. 'She may be having an interview with her solicitor. But that unmended glove – it's out of character, somehow. It's called *Lady* with a tattered glove. Not *Woman*. You'd expect a lady's glove to have a discreet darn. You know, genteel poverty was all the go. Governesses coming down in the world, like Charlotte Brontë . . .'

Would *her* pictures attract such intense speculation? Emma wondered. Debby hadn't said anything about how it was painted. She was evidently one of the many who *read* pictures instead of looking at them. Really seeing them.

'She may be his cast-off mistress,' said Emma,

turning away fretfully. 'I must get out of the habit of calling this the waiting-room. But I don't want a dining-room with all Mother's things. Table, chairs, sideboard. It's so cluttered.'

'Well, you could sand the floor and have it polished and put up your pictures when you've got rid of this naff wallpaper.' Debby pulled at a loose strip by the fireplace and it ribboned off in her fingers. Emma noted with some amusement that slang outdated in London still throve in Wales.

'I'd like to sell all this lot and put in a plain wooden bench and hang up Shaker chairs on the walls.'

'They'll cost more than you'd get,' said Debby thoughtfully, but she did not shoot down the idea. 'Terracotta linen or hessian. Something rough and simple for curtains and a couple of cushions. Like a modern gallery. You get the morning sun in here and you could paint the walls chrome or white or – anyway, something pale to show off your pictures. You can eat in the kitchen with friends. You're not in the London suburbs now.' Before Emma could react to this dig she went on, 'Where's your studio? Don't you need a north light? What about the bedroom next to the boxroom?'

'That was going to be Charlotte's.'

'She can have the other. It'll be warmer, too, over the kitchen. You've got four to choose from! Then you can move all your stuff out of the old surgery and fix that up to eat in if you have a party or anything.' How practical she was! Emma recollected her as a managing child, it had always been restful to have someone else to think for you. 'If you do your painting down here, Emma,' she was saying, 'you'll get all the village popping by and peering through the windows. You'll be safer upstairs. Now I must go. Lovely of you to let me ramble on, darling. This winter's going to be fun. I'll send Ivor over, and Robert. You won't have a moment to brood.'

Ah, that was it. She evidently knew all about the divorce and this was her way of coping. She wouldn't stop for tea after all and Emma watched her unhitch her horse, mount it and gracefully canter off down the drive.

What a formidable old woman she would make. She had certainly expanded to fill her position in the valley, abhorring a vacuum. Emma went back into the kitchen, made herself a pot of tea, ate two delicious slices of Welsh cake and was filled with self-doubt. Should she allow Debby to take over? For years she had allowed her husband to do just that and was only now piecing together her own precarious identity.

Well, to begin with she wouldn't have the picture propped up in the front room. If it were to be a gallery it would be all wrong. Standing in the doorway she saw the room with Debby's fresh eye, and with grateful surprise realized that Debby took her painting seriously, as if she respected it as legitimate work. That was a hurdle vaulted: now she would have to be professional about it. She could almost hear her father's remark that a professional worked when he didn't feel like it and an amateur only when he did.

Switching on the light, she walked across and looked at the picture. The damp patch in the top right-hand corner was in the shape of a black crow. The house was very silent and she was held in a strange immobility, as if she were in the middle of a web, and the threads of other people's lives dense around her. What of the doctor's mother and her sisters with their mania for shells, and the people who had sat in this waiting-room hoping their coughs and rashes would be cured by the god who sat across the way in his surgery? The past had claimed them and she, Emma, standing alone, was real and the house and its ghosts would acknowledge her in their own time. For a house was true to itself, it could not lie because it absorbed the lives of those it sheltered. It demanded to be filled, for that was its purpose, which was why an empty house had such a sad air about it.

She found herself looking intently at the troubled woman in the picture. Something disquieting stirred in her memory: the tension and fear were not up there on the wall where she was looking through the eyes of a six year old. They were here, in this room where her mother and Dr Lewis had stood by the big round polished table with its piles of magazines and old comics. No-one else was in the room. And why were they here instead of in the surgery, the proper consulting room? As a child Emma had a strong sense of decorum. A doctor was not like other men; he smelt different, you only saw him sitting behind his desk, a lamp with a green shade at his right and a pencil and pad in front of him. By his hand was always a sort of tube with three dangles to it, two for his ears and one to be put coldly on your chest or back. 'Breathe in deeply.' 'Say Ah.' That was what a doctor said to you. He didn't stand there, in the wrong room, and look as if he didn't know what to do or say. He didn't call your mother by her Christian name, he didn't touch her hand, then turn abruptly away.

'Mummy's not going to die, is she?'

That was what the child had cried out in fear of the strangeness, and they had turned to look at her as at a stranger; a look of blindness and shock as if they didn't know she was there and shouldn't have been.

'Darling. No. Of course not. It . . . it's you we're thinking about. That nasty old sore throat.' A lie. But arms round her, her mother bending down. The doctor saying nothing, a hand splayed damply on the table, making five separate finger marks.

'Am *I* going to die then?'

A tiny satisfaction, an upsurge of self-importance; they were locked then, these two, in an intimacy of grief on her account. This was perfectly acceptable if she were destined to be a gift for Jesus. Jesus loves me.

Suffer little children. She had never understood the suffer-little-children bit at Sunday School. Why did He want little children to suffer? Emma, at six years old, didn't want that, whatever Sunday School taught you. She did the only possible thing; burst into loud satisfying tears and felt the tension go away and Dr Rhys Lewis change back from a man to a doctor and her mother, in proper concern, all hers again.

'Of course,' present-day Emma, the real grown-up Emma, said aloud to the past. 'You carried me upstairs and I was put to rest on the doctor's huge brass bed. That's why the room was somehow familiar. That wallpaper with the grapes. That's when you gave me the shell house to play with.'

What else could be dredged up? What other screens drawn back as if someone was playing a game of charades with her? It was a guessing game all right. The house was very silent; maybe, she told herself, it just seemed like that after Debby's chatter. All the same she made herself walk, not run, to the kitchen and the kittens and the radio and the gently breathing Aga with its heart of fire. She poured herself a stiff whisky and turned on the six o'clock news.

PART 2

The year turns more slowly in the Welsh Marches than further south, and in the handful of days that make up St Luke's little summer there is very little rain, the sky a thin blue, the air curiously warm and pure. There is a different kind of stillness, an expectancy in which one senses a pause between the heavy bearing of summer and the absolute dearth of winter. A kind of menopause, and, like it, making for spurts of irritability.

Or so it was with Emma. St Luke was the patron saint of painters and physicians, she recollected – a happy conjunction. She walked restlessly about the garden, gathered late apples which, when cooked, turned into a beautiful white froth to be mixed with beaten up white of egg and sugar and served with cream. Apple snow. Blackberries were long gone but the hedgerows quick with sloes. She must get a recipe for sloe gin. Marigolds unexpectedly bloomed in lost corners; evening primroses put on a second growth. Handsome thistles attracted the finches, which came by twos and threes in the early morning to feast on their seedheads. Silky seedpods of tangutica hung like powdered wigs from the walls of the vegetable garden. Time to put the clocks back. But she needed to escape from the house, where she had been stripping wallpaper and shifting furniture until her back ached. She needed to walk round the lanes and through the village, like an animal exploring new territory, with circumspection.

Bryntanat was near enough to the border for it to be both English and Welsh, a truth not entirely palatable to the latter. Welsh had, in Emma's day, been taught in the village school and there were two chapels and the English church. She and her mother had worshipped in the old church, which had a rare Jesse window. As a child it had frightened her, vine branches twining up from the loins of a recumbent man. She had expected Jesse to be a woman.

The local farmers and half the village attended Chapel and their fierce harmonies escaped into the Sabbath quiet like hot air from an open furnace. 'Nothing like a dose of hellfire and brimstone to start the week,' her father would say, returning from a visit to Bethel. 'We all felt purged. And don't forget that Handel got the idea for his "Hallelujah Chorus" from the revivalists shouting out *Gogoniant*!' He prized his Welsh ancestry, although it was only on his grandmother's side. It ran sweetly in his veins, melancholy and consoling. To it he attributed his powerful tenor voice which the English vicar privately thought should be uplifted in his church.

'I like to practise my Welsh, vicar,' Hugo frequently told him. 'But I'll come to harvest festival.'

As she walked through the village Emma expected to feel great surges of emotion – after all, she had spent the best part of her childhood here. But instead she looked about her with indifference, standing on the humped bridge over the sluggish river, resenting the loss of the bakery where she had been sent to fetch jam tarts and new bread. The old bakery was now a smart black-and-white cottage with geraniums and crazy paving. Bryntanat had come up in the world; there was an air of prosperity about it, and the boys she had been at the village school with were doubtless business men or farmers, driving Volvos or Rovers, married with wives and children. The station had been turned into a motel, the railway tracks long gone, and the stationmaster with a silver plate in his head from the war tucked away in the churchyard.

What had she expected? A time-capsule?

The Post Office was still there, next to the lychgate that led to the church. It had always sold groceries and she needed some now, but on impulse turned and walked through the lychgate. The church was smaller than she remembered, steeple intact. She liked church-yards, and there were two here, the old and the new. The old had something of a history. Centuries ago it had been kept for Sunday games like Ninepins and Fives. Fairs were held, and a 'dancing bank' provided, which must have made the village a much merrier place on Sundays. But stricter days had come and games forbidden. The ground was then used for the occasional gypsy burial, unbaptized infants and the excommunicated.

She turned to the left, where a path led to the so-called 'new' graveyard. Here were rows of stone or slate headstones, some smart with gold-and-black lettering mostly in Welsh, which she lingered to read. Some were of heart-shaped granite, with jars of flowers set before them. Davies and Hughes, Jones and Prys . . . familiar names.

Beyond stretched the new sports field, just over the hedge.

'Back agin then, are you?'

Behind her a man had come up with no noise. An emaciated man with a shock of greying black hair hanging over his ears. She smiled to hide her fright; he had appeared so silently as if from a grave. Indeed, raw earth shone damply on the spade he carried.

'I know you, Emma Forden from Glammon Lodge. But you don't know me.' His full dark eyes gloated at his advantage; there was no conciliatory twinkle, and Emma had never looked up (for he was very tall) into two such dull caverns. 'Give you a clue, then.' He started to sing in a curiously high sweet voice, 'My hen laid a haddock right up in a tree.' He stopped, and involuntarily Emma opened her mouth and repeated the phrase and tune.

'Pudding Harry! No, it can't be!'

Pudding Harry had been a shapeless boy whose fleshy arms and padded legs had quivered in and out of his sleeves and short trousers. In the school playground the smaller children had climbed up over his quaking belly like mice on a mountain and to the rhythmic clapping of the bigger ones he would run with them, panting and grinning, from the big ash tree by the lavatory block to the oak, shiny with climbing, by the school gate. There he stood while the children reached up for the lowest branch and sat in a row like starlings, shrieking out the first verse of the Welsh National Anthem. It was Emma who had made up the words before she could pronounce the proper Welsh.

> My hen laid a haddock
> Right up in a tree.

The Welsh children copied her, but she was unaware of any mockery. Her Welsh in those days was good enough to win her a red ribbon and half a crown at the local eisteddfod. She still had a small, breathy singing voice which beguiled the listener into protective smiles.

Her speaking voice had retained this misleading, hesitant quality quite at variance with her bold good looks. In fact, it might have been the cause of her unfortunate marriage, promising compliance where there was none.

Emma saw at once that Harry's good humour had dropped away with his flesh. Maybe it had only been a protective device, like a hermit crab's carapace. He was looking her up and down with sombre appraisal, yet his voice was judgemental. She felt the merest frisson of fear and distaste. The churchyard stretched emptily around them; walled off from the village street on one side and hedged about towards the open fields on the other.

'Climbed up me like mice you lot did,' he said.

'But what happened, Harry?'

'Tell you what.' He speared the spade into the turf and wiped his hands down his smeared dungarees. 'Time I knocked off, come you to the Cross Keys. I go there dinner-time. Buy you a drink.'

They passed a newly dug grave on their way out and Harry nodded to it. 'Terrible clay, hard digging that. All equal down there, though.'

'That's your job, Harry?'

'It is so.'

The Cross Keys was at the far end of the village, humbler than the Lion which liked to think of itself as an hotel. The bar was simple and there was a fire burning in an old-fashioned grate. Several farm workers stood drinking their beer slowly and playing darts. They turned when Emma came in and did not appear to know her. But Harry put an end to that, saying loudly, with some bravado, 'This is Emma Forden come back, her the doctor left his house to.' And winked.

'Let me buy you a drink, Harry, for old times' sake.' To hide her discomfort she said to the barman, 'I remember once seeing a tramp with wonderful silver hair toasting a kipper in front of that fire. I was with my parents, it must have been near Christmas, because it was snowing.'

'That'd be in my uncle's time. Died last year. Wouldn't change a thing in here.' He was about Emma's age, but quick and stocky with an observant eye. 'All real ales, missis. Which d'you want?'

'Ansells 'll do us both. My treat,' said Harry.

They sat down near the fire. 'Come on, Harry. What happened to you?' Emma couldn't take her eyes off those shrunken cheeks, the grimy, scrawny neck sprouting from the collarless, equally grimy shirt. He smelt of the graveyard, the rawness and newness of deepdug clay.

'Lost six stone just like that,' he said. 'Six stone! Fell off me. How many pounds of sugar, sacks of potatoes is that, eh? Six bloody stone of meat and bone and fat on my poor bloody back.' He slurped off the foamy head of his beer and grinned at her with decorated lips. 'Think of that.'

'But how, Harry? Were you ill?'

'Mam died. That were five year ago. They took me to the Infirmary. Well, went all to pieces, didn't I? Livin' at home all those years. Diabetes, they said. *I* don't know. Fell off me and never put an ounce back on since. Come on, how much d'you reckon I weigh?'

From the bar one of the men called out, evidently used to Harry's question, 'Fifty p. for guessing the weight of this cake. Roll up, roll up!'

'Eleven stone,' said Emma, wanting to be on his side, trying to ignore the taunting laughter.

'Eleven! Ten six – that's all I weigh. Ten six and I'm six foot two. It's against nature, but I feel so light I could fly.'

'Ooh hoo, fly away, boyo!'

But Harry was used to teasing. He enjoyed it as he had enjoyed carrying them all around the playground for sweets.

Dropping her voice, she asked whether he was married, and to her surprise he said yes, he was, to a nurse from the Infirmary.

'No kids. She had one already, see. But the little beggar buggered off to Australia. Didn't hit it off with me. What about you?'

She hadn't expected that, and, looking into his gaunt face which fat had once plumped into a false joviality she thought that fat wasn't a bad thing. A fat old woman had few wrinkles and a benevolence that Emma would now question. She gave him a brief edited version of her circumstances, omitting the divorce, spoke of her father's death, her mother—

'Corker, your mam,' he said, sucking his bluish lips

53

together. He shouted across to the barman, 'Pint and a half of the same, Dai,' and lumbered up to get them. 'You lot were too young to know Emma's mam,' he said over his shoulder to the darts players. 'Us lads'd wait to see her drive up in that trap to fetch you and young Debby from the Hall. Cunning old pony, had a fringe, fat. What was her name?'

'Beauty. She rolled me off her back once into a bed of nettles. She'd blow herself out while we were trying to tighten the girth. Cunning. Yes, you're right there, Harry.'

But Harry wanted to talk about Emma's mother. Emma was puzzled. She had had no idea – a child wouldn't – that her mother had been an object of admiration – even sniggering desire – to young boys.

She frowned into her glass, wanting to get away. There was a gloating overtone to his talk that made her uneasy. Then rescue came, in the form of a voice she knew, remembered, calling from the door.

'Ah, there you are, Harry. Thought I'd find you here. I wondered whether you'd look at that old tractor of mine?' Archie Wentworth caught sight of Emma and came straight over, glancing quickly from one to the other. 'Why, Emma! I was on my way to call on you, my dear. Deb told me she'd seen you.' Nodding down at Harry, he added, 'Harry's a wizard at engines.'

Emma seized the opportunity of rising to greet him, pushing back her chair.

'I'll be up after tea, Mr Wentworth. Emma and me met in the churchyard. Not like her mam, is she?'

Damning words. She was a let-down.

As they left the pub together, Emma slipped her hand through Archie's arm. 'You were the US cavalry back there, Archie,' she said. 'I didn't know how to get away.'

She had always called him Archie. He was Archie to most people, friends and family.

'You don't want to see much of him,' he said now. 'Odd blighter.'

'I didn't recognize him without his fat. Oh, I'm so glad to see you! I should have come over—'

'Nonsense, you're up to your eyes, so Deb tells me. It's wonderful to have you back. I'd give you a kiss if it wasn't in the middle of the village. Some things change, but gossip doesn't.'

'It's a change from Highgate.'

'Will you stay or is it too soon to ask?'

'I hope so. But yes, it is a bit too soon to ask. Time seems to be knocked sideways. I don't know where I am, past or present. Maybe we should never have left. My father was never happy in London, you know. But of course you do.'

'I missed him. We were good friends. Lovely man, Hugo.'

They had reached the top of the hill and turned in at the gate to Domengastell. She let Archie walk ahead so that she could study him. In an odd way he was less changed than anyone, than Debby, than the village itself. It had struck her on hearing his voice at the door of the Cross Keys, noting his swift, almost youthful approach. As a child she had responded to him as if he were nearer her own age than her parents'. He never spoke down to her, answered her questions directly, joined in her games of inventing fantastic kingdoms out of the clouds as they drifted, hovered, or sped across the hills.

The high-bridged jut of his nose gave a cutting edge to a face that fell away from it. He could never quite live up to that nose as his grandfather, the Admiral, had. It should have carried him through life like a spinnaker in a spanking breeze. But he was not really a man of action, and to emphasize that he was growing an egg-shaped stomach that sat above his long legs, still elegant in his plus-twos and the dark-green stockings his sister knitted for him.

He was stepping up the drive now like a questing heron, vague blue eyes taking in everything, soft sparse sandy hair blowing in the lifting wind.

'Ivor not come up yet?' he asked as they went through the front door. 'Time you made a start on the grounds.'

'No. I've been busy in the house. Trying to get this room cleared so that I can put up my pictures and—'

'And what?'

She pushed open the door of the old waiting-room. It was quite cleared of furniture. A bucket of water and a couple of brushes by the fireplace. Tatters of wallpaper in a great heap in the middle of the floor. Half a wall painted white. Cans of vinyl white emulsion, eggshell white on sheets of newspaper.

'And what?' repeated Archie, taking it all in.

'Oh, assess them. See them *en masse* and have second thoughts, I suppose. You know.'

'Let's get this paper cleared away to start with. Where's your wheelbarrow?'

Without waiting for an answer he disappeared outside and she heard him routing about in the lean-to next to the stable. He was back within minutes and loading a heavy old wooden barrow with the damp mass. She left him to it, too surprised to speak, and went off to the kitchen to cut some cheese sandwiches and put the kettle on for coffee. A pint of beer midday on an empty stomach was making her feel slightly whoozy.

Archie reappeared after ten minutes, flushed and panting.

'I've found a good place for a bonfire and dumped it all there. I'll have another word with Ivor, you can't do everything yourself. Debby's a great one for ideas but she leaves it there. Thanks.' He reached for a sandwich, sank down on a chair, drank his coffee. 'Peaceful. I like it here. You will too.'

'I liked Robert,' said Emma. 'They make a great team, those two.'

'He's not soft,' said Archie. 'He's got balance. Deb's like Prue—' Why, Emma wondered with irritation, did he shorten everyone's name? 'She needs a bit of handling. Like her mother, full speed ahead but as good as gold.' He caught Emma's quizzical look. 'Not that I could ever handle Prue, never tried.'

Emma remembered Prudence; she had been wary of her. Small, neat, dry and tart. She had once been bitten by one of the Hall's dogs, a crossbred Labrador puppy, and had come howling up to the kitchen door where Prudence was washing eggs. The dog had slunk away at once and as Emma sat on a chair Prudence washed away the tiny blood-beaded perforations on her knee and said briskly, painting on iodine, 'I do hope you're not one of those people who go septic.' Emma had shaken her head obediently; she had not gone septic, she wouldn't dare.

'You're in the Lodge, I hear,' she said now, trying to imagine them away from the great rambling house. 'D'you like it?'

'Glad to leave. Yes. Good thing. Time to hand the place on. Prue needed to slow down – won't admit to arthritis, of course – and it's warmer.'

'Have you slowed down, too? I can't see it.'

'I don't need to. I've lived in the slow lane all my life. You know me, Em.' (He was the only person who shortened her name.) 'Born potterer. Do what I like, always have.' He drew out a pipe, held it up for permission to smoke and sucked in the flame of the match through the tobacco with a sigh of pleasure. 'Let me have a go at those walls. You've got brushes, I saw, better than a roller. Damned stuff goes straight up your arm.'

After he had gone, pleased as a schoolboy on a jaunt, Emma washed up, full of amazement that after so many years they had taken up, renewed, a friendship

57

with so little effort. She spent the afternoon sorting out her pictures and at about four, when the light was fading, took two mugs of tea into the front room to see how he was getting on. He was finishing his second wall. The room looked almost luminous. Clean as a deep breath on a winter morning.

'Archie, it's marvellous.'

'Not bad, eh? I'll come up and finish it off tomorrow.'

'Don't forget Harry's going up to look at your tractor tonight. Let me drive you home.'

They sat on the floor, drinking tea, backs to a stripped wall. 'I mean it, Emma. Make myself useful. Yes, I would be glad of a lift back. Don't want to miss the blighter.'

That was the only clue to the long gap of years. Archie was tired.

Word got round the village that Emma had put up her pictures in the doctor's old waiting-room, that there was no carpet in there and the walls fairly blinded you. It wasn't hard to guess who had been talking. Mrs Hughes had taken it upon herself to prop up the Nicholson picture on the mantelpiece and Emma kept it there, partly because it amused her to see the expression on the faces of the casual droppers-in as their fresh country eyes reeled from the drab squares and sudden crudescences of colour of Emma's paintings to rest on the calm conundrum of the one picture they could understand. At least you could see what it was: a picture of a woman, sitting at a table, looking sad, but at least a proper depiction of something human, nicely done as well. The older women remembered it from the past.

'She's in trouble, I'll lay,' said Mrs Hughes. 'Letting herself go.' The retired district nurse, in her seventies, who had cycled up to bring Emma some homemade sloe gin, nodded sagely.

'Makes you think,' she said, in her frail singsong voice. 'I like a picture that makes you think. Up there for years in the doctor's day. There's funny, never noticed it then. Now it jumps at you.'

Emma's paintings weren't supposed to make people think – only feel. What her visitors felt was revulsion. Young Blodwyn, Mrs Hughes's granddaughter, screwed up her eyes and asked, 'Do people pay money for them?'

'Some do,' said Emma.

Blodwyn wouldn't, though. She tried standing a long way off, then close up. The squares and rectangles made no sense to her. The hint of disaster that inhabited them got to her in the wrong way. 'Where's the coffee, then?' she asked, looking at one with the title written in one corner. *Coffee Bar.*

There was a long brown slab of counter, she saw that much, and a hunched-up figure of a girl in a shapeless green coat, back to the viewer. Cigarette smoke made a grey cloud round the sitter's head, a shoe curled round the leg of the stool. Blodwyn couldn't take her eyes off it. She walked round the room, then stood in front of it again, frowning.

'At least you can see that it's someone sitting up there. I'd say she's waiting for her boyfriend and he hasn't turned up.'

So it had got to her, and Emma looked at the picture with some affection. Why shouldn't people take what they wanted from a painting? She had finished with it, after all. Technically it wasn't all that good. She had a brief wish to give it to Blodwyn, but could imagine her horror at having to pin it up on a wall and look at the dull colours every day.

Myfanwy came, looking for a picture for the Lion, hoping for flowers or kittens. She'd even pay Emma, for old times' sake. But she went back to Tom with a long face.

'Why bother to frame them, I say!' she exclaimed.

'You might as well frame one of your muddy footprints on my nice clean carpet . . . look out, will you, Tom, where you tread!' She was cross, she'd thought better of Emma. Real nasty, some of them were. Living in London, that's what did it.

When she was alone one evening, Emma pulled the curtains to and sat crosslegged in the middle of the bare floor on a cushion. By the harsh light of the centre bulb (she'd have to do something about that) she looked slowly round at the walls. What was her object as an artist? To impose order on chaos. But her pictures looked as if the opposite were true: she had imposed chaos on order. Wasn't that the business of art, though, to make people see round corners? Reality was a springboard, where you landed when you leapt off was surely up to you.

But, by God, they *were* ugly. Ochres and browns, greys, purples and dirty pinks. Slabs and cross-hatches. Foggy, indoors and out. They were pictures painted by a creep. A creep who couldn't cope. All right, Camden Town was nothing more than a grey slab of streets set between green parks. But it had its own colour: markets, people. She'd been obsessed by Camden Town. And the Regent canal: the green murk of it, the condoms and empty tins and bicycle wheels eddying in the water. No wonder Alex had beetled off to a nice girl of his own kind.

Her legs were getting pins and needles. She straightened them. She had once gone to meditation classes where a circle of women sat crosslegged like this round a candle. Hands on knees, palms upturned. They were told to stare at the flame, then close their eyes and carry the triangular image to the centre of their foreheads to the third eye. The incandescence and warmth of the flame would then penetrate their whole being, bringing absolute peace. But hateful reason obtruded; the flame became a black triangle; being the imprint transferred on to the retina of the eye, like looking away from a waterfall and seeing the movement again on the side of the mountain. She had always failed to find the inner peace that was promised, and the lotus position was agonizing.

She found herself thinking of Alex again. Her own behaviour hadn't been beyond reproach, if the pictures that surrounded her reflected her state of mind at the time before their breakup. And they did. God! But all the same, he'd no right to send her flying across the kitchen to crash into the washing-machine, then walk out.

St Paul's revelation on the way to Damascus must have been something like this, only he had fallen down in a faint. A pity she couldn't. She felt more like the Troll-King's daughter in *Peer Gynt* with a cast in her eye, which made everything ugly.

A kind of persistent tapping had been going on for some time, and she got up and pulled aside the curtains. In the fading light she made out a dark head. It disappeared as she looked, and then a strangled peal at the doorbell summoned her into the hall. Her head was full of extraordinary lightness as she opened it.

'Bell's broke, is it, missis?'

A grin, half tentative, half sly, showed, for an instant, large flat teeth, white and young. The face was young, too, downy and fair-skinned. He was tallish, long legs in jeans, an anorak slung over his shoulders against the fine rain. One ear-ring.

'They sent me over from the Hall. Ivor Thomas.'

He took it for granted that she would ask him in, and stood in the hall looking about him with frank curiosity. After a moment's hesitation she led the way into the sitting-room at the back. At once he crossed to the French windows and looked out into the long dark garden.

'Said you could do with some help here, missis.'

So this was Ivor, out of a job again. Barely into his

twenties, at a guess. She glanced down at his hands; big for his size. Clean nails. She smiled.

'Why yes. I want to have a clear-out, there's a lot of stuff needing to be cut down in the garden. We'll have a huge bonfire, see what to keep and what's to go. D'you know anything about gardens?'

'You could say I know a nettle from a strawberry. But I'm a dab hand at tree-cutting.' He looked at the fire. 'You'll want logs.'

'Yes. OK. Tomorrow afternoon suit you?'

He nodded, looking slowly round the room, edged off his anorak.

'Tell you what, Ivor, let's have a drink on it.' She went out to the kitchen to get a couple of cans of beer and found he had followed her. Miss Matty had escaped from her kittens and was eating her supper by the Aga. Before Emma could stop him, Ivor had reached down behind the guard and caught up two of the kittens, cradling them against his cheek, making a purring sound with his tongue and lips to stop their cries. They sprawled, starfishwise, in his big hands.

'Pretty, I'll say. You keeping all of them, then?'

'They're having one up at the Hall. I'll have to see about the others. Why, would you like one?'

His face, which had been all smiles, dropped into anxiety.

'Have to ask my dad. There's cats all over at home. Live in the barn for the mice.'

Back in the sitting-room he fed the fire and dropped easily into the low stool near the old armchair, clicked off the disc of his can of beer and took a long drink.

'They told me you'd come back from Aberystwyth,' said Emma, doing the same, although she preferred to use a glass. 'What were you doing there?'

'Butcher's apprentice, but I can't stand blood. So I went into a squat with some mates until the money ran out.'

He didn't have a strong Welsh accent, only a lilt

which made his voice musical. For a cowman's son he was easy in his manner. He looked across at her with a hint of impudence. 'Did you think I was a college dropout, missis?'

Emma pushed back her hair, laughed in some discomfort.

'Well, why not? My daughter's friends are just like you – in and out of jobs, not wanting to go on learning after school. I think it's good to do things with your hands. I do.'

'Oh aye. I've heard you paint. Why do you do that?'

'I enjoy it. I did, that is. Now I'm not so sure.'

Honesty came easily when talking to the young. You owed it to them.

'So you'll be out of a job too.' He shook his empty can suggestively, and she fetched two more.

'They said you used to live here before I was born. Your dad was a schoolteacher at Llandryssil.'

'That's right. He died nearly three years ago. We loved it here.'

'Folk move on,' he said, staring into the fire, shifting a log into place with his feet. 'I shall. I fancy the States. Driving an old jalopy along all those highways.'

'Route 66.'

He began to sing it, waving his beercan.

' "By the time I get to Phoenix",' he said. 'Know that? I like all that old stuff.'

On impulse she got up and searched for the 45. Put it on the turntable and they listened to Glen Campbell.

They sat in companionable silence. When it finished, he got up, said, 'It'll be a treat working for you, missis.'

'Emma,' she said. But he shook his head.

'Mrs Rowlands. Or my mam and dad'll have a fit. See you tomorrow.'

After Ivor began working in the garden the weather changed. High winds tore the last leaves from the fruit trees and maples, tussled with oak and sycamore and horse chestnut, so that they stood half shorn, their branches fidgeting in the troubled air. Leaves lay thick on the ground and Emma shuffled through them with the same pleasure and abandon she remembered as a child. Only the beeches hugged their dry leaves closer, like burning shrouds. Here, she thought, looking up at the swift clouds, you really noticed the seasons changing.

They built bonfires, she and Ivor, the smoke leaning lazy against the wind which kicked up yellow flames from crisping leaves and smouldering rubbish. They discovered late-flowering pansies sheltering behind a mass of goosegrass. They cut back a shabby avenue of laurustinus and buddleia to reveal a grassy walk that led up to the stone seat Mrs Hughes had mentioned, flanked by two huge lolling half-dead lavender bushes. These she trimmed into round balls to set off the classic curve of the seat. When the wind dropped she took her morning coffee out and sat looking across the fields to the Berwyns shouldering away to the west. Black-and-white farmhouses inched up the lower slopes and the sun picked out white scurries of sheep, a square churchtower, a glint of river. A landscape empty of people, pleasingly so. She thought about her mother, about Dr Lewis, and felt grateful, felt blessed.

Sometimes, at dusk, on her way back from the vegetable garden with a snipping of herbs, potatoes that she had dug up like buried treasure, rhubarb, the last of the spinach, she would stop and look up at the sky. The sunsets were biblical; the sinking sun shafted bright needling rays through dark clouds over the western hills. Then, dramatically, like scorched paper burning on a fire, the dying light fringed the grey mass with vivid red.

She pruned every rosebush brutally, although it was probably the wrong time of year, talked to Ivor about laying the hedge properly. Did he know how to do it?

No, he told her, but he could ask the older men who'd been hedgers and ditchers in their time and hated the great mechanical machines that sliced off the top growth and left bare gaps at the bottom. Emma felt mentally invigorated by all this physical exertion, revelling in destruction as she scythed down swathes of great seeding nettles for Ivor to pile into a compost heap.

One morning she took down all the pictures from the front room and carried them upstairs. The room was now like the inside of a white shoebox. Was white the colour of silence? Closing the door on it, she took a stick of charcoal and her sketch pad and wandered out into the garden. There was a particularly spectacular giant hogweed she wanted to sketch before Ivor cut it down. It stood with its bold seedheads set with architectural symmetry, and boldly and cleanly Emma transferred it to paper. Her hand seemed to have discovered a new fluency.

'Don't you ever draw people?' asked Ivor, coming up behind her.

'People?' Never since art school. No, she'd never really wanted to draw people. Shapes, she realized, emerging from shadows, these were her people. Like the girl in the coffee shop that had floored Blodwyn. But she thought about it now.

From the front of the house a bicycle bell tinkled. 'That'll be Megan,' said Ivor. 'You've got some post.'

Emma caught the postgirl before she reached the front door and took letters and cards from her. India, she noted with a jump of the heart. Ivor came up, put his hand on the saddle of the bicycle and said, 'Late, aren't you, today?'

'Oh, you! And get your hand off my bike!'

They grimaced at each other in a sort of complicity, and Megan pushed his hand away.

'Are you bringing all that lot down to the bonfire on the fifth, then?' She gestured to the slaughtered holly bush lying outside the far front window, a great prickly heap of green. 'Or is it bad luck to burn holly?'

'Not if it's as prickly as you, it'll burn up fine. Shall we take it down for the bonfire, missis?'

Emma was already making for the house and half turned.

'Why not?' she said and went indoors.

In the kitchen she made herself a cup of coffee and sat down to decipher the writing on the postcards. Two of them, and a letter as well. Exotic Indian stamps, redirected from Highgate. Her neighbour, Madge, was a good friend, she ought to ring her up. One couldn't just vanish without a word. A card from her mother, too. From Jordan.

> I've been bobbing about in the Dead Sea, darling. Someone took a snap of me lying in it (so warm and bitter) reading *The Times*. Rode through a narrow gap (Siq) in the mountains to Petra. Rose red as promised but just a façade. Sad really. See you before Christmas.
>
> Love Mother.

Putting it aside, Emma settled down to let some of the heat of India seep into her. A picture of some holy man in a saffron robe.

> Rajneesh's Ashram at Pune. Had to have an AIDS test to get in (which is no fun). We pay £12 a day for awareness courses, meditation under the trees, harnessing our chakras. Everyone loves everyone. 'Beautiful' people of all nationalities looking for their 'bliss stations'. No beggars allowed, no dirt, pollution or poverty in this celestial spirit tank, which is quite cut off from the real India, which we return to tomorrow on our way to Goa. Miss U, lots of luv C.

AIDS test? Free love? Was she still on the pill? Why had Emma allowed her to make this trip?

The other card. A temple. Golden Lily Tank at Madurai.

> Lily tank empty! At 4 p.m. entry free and a crowd of women rush in to make puja with flowers, butter and fruit. Goa was beautiful but mad. Disney-on-sea. Fishing-boats caught sharks at night. Beach parties started at 2 a.m., neon-lighted palm trees and fluorescent painted sand. Deafening Acid House music. Trendy people out of their heads, dancing 6 hours nonstop (not me). Leaving for Madras. Love U. C.

Emma sipped at her cold coffee, threw it away, poured out another cup. Opened the letter. There was a snapshot in it. Who was this self-composed beautiful stranger sitting on a rough wall? Long sun-bleached hair, wearing a brightly patterned silk jacket and a minute skirt. Black night behind her and that huge smile for the camera – or the man behind it. A flashlight photo, evidently, and that pointed to Goa with all its goings-on. Where were her daughter's nice serviceable jeans? She was thinner.

The letter was dated about a fortnight ago. Again tiny cramped writing on the thin airmail paper.

> Writing this on a 40-hour train journey from Madras to Delhi. Over 105°F. Every card game exhausted, now playing a board game called the Geeta. Old lady next to me insists on shutting window to keep *out* the heat. I had hysterics getting on the train. Hundreds of shouting angry people trampling over each other, squashing babies, to get in the narrow door. A porter laid about them with a stick, Sammy and Dirk hauled me aboard by my hair, Beth and Linda were shrieking and fell on to my lap . . . I thought we'd be killed.
>
> Now trying to sleep, squeezed like sardines. This is the real India!

Later.

We made it. Now paying £1.50 a night to lie on a roof in the middle of Delhi in the heat and get eaten by mosquitoes. Missing home comforts but becoming a hardened traveller. Crazy country. Everybody spits everywhere, has six fingers. Reams of red tape . . . no efficiency.

What I LOVE. The sun, sea, banana milkshakes, temples, Indian sense of humour – Hindi films and music – saris – BEING HERE.

What I HATE. Cockroaches – awful loos and no loo paper – everything tasting of curry – hard beds, the runs.

MISS your sausages and mash – tap water – my bed.

Haven't slept for three weeks, too hot, too crowded, can't get things together and have ripped my nice spotty Jigsaw trousers. My Walkman was pinched.

Dirk gave me this gorgeous jacket I'm wearing in the photo, d'you like it?

We've met some film people and might go on to Thailand with them. Thanks for money waiting for me here in Delhi. On to Varanase after we've been to Agra (can't miss the Taj Mahal). Why don't you write?

Emma leaned back, breathless. The energy that pulsed from two thin pages in her hand filled her with heat and guilt. Write to her? Where to, for God's sake? Charlotte Rowlands, travelling with two boys and two girls (or should she say young men and women?) somewhere in India – or was she now in Thailand? Long blond hair, ripped Jigsaw pants, liable to hysteria in claustrophobic conditions. Please forward.

Wasn't there an address in Delhi? A relative of one of Charlotte's schoolfriends? She'd ring up Beth's mother, that was it. They could exchange catastrophes. She had forgotten India, her own daughter, in the excitement and strangeness of the move, of the past edging its way back into her life. It wouldn't do; family was important. How could she have let time slip by so disregardingly?

Hang the cost, she thought. I'll telephone Mary right away and get the Delhi number from her.

'Mary?' she said. 'It seems ages—'

'Is that you, Emma? I've been trying to get hold of you for weeks. Where are you? Beth rang me last week—'

Mary was put out. Emma could tell from her voice. She wasn't a close friend.

'I'm sorry, I'm in Wales. Yes. Wales. Yes, it was unexpected. I've sort of moved here – look, I've just heard from Charlotte. Yes. Two delayed cards and a letter from Delhi. Are they still—'

'Charlie's all right now,' said Mary maddeningly. Charlotte was Charlie to her schoolfriends. 'She had a nasty fall in Goa – off one of those scooter bike things they hire. Bad gash on her leg. Didn't she tell you?'

'No,' said Emma faintly. 'She didn't mention it. Can I ring her in Delhi, d'you think? Why are they sleeping on a roof? I thought they would be staying with a relative of yours.'

'Yes. Well. I thought so too. But my brother's engineering firm moved to Varanase and he had to go as well. I'm sorry about that. Beth's staying with him now. I believe the others have gone on to Rajasthan. I don't know where you can reach them.'

The flawless mother of Beth was discomfited, which gave Emma courage.

'Are you sure Charlotte's all right?'

'Oh yes, Beth said her leg had cleared up nicely. She had to go to hospital, pretty awful conditions, but a good doctor, thank God—'

'Charlotte doesn't go septic,' said Emma strongly, remembering for some reason Prudence's adjurations long ago.

'Well, she's lucky. Now, have you got paper and pencil? Here's the Varanase address and number.'

After repeating it all back, Emma thought of something else.

'Charlotte said something about going to Thailand with some film people—'

'Beth definitely won't be doing *that*. I think she's found the whole trip rather exhausting. I've told her to fly straight home.'

Obviously the little group had fallen out. Conciliation was needed.

'Look, Mary, let me give you my address and phone number here. I may not be going back to Highgate just yet. If anything happens, will you let me know? At least Charlotte collected the money I left for her at the bank in Delhi.'

'Right. I've got all that,' said Mary, after Emma had spelt out the Welsh names for her. 'This call must be costing you a bomb in the middle of the day. We'll keep in touch . . . by the way, Dirk's mother rang yesterday. She doesn't seem worried. But they've always let that boy run wild. Don't forget the time zone. Six hours ahead. Give my love to Beth when you ring. Bye now.'

No, Mary definitely was not a close friend. All those subtle digs! She felt sorry for Beth, clever and mousy, drawn along in the wake of extrovert Charlotte. And with a domineering mother as well. But she was the only one of the group to be accepted by Cambridge. It would be good for her.

Six hours ahead. Was that India or Wales? She'd take a chance anyway. She got through quite quickly, unbelievable to think her voice could travel all those thousands of miles . . .

'Mrs Rowlands?'

Yes, it was Beth's voice.

'Oh, Mrs Rowlands, *hullo*. Mummy wondered where you were . . .'

Emma explained, and the little clear voice went on, 'They've all gone off on a sort of camel trek.'

'Camel trek? Where?'

'Rajasthan. Somewhere. But I got the runs quite badly – well, we all did. I felt awful, so I'm staying here with my uncle. There's a swimming-pool. What? No, I'm OK now. I'm flying home soon. I can't wait for a nice cold rainy day and porridge and the buses along Regent Street.'

'What's all this about Thailand?'

There was silence for half a minute. Beth was choosing her words carefully.

'Well, there was this small film unit making a documentary about students travelling around. You know, using the *Rough Guide* – and all that. Charlie's dead keen. They'll pay the fare to Bangkok and living expenses. I'll get her to ring you.'

'It sounds dodgy to me. I don't think Bangkok is all that healthy . . . Anyway, how are the others, Linda, Sammy and Dirk?' Emma realized that she didn't know her daughter's friends all that well, and was alarmed to hear a break in the voice at the end of the telephone.

'Sammy's fine. Yes. He's – he and Linda – look I must go. I'll get Charlie to ring—'

Just in time Emma stopped her hanging up to give her the number to call. Hope she's got it all right. Well, what could you expect? Three girls, two boys. Shake them up together and one has to be the loser in the throw of the dice. Poor Beth.

Next day Emma bought an airmail letter and wrote to Charlotte, explaining the reason for her move from Highgate. She would write a longer one later, she told her. She was glad to have all her news but did Charlotte really think that going on to Thailand with people she'd just met was really such a good idea? Please telephone this number.

What a stupid thing to say, just what you expected from a mother. Charlotte would shrug it aside without a thought. So Emma finished by saying how much

Charlotte would love the house and the surrounding country. Her room was ready for her. If she wanted to write to her father he was in South Africa, staying with his parents. She gave the address. Then made a tiny drawing of Domengastell on its hill, with the far-off mountains behind. She added, 'We're having a firework party on the 5th.'

That was pretty small beer compared to camel trekking in Rajasthan or dropping in on the Taj Mahal, but it suited Emma.

On Guy Fawkes Day she awoke to see the grass brittle with frozen dew, the hedges laced with frosted spiders' webs. Ivor arrived early to help her fold down the seats and load the back of her car with the last of the holly bush and the pruned branches of the buddleia. They drove to the football field where a great bonfire had been prepared. It was already six feet high and small boys were tossing up old cardboard boxes which tumbled down the other side. Ivor took charge, methodically forking in holly around the bottom of the pile. A guy lolled in a wheelbarrow, ready to be strapped into a wooden chair.

'Ten p. for the guy!' they demanded, waggling its limp arm at Emma. In North London the custom seemed to have died out. She hadn't seen a guy touted round the streets for years. Maybe because someone might think it had racist overtones or made an unacceptable religious statement. It looked horrible, a turnip face with someone's old discarded woollen hat on its head. The overstuffed body a deterrent against unhealthy eating habits.

She left Ivor down there and drove back alone, for there was work to do.

Yesterday morning there had been a letter from her publisher. He wanted some rough sketches – bold and in colour – for the enclosed children's stories. Her black-and-white abstracts for the small book of poetry

72

she had illustrated the year before had been a success. Even the poet had liked them. What he wanted now was very different. 'I'll leave it to you, of course,' he wrote, 'but children like realism. It might be fun for you in the depths of Wales, with all that healthy greenery around. Look forward to your ideas.'

It was a small publishing house, run on a shoestring, but the books Mark Ingrams published were all well produced. Arcadia Books, a survivor swimming out of range of the snapping jaws of the giant conglomerates. What he really wanted, she realized, was a lay-out he could use, to cut costs. She settled at the kitchen table when Mrs Hughes had gone home and read through the manuscript. Long after, when she opened her first copy of the published book, the smell of the kitchen would come back to her. The clean soapy dampness of the floor, the ridged damp of the table, scrubbed to whiteness by Mrs Hughes.

They were curious stories, somewhat old-fashioned for today's knowledgeable children, but Mark always knew what was round the corner, that was why he kept afloat. Fantasies, charming. The one she liked best was about a peasant girl who planted a tree which bore four fruits: pears, apples, peaches and plums. There was a king's son, of course, who fell ill and she cured him by giving him one of each fruit to eat. The stones and pips from these must then be planted in one hole at full moon, and then he would have a tree in his garden similar to hers. But the tree must never be cut or harmed or it would bleed to death. Her tree too would die, and so would she . . .

The idea of using colour was exciting and she tried out several drawings. They looked feeble. Water-colour then? Charcoal, gouache with a wash? The tree must stretch up off-centre, through the text, so that the fruit hung temptingly above the words. Words could be chased through the branches. She'd always liked that as a child.

She worked through until late afternoon. Then the telephone rang. It was Debby.

'They're lighting the bonfire at dusk,' she said. 'You're coming, aren't you? The boys are home so we'll all be there with fireworks. Don't be late. We're baking potatoes in the ashes and I'm bringing soup and coffee.'

When she walked down, well muffled up against the cold, Emma saw that the fire was well away, flames already crackling above the spitting holly. The field was crowded with dark figures. Children, wound round with woollen scarves, zigzagged in and out waving sparklers. Firecrackers and squibs enlivened the darkness, making nervous adults jump back angrily, the children shout with laughter. Emma stood on the verge of the field looking round for Debby, then, on impulse, ran back up the hill. She must get all this down on paper. The habit of work was strong because of the intense concentration of the day. She grabbed a pad, charcoal, pencils and drove down to save time.

Flames were creeping up the chair the guy sat on, wickedly devouring his old boots. Pathetic and grotesque as he was, she stood noting it all down, quickly and surely. Sparklers had been stuck in the woollen fingers of his gloves, and now they all caught fire; a statement of frenzy, as if he were celebrating his own death by burning. A small explosion startled Emma. Someone had put a banger in his chest and the body split apart and burning strips of cloth flew off on the night wind all over the crowd.

Archie came up beside her. 'Dangerous, that. Idiotic thing to do. Someone's sure to get burnt. Rhys used to carry stuff round to deal with burns on the spot.'

They could hear scoldings and cries from the scattered crowd, but Archie steered her away to where Debby was keeping an eye on her sons who were setting off rockets stuck in wine bottles. She was annoyed.

'Who did that?' she asked Archie. 'Is anybody hurt?'

'Nurse Gwyneth is coping, as usual,' said Archie with a grin.

'Well, that's something. What we'll do when she dies I don't know. Here, Emma, have some soup. This is Davie, and that's Robbie. Boys, meet Emma. We were at school together.'

They smiled, nodded, lighted their rockets and stood well back. The rockets arched up, then exploded into streams of glittering fragments like a shattered stained-glass window before their slow fall into extinction. Higher still, in a clear sky, the moon rose with its own attendant stars. Good-looking pair, the boys, thought Emma, drinking her soup. Davie's like his father. Robbie has his mother's cheek-bones and dark eyes. Beyond them she noted the shifting shadows; firelight on a cheek, women bending over their children. More rockets hissed up.

'Isn't your mother here?' she asked Debby.

'Too cold for her. She's stayed indoors. Try this potato, but it might taste of paraffin. Some joker poured paraffin on the fire to get it going. Seriously, Robert,' Debby went on, touching Robert's arm as he put a match to a Catherine wheel on a stake, 'this gets rougher every year. Just look at Pudding Harry!'

'Pudding Harry! You can't call him that now!'

'Just look at him, poking about in that fire and his wife trying to pull him back!'

'He's after potatoes.' Archie gave a high neigh of laughter. 'And this one's disgusting, Deb. I'll light my pipe instead.'

Emma saw a fat woman, half Harry's height, throw her arms round his waist from behind, dig her heels in and pull. They fell backwards in a heap.

Across the field three fountains of light started to play; gold, silver, multicoloured. It was a long time since Emma had seen Roman candles – or were they called golden rain? She hadn't celebrated Guy Fawkes

Day for years, since Charlotte was little. Family occasions had been rare.

'I've heard from Charlotte,' she said to Debby now. 'She's having a wonderful time. All sorts of adventures. They might go on to Thailand.'

'Oh, but she'll be back for Christmas, won't she? You're all to come to us, you know. Your mother will be here as well. It'll be like old times.'

'Not quite.' Emma's throat tightened. Nothing could ever be quite like the old times.

'My sister's coming, too,' said Archie, taking her arm in a comforting grip. 'We'll be quite a party.'

'Oh yes. Aunt Letty. And you're not to tease her, Dada. Ma's bad enough.'

The field was clearing and all at once grown-ups and children were aware of the darkness and the cold. Tomorrow small boys would be gleaning the burnt-out fireworks to treasure, boasting that theirs had been the best. Fifty-pence rockets, eighty-pence Catherine wheels. Thrilling to see money burning.

Time to go home. Waving goodbye, she watched the family with a kind of envy. Was it home, that dark house on top of the hill? At least she had her work and that was home enough.

To her surprise Archie and Robert appeared the following afternoon with a rabbit, considerately skinned. She was working upstairs in her studio (for she had taken Debby's advice, and found it safer) on the bonfire party. It was going well. It had a primitive savagery about it that pleased her. She had chosen a large sheet of grey cartridge paper and used chalk; red and yellow, white, gamboge, charcoal. She called to them from the window that the back door was open. They had laid the rabbit on the kitchen table when she came down, bringing the sketch with her.

'Wonderful! Thank you – I love rabbit stew! How about a cup of tea and some bara brith? I made it myself.'

She laid the sketch on the table.

'That's it?' said Archie. 'Bonfire night, eh? How did you get it all down?'

'You can work from a sort of shorthand.'

'You've hit it off.' Robert squinted down at it. 'Hey, it looks as if Harry's wife is pushing him into the fire . . .'

'Don't do any more to it,' said Archie. 'It jumps out at you, like the flames of the bonfire. The guy seems to be crying out.' He looked closer. 'It's as crowded as a Breughel. Have you noticed that people's faces don't really change over the centuries? Walk through any town and you'll see an El Greco or a Hogarth . . . Isn't that young Ivor? You've caught the cocky way he thrusts up his chin.'

'You're right,' said Emma. 'I'll fix it straight away before I spoil it. Mind, it's only a sketch. I don't consider that a finished picture.'

'Pictures,' said Archie, shamelessly wheedling. 'We must be the only people in this village who haven't seen your pictures. How about it now we're here?'

'So that's what the rabbit's for!'

Smiling, Emma led the way along the hall and flung open the door of the old waiting-room. She must stop calling it that, thinking of it as that.

'You can admire your own work, Archie,' she said.

A white shoebox faced them. Immaculate. Nothing except a square cushion in the middle of the floor.

'I say,' Robert exclaimed. 'The Emperor's clothes, eh?'

'Just so.'

'Where are they? What's this?' Over the fireplace, as a concession, Emma had pinned up her study of the giant hogweed.

'Country style. Fresh start. And guess what, Ivor's promised to let me go along on a rat hunt.'

'You know what you're letting yourself in for, do you?' Robert was shocked. 'Rough and gory. I'd have thought—'

77

'Townee too squeamish? Yes I know. He was daring me in a way.'

'And just for that, you'll go.'

'Why not? That and other things.'

She led the way back to the kitchen, put the kettle on to boil.

'I'm sorry, Archie. I've shoved them all upstairs again . . . Later on perhaps, I may . . .'

But it would be a long time, she knew. She had no wish to return to her own vomit, and it occurred to her briefly that had she been a Navaho Indian, making pictures in sand, she could merely have blown them all away.

Some days later Emma picked up Ivor at the bottom of the hill just before seven o'clock. He was leaning against what had been the old school wall, by the little garage. She was all right for petrol, she'd filled up the day before. How far this barn was she didn't know.

'Heavens, Ivor,' she said, as he came towards her. 'You look as if you're going into battle!'

An old ex-Airforce flying helmet gave him a rakish air. As did the scratched leather jacket zipped up over thick denim jeans and high boots. He carried a pair of red agricultural gloves and a heavy iron bar. Grinning, he opened the door and climbed in.

'I am,' he said, licking his dry lips. It was cold. A grey mist curled up from the river, so that the road was half obscured. 'It'll clear up later, so let's go.'

They drove about a mile and then turned up through a farm gate along a rutted lane, dinted with half-frozen ruts and the footprints of cattle. On either side the hedgerows shone black with dew and ragged briars and blackthorn spikes reached across to the car windows. At the top of the lane a farmhouse showed lights in the kitchen and a dog barked dismally at the end of its chain in the yard.

'Carry on,' said Ivor. 'The barn's on the top, across that field.'

Ahead the lane petered out on to muddy grassland. The car bumped over tussocks and Emma put it into lower gear, praying that no random rolls of barbed wire would give her a puncture.

'Land-Rover'd be better,' he said. 'But you'll do.' Thanks very much. Her little Fiesta had been fine for London streets, but this! Ahead the barn loomed black against the white ice of the higher, starved ground. The sky polar-ice blue, colour of cold, not a summer depth. Some half a dozen men and as many half-grown youths in wellingtons, heavy sweaters or Barbours held their dogs on leashes. Jack Russells mostly, keen and speedy. She stopped the car by a battered old Ford with a trailer. Others, of similar age and caked with mud, had been parked in a random mass by another low building. Pigsties, deserted now. There was a smart black saloon, a Land-Rover and a tractor among them.

'That's Glyn's. Particular, he is,' Ivor nodded towards the saloon. 'You want to watch him. He's magic.' He jumped out and shouted. Glyn came over. The son of a German prisoner of war who had worked at a camp in the area, and stayed to marry a local farmer's daughter, so she'd been told. He ran these hunts, it was good business. His father now owned his own farm up at Tregaron.

Glyn was a stocky man with powerful shoulders and a flat, tight face, pink with chill. He flung his arms across his body and stamped as Emma stepped out, carrying a canvas bag with her sketching things.

'Looks smart among this lot,' he said, nodding to the little red car. 'Soon warm up when we get going. Pleased to meet you, but keep out of the way, missis. Women don't like rats.'

'I've never met one,' said Emma coolly, shaking his huge red hand. 'But thanks for letting me come along.'

'Right then, let's get started. Where's Harry?'

There was now a restless mass of dogs in front of the barn. A brown-and-white surge of Jack Russells with a scattering of sharp lean terriers. Whimpering and barking in anticipation, they strained at their leashes, tails going, paws scrabbling with excitement.

Ivor had told her that a pack of twenty could kill as many as a hundred rats on a good day.

It was a big storage barn with a tiled roof and openings on either side, room for haycarts to be driven in back in the old days. Three hundred years old, at a guess. Nowadays it was used for grain storage, in bins.

Emma shivered at the thought of the carnage to come, wandered inside, leaned against the wall and looked around her. It had a gloom and quietness that cut off the confused din from outside. A sturdy geometric symmetry of huge oak beams supported the length and breadth of the walls and the soaring inverted Vs that braced the shadowy roof. Daylight shafted in through cubes and rectangles left by a few shattered tiles. Long rods of dusty light pierced the upper darkness and diffused into daylight halfway down.

Harry passed her, an executioner's figure in his red rubber gloves and black knitted cap pulled well down over his ears. His black sweater had one scarlet word knitted into it. HOSANNA. He carried a chainsaw without the blade; instead a pipe had been fixed.

'This'll smoke 'em out, see?' he flung over his shoulder as he made for the further wall.

A group of youths ran in and started beating the huge grain containers with staves. It seemed as if a heavy-metal band filled the barn. Emma slipped out before she was ordered to do so. She was nearly tripped up by the dogs, now released. And all hell broke out. Rats were suddenly everywhere, swarming over the tops of the containers, running across the floor, leaping up at the walls, dashing for exit holes.

The dogs were on them, urged by the shouts; they

pounced, shook, left the dead and went on joyfully to despatch the living. The floor heaved with a black, white, brown tide, splashed with red. A shout from above as Glyn, astride a beam, flailing an iron bar, beat down rats on to the men and dogs below. Yelping, squealing, savage laughter, fear and a hot excited rage and exhilaration filled the barn from floor to roof as the sun rose higher and the frost melted on the ground outside.

Emma's hand trembled as she slashed swiftly at her pad with a stick of charcoal. It was a hopeless task, but it kept her from being sick. She retreated further from the opening and watched a line of four youngsters with their dogs, who had been set to stop that escape route. As a squealing tide of terrified rats poured out they beat about them with pitchforks and heavy sticks while their dogs finished off the crawling wounded. One boy had an airgun and pot-shotted dangerously at escapees.

'Daft bugger, leave it to Scorcher or you'll hit him!' yelled an undersized lad with huge kicking boots. The boy with the gun had RATS painted on his motor-cycle helmet and out of bravado fired up into the air.

'Scares 'em, though, dunnit?' he yelled back, hate blazing in his eyes.

Then a huge rat, as big as a size-twelve wellington boot, ran across Emma's foot. From its pointed muzzle came blood and a keening sound. Up dashed a small Jack Russell and seized it behind the ears. He got it down on the ground, but it gave a convulsive jerk, and twisting upwards bit hard into the dog's throat, hanging on as it was thrown from side to side.

'Come on, Scorcher, shake 'im, boy! Kill 'im!'

But the rat was nearly as big as the dog and Emma watched, terrified, unable to move. This was a nightmare. At that moment Ivor ran past her and she grasped his arm.

'That dog will be killed, oh—'

Ivor snatched the pitchfork from the yelling boy and neatly skewered the rat as it clung, not touching the dog. The jaws relaxed, the rat twitched in its last agony on the prongs and the dog sank on to the ground, shaking its head groggily.

'It's a monster and Scorcher got it. It's a monster an'—' The lad was pulling the rat off the prongs of the pitchfork by its tail, when Ivor, his face mottled with anger, hit him hard. The lad toppled over sideways, rat in hand, landing by his coughing dog.

'What's that for then?' he asked. 'Scorcher got it. It's Scorcher's.'

'It damn nearly got Scorcher, you young fool! That dog's too young for the hunt. I told you not to bring him. Glyn'd say the same. Now he's bitten. He might die. Stupid little git. Now get him to the vet.'

The boy's mouth drew down at the corners. He couldn't be more than twelve. He stretched out a hand to the shivering dog, looked up at Ivor. But Ivor flung off back into the barn.

'I'll miss the rest of it—' he said, torn. Emma saw that the little dog was only half grown.

'I'll take you,' she said, helping the boy up. 'What's your name? You carry Scorcher.'

'Scorcher would've finished 'im off. We get prize money for the biggest rat. I'd better hide it else someone'll pinch it off me. I'm Dewi.'

He shoved the rat under the stone wall and piled stones on it. Then he picked up his dog and followed Emma to the car. It didn't cross his mind to thank her, but as he sank on the seat, the dog in his lap, he caressed its head and gave a long sigh. There was blood on his boots.

'You won't peg out, will you, Scorcher? Not you. You're a champion you are. In't he, missis?'

They were driving at a fair pace across the field. Emma could have kissed Dewi. She had been able to retreat with dignity, with a purpose. They negotiated the overgrown lane, and the chained-up dog gave its mournful greeting as they passed the farmhouse. The day was clear and blue now, warm for November. Across the fields the sound of church bells blew towards them. Sunday, a day of prayer.

She followed Dewi's directions, hoping the vet was in, his midday Sabbath dinner finished. The time had fled.

'Ivor probably saved his life,' said Emma, and Dewi grunted.

Morgan Griffiths was in, playing a small harmonium in the front room for his mother and sisters. One of those born to bachelorhood was Emma's first impression as he led the way to the surgery. He looked well-fleshed and docile, but his manner changed as he closed the door between his work and the rest of the house. He looked keenly through his spectacles, his hands touched the little dog with professional firmness.

'Put him up on here, Dewi,' he said. 'Ratting, were you? This fellow's got a bit to go to his full strength. He's like you, bach, got to fill out, get some muscles.' He reached over and squeezed Dewi's upper arm. 'Get some biceps, man. Duw, plenty of porridge.'

He cleaned the torn throat. 'Nasty bite that—'

'He near killed a monster, big as your boot—'

'I'll have to give him an injection. Hold him still now.'

While he swabbed a place on the dog's backside, then deftly slid in the needle, pushing the plunger down, Emma asked whether a rat's bite was poisonous.

Mr Griffiths withdrew the syringe, swabbed again and looked at her directly for the first time.

'Ever heard of Weil's disease?' She shook her head. 'Carried in rat's saliva, and its urine. A rat urinates every thirty seconds. Contaminates everything it touches.' He turned again to Dewi. 'Come you now, boy, and wash your hands while I wash – what's this fellow's name?'

'Scorcher,' said Dewi.

'Scorcher's neck and head and belly. See what I'm doing? You do the same, soap around the nails, now, then use a paper towel. Particular you have to be. How about you, missis?'

'I'm Emma Rowlands. I've moved back to Bryntanat.'

'Good of you to bring the lad here. Better wash your hands, just in case. And you, my lad, should be wearing rubber gloves.'

As she and Dewi did as they were told, Mr Griffiths dried his patient with paper towels and went on talking.

'Rats. Need a Pied Piper to get rid of them. Warfarin's meat and drink to them, especially now some farmers are growing maize. Love maize, those creatures, makes 'em immune to warfarin.'

'It's good fun, ratting,' said Dewi. 'We'll get near a hundred today, counting the old pigsties after the barn. You should have seen Glyn, Tregaron, up on the beam. Grand he was.' He looked at his dog lying obediently on the table. 'Scorcher'll be a champion, won't he, Mr Griffiths, when he gets better?'

'*If* he gets better, Dewi. If luck and the Lord agree. Then he won't get poisoned again. Once bitten, no more trouble. Have to watch, mind. Keep him quiet, warm bread and milk.' Abruptly he turned to Emma, adjusting his spectacles with a large, soft very clean hand. 'Know why the men carry pheasants home from a shoot by the necks, Mrs Rowlands?' So he had spotted her wedding ring. Should she after all keep it on? Looking down at it now, as she dried her fingers, it seemed like a forged passport. 'Dewi knows, ask him. His father beats for Talycoed.'

As they left, Mr Griffiths said again, 'Straight home with him now, and let me know how he goes on. Quiet and comfy he needs to be for a day or two.'

There seemed to be no mention of money.

'He was nice,' said Emma as they drove on down to Dewi's father's smallholding. 'Didn't seem to mind working on a Sunday.'

'Animals don't know it's Sunday,' said Dewi with a child's logic.

'What about those pheasants? Why do—'

'Don't want to touch their feet, see? Rats pee in ditches, dirty the water. Birds get it on their feet, drink it too.' That put Emma right off eating pheasant.

At the cottage Dewi's parents were sitting down to their dinner. When they saw the car draw up, they both came to the door. They were as small-boned as their son, the mother as pale-eyed. She stood with bowed shoulders by her husband, who was still chewing.

'You've got your treacle butties for dinner,' she called out in a complaining voice as Dewi ran up with the dog in his arms.

'What's wi' Scorcher, then?' asked his father. 'And who's this?'

Emma had followed, after waving from the car in what she hoped was a friendly manner. She introduced herself and explained what had happened. They stared at her in silence, then at their son. Emma feared for Dewi. Would they hit him as Ivor had done?

'It was a very big rat,' she said.

'Aye, an' Scorcher had it by the throat, but Ivor got it off him with a pitchfork. It was as big as, as big as—'

'Never mind that,' his mother interrupted. 'Our dinners are getting cold. Put the dog in his kennel. I'll get a bit of blanket.'

'And vet'll be paid out of your earnings,' added his father. 'Going back now, are you?'

'Yes,' said Emma. 'And Mr Griffiths said the dog will need some warm bread and milk.'

'Did 'e now? Off you go, then.' And the door was shut. After a moment, as they walked down the path, it opened again and the mother called them back.

'Come you here, Dewi. Here's a bit of blanket. He can lie by the fire when you come back. Go on now.'

'Ta, Mam,' and Dewi ran back to the kennel, tucked up his dog and got in the car. 'He's near enough asleep,' he told Emma. 'Mam'll see to him. Bark's worst than 'er bite.'

They looked at each other and burst out laughing.

When they arrived back the hunters were taking a break and sitting about eating cold sausages and sandwiches and swigging cans of beer. A crate of cans stood by the pigsties' wall.

'Them next,' grinned the youngster who had been showing off with his airgun. 'We've scooped up the buggers we got in the barn.'

A trailer full of grey and black bodies sleek as fish stood at a distance, for which Emma was thankful. Dogs lay panting on the ground, some bleeding from scratches about the neck and nose, some drinking from a large shallow basin of water that had been brought for them.

'Gives 'em a thirst, like us.' Ivor came up to Emma with a couple of cans of beer. 'How's Scorcher?'

'Sorry for himself. The vet gave him an injection. We took him home. He's tucked up in his kennel.'

'He'll be all right in a day or two. Strong little beast. If he gets over this he won't get Weil's again.'

'Isn't it a killer?'

'Can be.'

They drank in silence. The beer was nectar.

'I can't get over your enjoying all this when you told me once you couldn't stand the smell of blood in a butcher's shop.'

Ivor laughed.

'Well, this is different, in't it? Cutting up dead animals is disgusting. Never had a chance, did they? Turned me off meat. Hunting live ones is all right. Specially rats.'

'What will you do with that lot over there? The dead ones?'

'Feed 'em to the pigs. Nothing's wasted. Farmers pay us to keep 'em down. They're happy. We have a good day's fun. We're happy. There's a hunt ball at Christmas. Praps you'll come.'

Emma sat stunned. A Ratcatchers' Ball. Did they wear hunting pink?

Men and boys started to move towards the pigsties. She had had enough and walked into the empty barn. Were all battlefields as quiet after the slaughter? She sat on some piece of agricultural machinery and made a more detailed drawing of the interior, using charcoal and smudge-stick. What a setting for the old mystery plays! All the austerity and simplicity of the early churches were echoed here. Perhaps it was a tithe barn, that might explain it.

In a far corner a rat rustled quietly away and she was glad of it. She was all for survivors.

Much later that evening, while Emma sat in the kitchen drinking cup after cup of tea, she began to shake uncontrollably. The cup dropped out of her hand and she watched the liquid spilling down to the floor, dripping off the table edge. Like blood.

Since returning home she had been in a state of hyperactivity, restacking logs that had fallen to the back of the outhouse, carrying armfuls into the house, lighting fires against the insidious chill. Her mind was full of pictures which she tried to shut out by cursing the cold, working out how she could instal central heating – and all the time aware of a shameful excitement, self-disgust and a pumping of adrenalin that would not let her rest.

Was this how war reporters, war artists felt, noting the slaughter, not taking part? Watching the precise mechanics of dealing out death and suffering it – but vicariously? Was cruelty the oldest of tonics? Violence

– except on the few occasions when Alex had lost his temper in infantile tantrums and slapped her – had never been part of her life. Her mind felt clear and empty as she watched the spilt tea settle in a puddle at her feet. She no longer wanted to think about Alex, but the stamping and shouting and beating sticks of the morning had somehow stirred him up again; brought him to the surface like a dead fish, belly-up in a pond.

Maybe she was the kind of woman who craved violence, and so provoked it. But she didn't think so; the sad sobriquet of a battered wife did not apply to her, for between victim and attacker there was so often a tight if unacknowledged bond of compatible provocation, an undertow of sexual excitement that engendered pleasurable fear. In the papers she had read about women putting up with such treatment for years. What made men behave this way? Did they hit out under the goad of failure, the fear of being left alone? She had made all these excuses for Alex, but in the end had recognized it was something much simpler; Alex had feared social opprobrium more than anything else.

He had simply wanted a wife who fitted in, set him off, did things the way his parents did. He required an ordered home life with the spotlight on himself and the male privilege of one or two brief affairs; a competent tennis partner, a presentable hostess adept at social chat. Within such a framework Alex could thrive and give a good account of himself. As such, of course, he was an anachronism.

'I must have a bath. Wash all this off.'

The kittens looked up at the sound of her voice. How they were growing! Prowling about, tonguing the spilt tea and veering away to bat at each other.

The bathroom was cold, of course, with no heating. She turned the taps on full and watched the water running into the noble bath. Scented steam rose as she poured in a reckless dollop of Badedas and noted with pleasure the slow greening of the water. The bath was as commodious as a Roman sarcophagus. She fetched her portable radio from the bedroom and made up her fire, noting how the little shell house gleamed on the shelf over the fireplace. She was becoming used to living alone; enjoying the freedom it gave her. Would her mother ever come to terms with it? Probably not, she was of a different generation and had not suffered the steady growth of antipathy that had eroded Emma's marriage. Yet they were both in the same situation, women without men; opening their front doors on to silence and emptiness.

As she peeled off her clothes, discarding the dirty layers of the day, it occurred to Emma that she had never been able to discuss this aspect of their common condition with her mother. Maybe, when she saw her, there might be an opportunity. Just now she needed the voices on the radio, however trivial, to keep her company. She sank into the warm water, noting how steamy the bathroom was, and sat soaping and sponging her shoulders and breasts, relaxing from unbidden memories and tired out with the energies of the long day. Lying back, her hair floating on the water – later she could shampoo it in the bath as she used to as a child – she thought of Ivor. He had cut quite a figure in his flying helmet, his face innocently alive with laughter, photographing the scene before joining in the action. He had told her once that he had shared a tin bath with his sister in front of the kitchen fire when he was little. An absurd thought crossed her mind as she watched her feet floating free. This bath was big enough for two, as she had once mentioned to Debby; and for a moment she imagined Ivor sitting at the other end, his thin young shoulders white against the weathered red of his face and neck, big brown hands at the end of pale arms, like the big work-a-day hands of Michelangelo's *David* she had seen in Florence. She remembered the gentle way he had picked up the kittens that first day in the kitchen, the swift despatch of Dewi's giant rat. It crossed her mind that she might, possibly, make a drawing of him. He would be sure to have a dramatic photograph of himself to show her. At this moment, she thought, idly washing her hair, he would be with some girl. Who? Megan, perhaps? And what would become of him? Would he ever make it alone to America, drive a jalopy along Highway 66, or settle for a local girl, those endless horizons merely a dream?

Later, swathed in a bath towel, watching the water vanish, the bathroom clear of steam, she thought fleetingly that it would be a better ending to the day if someone else was doing the drying, someone else brushing her hair as she crouched in front of her bedroom fire, spreading out the bright strands between her fingers. A philosophical acceptance of the solitary life, after all, went only so far.

Ivor came the next day, out of a bitter, darkening afternoon. Emma heard the strangled peal of the bell and went to open the door, glad of an interruption of her work. He stood there, his flying helmet a protection against the nipping wind. The weather blew in with him, and she motioned him into the hall and shut the door.

'I could fix that bell,' he said, as they went through into the kitchen. Her work was spread over the table, and she pushed the sketches aside. 'But you'd be better off with a knocker. See, I've got a present for you.'

He reached into his pocket and brought out a heavy parcel, wrapped in newspaper. 'Got it off a mate at the market. There.' He pulled out an old brass lionhead door knocker, dark with years, heavy and enduring.

'Oh,' said Emma, reaching out to touch it, 'it's handsome, Ivor! How good of you. Why, thank you—'

'I came round last night to show you the polaroids, but you didn't hear that old bell,' he said accusingly.

'There wasn't a light downstairs, so I thought you'd gone to bed early.'

'I was having a bath.' In spite of herself she coloured up.

'Aye, we all needed one. Good day out. You did well, missis. Anyroad, I thought you could do with this. I'll screw it on tomorrow.'

Emma filled the kettle, put it on to boil. Ivor stood by the table, looking down at the layouts for the children's book. Delicate drawings tendrilled across the text she had sketched in. A black cat flew above a chimney, chasing a flying mouse. He put out a hand, drew it back.

'Thought you'd be drawing rats not cats,' he said, and pulled out a packet of photographs. 'But they're pretty.'

'They're for a book of children's stories.'

'These aren't.' He grinned, and spread them on the table. Bringing their tea over, with slices of fruit cake, Emma glanced down at them. Mostly of men and boys, posturing outside the barn with dead rats tied by the tails to long sticks, boastfully grinning. One dramatic shot of Glyn up on his beam, a rat dropping from it.

'That's good,' said Emma. She could use that. The others were disappointing; blurred because of the movement. Instant photography had its limits. 'What about this, then?'

Naturally, a picture of Ivor with a pitchfork in one hand, a rat in the other, pure joy on his face. Bold the pose, shoulders back, one foot forward like a warrior. She looked closely at it, Ivor breathed over her shoulder.

'Would you feel like doing me proper? With pencil or paint. You could use that photo.' He was watching her face. 'Look, I took this one of you.' When had he taken it? She thought he had vanished into the barn while she was bending over Dewi's little dog. 'You didn't puke, nothin' like that. Glyn was waiting for you to puke.'

Puking took a time to catch up on her. Lucky, that was.

'I do hate being called missis,' she said. 'We're friends, Ivor. Call me Emma and I might do a smashing charcoal sketch of you that you can show everyone.' She saw that the door knocker had been a sweetener and so had the photographs. Well, she could play that game too.

Now he shifted uneasily, eyed her with trepidation; enough of a village lad to know what people would say.

'Well, only when we're alone. The Hall wouldn't like it.'

'They're twenty years behind the times, Ivor. Anyway, Mr Wentworth is years and years older than I am, but I've always called him Archie.' She sorted slowly through the photographs to give herself time. 'And if you're going to the States, it's all first names over there.'

He brightened up.

'I could backpack with a mate once I've saved the fare.'

'Come on then,' said Emma firmly. 'Let's put on the Glen Campbell nice and loud and you can pose for me in the big room. There's a good central light.'

As she started to draw him Ivor looked round the white empty room, down at the floor, shifted his legs. He was hopelessly self-conscious, which surprised her.

'Can't you just copy the photo?'

'No. It's better from life. I'll use the photo for details later.'

'I feel a damned fool, that's what,' he said. 'What shall I think about?'

'Oh,' said Emma, concentrating on her work, 'think about going to bed with some nice girl. But keep still, do.'

He was still. His arms dropped to his sides with shock.

'Well, missis – Emma – that's a funny thing to say – I'll think about your floor instead, if you don't mind. You were going to sand it, you said. I could sand it for you, make it smooth.'

'Why, thanks very much, Ivor. I'll hold you to that.'

She hummed along with Glen Campbell, blaming herself for such a crass suggestion. One should respect the reticences of the untried. What was the matter with her?

As she glanced at his face to check that his chin was up she caught his eye. It was fixed on her in pure fright.

'I'm sorry, Ivor. I didn't mean to embarrass you. Trouble is, at art school we always talked like that. It gave us all a laugh, and made the model relax.'

'How much do they get paid? Models?'

'A life-class model would get between six pounds and seven fifty an hour. If you posed six hours a day, that's about forty pounds. Not bad.'

She'd got the right stance now. She could sketch in the barn as background later. It was that face. It didn't fit. In the photograph he'd been laughing, reckless. Here he looked hangdog in spite of his one jaunty earring.

'I'd rather do your garden for five.'

To make amends she said, 'I'll pay you thirty a day if you'll sand this floor for me, if that's what you'd like. There's nothing to do outside in this weather.'

'Right, you're on. There's this mate of mine. He'll let you hire a sander from his shop.'

That was better. The expression on Ivor's face was now more the hunter than the hunted.

'Look a bit triumphant, Ivor. Think about that whopping rat you've just skewered. That's better.'

She worked on and watched those flat teeth show in a smile. Now he matched the flying helmet. Had the original owner smiled in such a way, and had he survived?

She went through to the kitchen to fetch a couple of cans of beer, hunted through her records and found *The Planets*. Put on 'Mars' and as the first swelling chords echoed through the house, handed Ivor his beer as he looked greedily at himself, the warrior.

'Ivor,' she said, 'this is no longer the waiting-room. Its waiting days are over. I'll just call it the big room. Not the Enormous room, just the big room.'

So they clashed cans to toast the new name. But she wondered about the ear-ring he wore. It seemed out of character somehow.

'I did warn you,' said Robert.

They were sitting round the kitchen table, all of them. Debby and Robert, Archie and Prudence. Emma had judged it time to return some hospitality. She had, with Mrs Hughes's help – for the Aga tended to be temperamental – cooked roast lamb, and the roast potatoes had been perfect. Roast parsnips with garlic. The last of the perpetual spinach from the garden for she had set herself against frozen peas. A good old-fashioned bread-and-butter pudding or plum-tart. Mrs Hughes had made the pastry, providing her own bottled plums. Cheeseboard with Bath Olivers.

'Them up at the Hall knows good food,' she had said threateningly when Emma suggested a lemon mousse. So it had to be good nursery food and Debby had enthused over the pudding.

'Our weekenders might like something really English like this,' she said. 'But it can be tricky.'

'Not if you use a bain-marie,' said Emma, who had not wished to try to outdo them up at the Hall by serving a sophisticated meal. She didn't regard herself as a good enough cook. 'Some London chefs put whisky in it.'

'I wouldn't care for that,' said Archie. 'I dote on

94

bread-and-butter pud just like this, especially with cream.'

'We'll have coffee in the little sitting-room,' said Emma. 'It'll be a bit of a squash, but there's a fire. I promised not to talk about the rat hunt until we'd eaten.'

'Do we have to, now?' asked Prudence, making a moue. 'I don't really approve of all this fraternizing, Emma. They're rough types.'

That was when Robert had said, 'I did warn you.'

'Yes,' she said, bringing in the coffee. 'It was pretty horrible, but so – dramatic. I managed to get something down. That was why I went. I know Ivor meant it as a kind of dare. And I wanted to ask you about the old barn up there. Is it a tithe barn? The proportions are marvellous.'

'I believe it was part of an old priory a hundred years ago. Not a lot of it left now, of course. The locals always carted away the stones for their own buildings.'

Archie's long legs took up most of the space in front of the fire. Prudence had the other armchair and Robert and Debby sat in the small sofa, Emma on the Lloyd Loom chair she had brought from the boxroom. Tidied up, the room wasn't too bad, there was even space for a low table on which she put the tray. All the same, the walls could do with a coat of paint.

Debby said, 'I don't want to interfere, Emma, but what if you knocked down the wall between this room and the surgery? You'd have a sitting-room this side and a dining area at the other end.'

'This was Rhys's private den, wasn't it? He used to keep his poisons cupboard in here.' Archie was looking round with lively interest. 'Over there, on that bookshelf.'

'Mrs Hughes called it his snuggery. He used to play his records on that wind-up gramophone. I wonder she didn't take it when he died. I've just put my record-player on the top.'

Prudence looked up from her coffee. 'But there's a perfectly good dining-room already, surely? What about the waiting-room?'

At once on the defensive, Emma said, 'Well. No. It's too big, Prudence—'

'She keeps it for her pictures, Ma.' Debby, protective as she had always been, covered up for Emma. 'But what about an archway through that wall into the old surgery? Or a sliding door? Or—'

'Let's just enjoy our coffee, shall we? There's plenty of time for Emma to decide what she wants—'

Emma smiled across at Robert. It was good to have allies.

'You see,' she said, 'I thought Charlotte might like to have a room of her own, apart from her bedroom. If she brings friends to stay . . . Well, she could have the old surgery.'

She hoped her daughter would bring friends to stay. It had only at that moment occurred to her. 'I'll have to do something about it, of course.' She caught Archie's eye, and he winked.

'When do you expect her, then?' Prudence was only half satisfied. 'And when will Adela be coming?'

'I haven't heard. But Mother will be here in December, of course.'

'I want to hear how you got on last Sunday. Any more coffee? It's good.'

Archie passed his cup to Emma and at once she said, 'Oh it was – well, it was exciting. All that energy, that's what got to me. I've never seen anything like it.' She ignored Prudence's shudder of distaste. 'They were bursting with it. But isn't there any other way of getting rid of rats?'

'Not really. They're getting immune to warfarin—'

'That's what the vet said. Meat and drink to them, he said.'

'Morgan Griffiths? Don't tell me he was there!'

'No, I had to take a boy and his dog to him. A rat bit

him – the dog, not the boy. Dewi. His father's one of your beaters.'

'Prys the Gelli. I know him. Yes. Surly chap.'

'I'm not against rat hunts,' said Archie. 'They've been going on for hundreds of years, like foxhunting. Only way, face-to-face combat. Lets off lots of steam. Good day out for the lads. Dogs enjoy it, keeps 'em keen.'

'They got well over a hundred.'

'Archie's right, gets rid of a lot of aggression,' said Robert. 'I expect your London streets would be safer if the local councils organized rat hunts for the young-sters. Regular employment. Sense of achievement. Better than hanging about in alleys waiting to mug old ladies. People are full of anger.'

'Think of all those warehouses – the ones that haven't been turned into fancy flats.' Archie pursued the idea with relish. 'London's swarming with rats, they come up out of the sewers, out of the river in a black tide. Read your Dickens—'

'Oh, stop it, Archie! It's not a joke. You can't have gangs of ruffians armed with sticks or whatever, roaming about the streets.' Prudence was flushed with annoyance.

'Why not? It's a novel idea. People shouldn't bottle up their anger. Think of all the battles fought over this border country. Round this village. English against Welsh, and before that Romans against British. Robert's got something there. I wonder we don't plough up centuries-old bones. I always think of it when I walk across Offa's Dyke.'

Emma thought it time she cooled the atmosphere with a joke.

'I couldn't believe it', she said, laughing, 'when Ivor told me they held a Ratcatchers' Hunt Ball at Christmas. And a stirrup cup—'

'Stirrup cup! Hunt Ball! That's pushing it a bit far. It's a travesty. Archie—' Prudence appealed to her husband, at a loss.

'I expect Emma will enjoy the Boxing Day Meet much more, Prue. There aren't any hunt saboteurs round here – not yet. And there's more style in hunting foxes than hunting rats.'

'I remember it, you know, from when I was a child,' said Emma. Tonight was not the time to argue the rights and wrongs of hunting. 'My mother rode one year, didn't she?' Her father had kept away.

Safe in the past, Prudence nodded. Arthritis had forced her to give up riding, but the thrill of following the hounds even in memory revived her.

'Mind you,' Archie said thoughtfully, 'there are some so-called country sports I do hate. Otter-hunting and hare-coursing, for instance. Oh, and that reminds me, Emma. I was looking through those notebooks of your father's which Adela brought when she came to the doctor's funeral. Fascinating stuff—'

'What notebooks?' Emma was mystified and slightly put out.

'Research notes, mostly on the history of this parish. He'd nosed out some curious facts. There used to be what was called an annual hare-mobbing on the third Sunday in October, to celebrate the festival of dear old Garmon, our patron saint—'

'Hare-mobbing, what on earth . . . ?' Robert had sunk back, his eyes closed. He felt he had contributed enough to the conversation. 'There aren't many hares round here, not mobs of 'em, surely—'

Debby nudged him sharply, then grimaced at her father.

'Robert's half asleep. He was up at dawn, worrying about the cows. Do go on, Da. Don't you mean hare-coursing?'

'No. But it sounds a barbaric variation. The wretched animal was beaten out of its hide and greyhounds set on it. All the villagers yelled and chucked their hats and stones at it to scare it out of its straight run. Half of them were drunk, of course. Hugo quoted from the rector of the time as saying it was "an outrage upon humanity".'

'Like birds mobbing an owl in daylight,' said Debby. 'How horrible. When was it stopped?'

'Hugo doesn't say. Sometime at the beginning of this century, I imagine. So you see, Prue, cruelty has always been part of country life. We're all born with a streak of it.'

His wife stirred restlessly.

'Don't include *me*, Archie. And why St Garmon's Day should ever have been celebrated – if one can use such a word – in that horrible way I simply cannot understand. I think this conversation has gone far enough. I'm sure my digestion won't stand any more.' With practised ease she began to speak about Adela's trips abroad and the charming cards she had sent; how interesting it would be to hear all about her adventures at Christmas.

So the rest of the evening passed off pleasantly enough in harmless small talk. But when they walked through the hall on their way out, Prudence paused.

'This was the waiting-room, wasn't it?' she asked, touching the handle. 'Do let me see what you've done with it, Emma.'

Emma opened the door and stood back.

'I've still got to sand the floor, it's so rough,' she said.

The big white empty room confronted them, harsh in the centre light. Just one charcoal drawing over the fireplace, Ivor triumphant, outside the barn brandishing his rats. Pinned up on the walls were sketches of rats – leaping, running, climbing, lying dead. Men's faces emerging from shadows, boots trampling, pitchforks raised, sticks coming down. Dogs attacking. Quick studies of heads, paws, tails waving. The barn, interior and exterior.

As she heard the sharp intake of breath from her guests, Emma said gently, 'Just getting my hand in. I'm

99

out of practice with animals. I get a better idea of what's wrong with them when they're up on a wall.' And closed the door.

'It seems such a waste of space, my dear,' was all that Prudence could find to say, faced with such horrors. The others said nothing.

'I like wasted space,' said Emma, suddenly angry. She had not wanted them to see these working sketches, unfinished as they were, and anyway part of a much bigger project that excited her. 'I think space should be wasted, otherwise it isn't spacious.' There was a ring of truth about this off-the-cuff pronouncement that delighted her.

On the doorstep Prudence kissed her and said, 'Thank you so much for a lovely meal, dear.'

But in the car on the way home, Prudence spoke her mind. Her words were brief and to the point.

'I do hope', she said in even tones, 'that Emma is not going to set herself up as an oddity and regard it as a duty to shock us. That would make things very difficult.'

Archie, concentrating on his driving, wisely said nothing.

PART 3

December brought flurries of snow and a white light that cast a clear reflection into each room at Domengastell. With Ivor's help, Emma lifted the old cracked lino from three bedrooms and asked him to sand the floors. He had brought his mate Mervyn to give him a hand with the sanding of the big room.

Mervyn was one of the black Welsh from the south: small, dark-haired, sharp brown eyes and quick on his feet. He showed Ivor, who against him seemed slow and cumbersome, how to work the machine. Emma, coming into the room with coffee for them at midmorning, had reeled back at the noise, the fog of fine dust and the two masked men, goggles on and white scarves wrapped round their heads and ears.

'It's the dust, missis,' Mervyn had coughed at her. 'There'll be dust on that coffee. We'll come out for it.'

In the kitchen Mrs Hughes told them to shake their wrappings outside before they sat down or the dust would be all over everything. But Mervyn soon had her in a better humour, offering her cigarettes and telling her of the great bargains he had on his market stall come Thursday.

'You'll be wanting rugs for them rooms upstairs, doubtless,' he said. 'Else the cold'll strike through the floorboards. Cold old house, this. And shall I be on the lookout for some radiators?'

'You watch him, Emma. He's so sharp he'll cut himself . . .'

But Mrs Hughes shook her head at him almost flirtatiously. Good women never could resist a rogue.

He winked at Emma, looked at her out of his bold eyes and asked how she liked the door knocker. Ivor had told him she hadn't heard the old bell because she was still in her bath. Pity, that.

'I've done that door knocker with half a lemon, and given it a good polish. Come up lovely, that has,' said Mrs Hughes, who did not approve of baths being mentioned in mixed company.

Emma intended to stain and polish the floors in the two smaller bedrooms to get them ready for her mother and Charlotte. The wallpaper in the room she had chosen as a guestroom would do for the moment, it had faded into quite a pretty primrose stripe and she had made curtains to enhance the colour. She would have to think about her daughter's room. There was no hurry. Beds could be made up at the last minute, fires lighted.

She had a surprise when she went into the big room off the hall that evening, when Ivor and Mervyn had finished. She had forgotten to take down the sketches of the rat hunt and each one was filmed over with fine wood dust. The dust clung to the coats and ears of the animals, giving them a furry look. Almost *trompe-l'œil*. All at once she knew what to do.

She spent more than an hour, working carefully. Using her fixing spray and a fine brush, she cleaned off the dust from the background in some sketches and left it on the bodies; then sprayed them. It was extraordinary, almost a new medium. Cleaning dust from the eyes gave an alert shine to them; the animals looked alive. Leaving a dusty film in the interior of the barn so that the sunlight caught dust motes, made them shimmer in the gloom. Cleaning the dust off the dogs' white-and-brown bodies made them stand out against the faint haze.

Tomorrow she would take them upstairs. Just now a glass of whisky and the concert on Radio 3, a hot-water bottle and bed.

The telephone rang, loud and clear. Charlotte at last?

Not Charlotte. A familiar voice though. She recognized that worried gabble pouring into her ear.

'Madge? How are you? You got my letter, then?'

'Yes, oh yes. But Emma, something awful's happened. You've been burgled. The police—'

'Burgled?'

Emma slid down to the floor, cradling the telephone on her lap.

'I went in yesterday to collect your post and check up, you know. And it's bitterly cold here, Emma. I thought I might switch on your heating. Damp, you know, it gets into an empty—'

'Madge, how bad is it? Is the flat messed up? What's missing?'

But how was Madge to know what was missing? Emma had taken most of the furniture herself. What was left belonged to Alex: clothes, shoes, hi-fi, video recorder, TV, radio, books . . . she had locked them all into their bedroom.

'Missing? I don't know. The police wanted your number. I rang the police. When they came I let them in and two boys and a girl climbed out of your kitchen window and ran off. That man at the bottom of your garden still hadn't mended his fence, so they must have got in from the road—'

'All right, Madge. Tell me tomorrow. I must pack and arrange things this end. You've been wonderful.'

Madge thought so, too. Emma could hear pride in her voice. And why not? She wasn't young, and nowadays the elderly were all at risk. Suppose she had been coshed in the hall?

Emma rang Mrs Hughes and arranged for her to look after the cats and the house. It was a choice morsel for her to spread round the village. Emma Rowlands' London flat broken into . . . didn't know she had one . . . what, two homes? Think she'll come back, then? Police want to see her . . .

She rang Debby, who would be scandalized to hear the news secondhand.

'I'm not taking the car,' she told her. 'You don't happen to have a timetable of London trains from Gobowen? I'd like to catch an early one tomorrow.'

'There's a train at nine-twenty,' said Debby, after a pause. 'Yes. Straight through to Euston. Look, Robert can drive you to the station. You don't want to leave your car there, you don't know how long you'll have to stay. Then when you come back, ring us and we'll meet you.'

Robert came on the phone.

'What a beastly thing to happen,' he said. 'It's no trouble, Emma. I've got to call on a chap near Oswestry anyway. Pick you up at eight-thirty.'

The next day they drove through a dark wet morning and Robert had to use his headlights through the lanes. A thaw had set in overnight.

'D'you know what's missing? I suppose not.'

'I brought away most things when I moved here. It's Charlotte's things I'm worried about. Oh, and of course, Alex's. He never called back to collect them. That's what's made it difficult to sell the flat. He's in South Africa. He was born there and his parents have moved back.'

'What sort of a chap is he? I can't imagine him. That is, if—'

'Oh, I don't mind talking about him. I felt you and Debby were keeping off the subject.'

'Debby likes things to be clean cut. She doesn't go in much for talking about things she can't put right.' He slid a wry look at her. 'But I'm frankly curious. Pity you couldn't make a go of it.'

'What went wrong, you mean? Well, the marriage just went downhill, that's all. We simply had nothing in common. To begin with, his people never hit it off with mine – I know that shouldn't be important but it was – Mother condemned them at once when they expected her to play bridge and talk about golf handicaps. They lived in Surrey, we lived in North London. That was it, really.'

'What did your father say?'

'He thought it was up to me and refused to interfere.'

Her father had in fact warned her that Alex had his father's bullying charm, but she had put it down to the fact that the two men never got on. Alex's father despised schoolmasters. You never made money by dinning facts into the young. Robert said, puzzled, 'But you must have been in love once.'

'Oh, of course I was. We both were. I'd never met anyone like Alex; he thought nothing of flying over to Paris for lunch, for example. He liked sport and people and having fun. He was very attractive.'

Especially to someone like me, thought Emma, one of a quiet threesome, wanting to escape into a twosome. A lorry accelerated past, showering the windscreen with muddy water.

'Damn,' Robert frowned. 'You could have had fun, I suppose, without marrying him.'

'It was a long time ago, Robert. I was very earnest. I thought I could go on with my graphic art and so on, but his parents bought us a house near Epsom – and them. It was dire. But it's never one person's fault things go wrong. It's just – well – impossible propinquity. Look out, there's a tractor.' Robert slowed down as the tractor inched its way backwards out of a field. 'I was naïve enough to believe my marriage would be like my parents'.'

It was a relief to talk and there was something both restful and transient about talking in a car, to someone whose attention was on the road and not on her. She gazed out on the grey and drizzly landscape passing by and it seemed as if her ideas, idly translated into speech, were one with the dripping hedges, the farm gates, the occasional farm worker with a sack over his head. All passing.

Robert turned his head and nodded.

'That's understandable. I remember them so well, your parents. When he was coaching me, we'd see your mother walking past the window carrying a halter to catch that pony of yours. Your father would get up and look after her and smile. He loved to watch her.'

'Yes, he did.'

He spoilt her, Emma thought. They had come to the outskirts of a town, red houses on either side of the road and a grey church with a peeling board outside. COME TO J, it said, flapping in the cold wind.

'I've got Virgil's *Georgics* at home. Still read them. Your father said that all farmers' sons should know them. Best book on husbandry ever written – allowing for climate and place, of course. I must show them to you. Ploughing. Reaping. Manuring the fields, harvesting; it's all there. Marvellous stuff. Wonderful chap on bees, Virgil. Made me keep them.'

'We did the *Aeneid* at school. But I could never get along with all those gods and goddesses.'

'Arms and the man I sing – but I always think of Bernard Shaw, don't you? Mind you, Emma, it's Latin one side and English the other. A marvellous crib.'

Emma laughed. 'He used to get so cross when parents complained that Latin and Greek were dead languages and a waste of time. He'd tell them that the English language was being killed off every day, every time their sons opened their mouths to speak. He wrote articles about how the barbarians were at the gates and that English would be dead long before the classical languages. He was written off as an eccentric by all the new educational theorists. We're here. Thanks, Robert.'

'You've got ten minutes.'

Emma bought her ticket and found Robert still waiting on the platform, looking around.

'I remember a time when you could get a train through to Oswestry from here and then on to

106

Bryntanat,' he said. 'Now this seems to be the end of the line. The local went from beyond those palings.' He didn't like change. 'I hope you won't find things too bad up there, and don't forget to ring us with the time of the train.' He leaned forward and kissed her cheek.

As Robert put her case in the compartment she said, laughing, 'I'll pass on your idea of regularized rat hunts to the police.'

He stood waving as the train drew out and Emma waved back with the random thought that had the family not moved away from Bryntanat she might have married a man as pleasant as Robert. But as they left the mountains behind and then the Wrekin, and approached the Midlands and the outskirts of Birmingham, her thoughts began to move ahead with the motion of the train and she began to dread what she might find.

It was strange to be going back to a place she had lived in for ten or more years and now meant nothing. Parts of your life just fell away out of the main pattern. It was like driving over a route so familiar that miles went by without your being aware of them. Then a landmark would catch your attention and you couldn't understand how you had arrived at it. Odd to think that you lived your life forwards but only made sense of it backwards.

She was glad she had been careful in what she had told Robert. Anxiously she went over the conversation – for certain things could never be said. Epsom, she thought; pretty enough, with the downs and so on, but God what a no man's land, neither town nor country. They had both joined a tennis club, Alex a golf club and she had tried to fit in. But she could never live up to his mother's standard of entertaining; Alex's friends bored her and she gave up trying. Things had got better for a time when they moved back to London. Convenient for Alex's new job, so they sold the house and bought the Highgate flat. Blessedly uncosy, and she could take up painting again. She was back on home territory, for her parents had a house in Islington. Alex played squash and travelled to Surrey at weekends to play golf. Their sex life faded out; if he had other women, Emma didn't greatly care. She was not jealous by nature – anyway, not jealous of Alex – for it seemed to her that jealousy was self-defeating and soured a marriage. If you could neither condone nor forgive, get out quickly or both of you were diminished.

Her mistake had been in not getting out soon enough.

The din of Euston hit her as she walked on to the platform and then down into the Underground. So many people, all looking grim and tired; the air thick with their breath. She was hungry, having eaten only sandwiches and coffee on the train, but she had promised Madge she would be at Highgate and the sooner she got there the better.

To her surprise a policeman met her at the door.

'Mrs Rowlands? I'm Sergeant Jenkins.' He watched her as she opened the door. Her key must have lain in this handbag ever since her arrival in Wales. So strange to be walking into her own hallway; it smelt unused, so deserted. Sergeant Jenkins followed her into the dining-room.

'Lucky for you your neighbour came in when she did. We haven't touched anything here yet,' he said.

Maybe Madge had seen her arrive, she was sure to be on the lookout. She looked round the empty room. The bare floor was covered with muddy boot marks and one small female footprint, which looked unthreatening. The intruders had pulled down the curtains she had left at the windows and used them for bedding. When Emma went over and shook the untidy heap a used Tampax fell out, a grimy Kleenex, and something else.

'Wait a bit,' said the sergeant. '*And* I'm not

surprised.' He drew a plastic bag from his pocket and bent down. 'Two used syringes,' he said. 'They came in to give themselves a fix, most likely.' Carefully, without touching them, he slid them into the bag.'

'What about this?' Emma gestured to the Tampax.

'Best throw it out, missis. Just natural, that.'

Oh yes? Natural on her floor and in her curtains? What else would she find that was just natural?

'It's my daughter's room I'm worried about,' she said, and ran upstairs. The door to Charlotte's bedroom was closed. Knife marks round the lock, but . . . where had she put the key? Hidden it somewhere, but where? Had they found it? She tried the doorhandle in a sweat of fear and did not hear Sergeant Jenkins come up behind her, moving lightly for a stout man. His round face burst from his collar like a radish.

'You'll want this,' he said with a half-grin. 'Top shelf of the airing cupboard.'

She snatched the key from his hand and opened the door; nothing was touched. The wardrobe locked, the chest of drawers inviolate. Where had she put the keys? She looked at the sergeant, and he said, 'Probably took them with you. Slipped 'em in your handbag. My wife would.'

'There's the bedroom,' she said, not wishing to prove him right yet again.

'Well, not so lucky there. You'd left the key in the lock, see, or they found it. Your neighbour said there was a hi-fi system here and a TV and a video player and radio.'

Had she left the key in the lock? Surely not. The furniture van had been at the door as she was clearing the bedroom. Dressing-table, bed, carpet and chairs had been taken downstairs. Now had she locked the door or not?

'I can't remember where I put the key, Sergeant,' she said. 'But all my ex-husband's things have gone. There was a suitcase of clothes as well. I'll give you a list and get on to the insurance company.'

'May I ask where the ex Mr Rowlands is?'

'Certainly. He's in South Africa. He left his things here until we sold the flat. He won't be pleased.'

'I dare say not. But – don't quote me, Mrs Rowlands – it's been a bit of luck for your daughter. Not professionals, see? As I say, kids. Too busy pinching the things in the bedroom, flogging 'em, see? They'd have been back, mind, if your neighbour hadn't spotted them. Then they'd have got in somehow. Come and look at the bathroom.'

The bathroom was a mess. The bath filthy with watermarks, Emma's old forgotten bathrobe dragged over the taps, evidently used as a towel. The soap sat in a pool of water, softening into a mash.

"Well, at least they're clean now,' she said, suddenly laughing. 'I expect they had nowhere to go, Sergeant. And in this weather . . .' Outside the rain had started again, it lashed against the windows angrily. 'They haven't left any graffiti on the walls, or – how long do you think they were here?'

'Hard to say. Three or four nights. You should have let us know down at the station you were leaving it empty, missis. Risky, these days.' He led the way down to the kitchen. 'Like rats they are, creeping into whatever holes they can find. Look.'

Rats. That struck a chord.

The kitchen made her reel back. The half-tolerant thoughts she was indulging deserted her in a rush of fury. The sink was full of the unwanted dishes and crockery she had left behind in the cupboards. Grease skimmed the water like dirty ice on a pond. Chip papers were crumpled on the draining-board, plastic drinks containers on the floor, newspapers that had held fish or hamburgers tossed on the table with foil containers encrusted with half-eaten Chinese take-aways.

'I'd like to bring them back to clear this lot up, Sergeant! What kind of homes do they come from? I know teenagers are sloppy – but *this*.' Idiotically she said complainingly, 'There was plenty of hot water for washing-up.'

Sergeant Jenkins, evidently a family man, was delighted by her rage. She had been altogether too soft and liberal in her reactions so far. 'You should have turned the gas off at the mains,' he said. 'Dangerous, that, leaving it on.'

'My neighbour pops in to put the central heating on from time to time.'

'Look at all these milk cartoons,' he said now. Milk cartoons was how he pronounced the words. They were half full, some of them, with stinking congealed milk, their tops smashed. 'Must have been in for nearly a week, on and off,' he said, 'for milk to go as bad as this. Savages. Can't even open a milk cartoon.' In his face was the open admission that he hated the feckless young. Couldn't do with them. His kids would never behave like this.

Emma was looking at the window and the blood-stains on the sill. Glass shards on the floor. They must have been small to climb in there.

'Parents don't watch 'em, that's the trouble. I'd say these were teenagers, skinny ones at that. Maybe thirteen, fourteen years old.'

'And using drugs? How do you know they're not homeless?' She had caught the dislike in his voice.

'I don't know any more than you do, missis. But we get a lot of truanting round here, and it's my guess they're using your flat as a sort of den to shoot up, a hidey-hole like kids do.'

'Pity they can't find something more interesting to do, Sergeant.' And mischievously Emma put forward the idea of organizing rat hunts to sop up all the aggression floating about in Highgate and Camden Town. With a serious face, to show she wasn't joshing him, she said this is what happened in the part of Wales she lived in.

'Where's that then? You've moved away then, definite, have you?'

That had been a mistake. Quickly she amended her words.

'We haven't quite gone, Sergeant. I'm waiting for my daughter to come home first. And, of course, my ex-husband. We share the flat, you see. We shall be in the Border country. You're from the South, at a guess.'

'Cardiff. But I remember rat hunts as a lad. I'll tell the Super.' He was looking at Emma with approval. 'We'd better get along to the station and make out your lists of things missing. Not that we'll get anything back.' He sent a look of pure cunning in her direction. 'Don't really care, do you? Your ex's stuff? Insurance can take care of that, eh?' He nearly winked.

Emma rang her mother, hoping she was home, to ask for a bed for a couple of nights. Adela was delighted. She had recently arrived back from Jordan and felt in need of some diversion. Besides, she had taken lots of snaps and now was wondering why they no longer interested her.

'Come round, darling,' she said. 'Soon as you can. Serves Alex right. It's high time you sold that flat. Better ring him though, when you've made a list. Be on the safe side or he may turn nasty. Nastier than before. You don't want him nosing round Domengastell.'

The thought of Alex even putting a foot in the drive made Emma feel sick.

'I've got to go to the police station and make a statement, then I must call in on Madge. I'll be round to you about six. I'll bring a bottle of sherry.'

She bought flowers and added half a bottle of brandy for Madge's nerves, wished she had thought of bringing her up some Welsh butter. She boarded up the kitchen window more securely, turned her back

112

on the mess and spent an uncomfortable half-hour at the police station.

They seemed to think it was her fault, leading young people astray by leaving her flat empty and not telling the police.

'If you're so stretched, as you tell me,' she said, 'what would you have done about it? You couldn't spare two men to come round, my neighbour told me. If you had put a constable in the back garden, you'd have caught them as they ran.'

'Maybe. But the stuff'd be gone by then. Kids pinch videos every day, anything that isn't fastened down. They just laugh at the police. They know they'll get off easy.' They were annoyed, she could see that, and when the inspector spoke his final dismissal his voice had an edge. 'Think yourself lucky they hadn't peed all over the walls and floor, like tom-cats to mark their territory.' He relished the look on Emma's face as she left.

With some distaste she returned to her violated flat, pulled the kitchen chair into the hall and sat down to telephone Alex's firm to get his address. Maybe they could fax him the news?

'We could, but he'll be staying with his parents in Cape Town. You could speak to him direct, Mrs Rowlands.'

This, she realized, was what they preferred. Private affairs did not mix with business. How long would he be away? Due back at the end of the month. Well, thanks.

Just after six, in order to cut costs – South Africa was a long way – she rang his parents' number. Her heart bumped uncomfortably, anticipating his mother's thin voice, pruned like a thorn hedge. But an altogether different voice answered: breathless, young, a very clipped accent. Emma gave her name, asked for Mrs Rowlands.

There was a gasp. 'You're Alex's wife? Ooh, I've

been trying to get you on the phone. Where have you been?'

'Hang on, who *are* you? Why have you been trying to get me?'

'I'm Phoebe. I want to ask you to please hurry up with the divorce so that Alex and I can get married.'

She must be very young to be so direct. Emma shifted on the hard wooden chair, trying to put a face to the petulant voice. Fair, she'd be fair. Blue eyes or brown? Did she have the slender bruisable arms of young girls? Inexplicably she felt a rush of concern, as she might for her daughter or even, she realized, for her young self.

'Are you sure you want to marry him, Phoebe? He's—'

'Don't you dare say anything against Alex! He's told me all about you, how awful you've been to him. Of course I want to marry him. I . . .' The self-righteous shrillness stopped for a few seconds and Emma waited. 'I *have* to marry him, Emma. Why won't you let him go?'

'I have let him go,' said Emma wearily. 'The decree nisi came through six months ago. It's long over, my dear.' She felt a hundred years older than this distraught girl at the end of the line. 'Oh, my God, I see. You must be pregnant! Well, Alex is completely free. It's only financial things we've got to clear up. This flat. I want to sell it, but he's never here—'

There was a cut-off wail in her ear. 'But where will we live when we come to England if you sell it? Alex promised – are you sure he's free?'

She made it sound as if Alex were on special offer.

'Yes, I'm sure. You can tell him so from me. And where you will live is surely your affair. Oh, I rang to tell him that we've been burgled. His video and the other things he left in the flat here have gone. Does he want me to get on to the Insurance or will he? I've left a list with the police. Have you got all that?'

114

'Emma? What's all this about, what's the trouble?'

Alex's mother, evidently having snatched the phone from the nerveless Phoebe who had so nicely netted Alex, came over loud and clear, as in the past. Emma explained.

'And do tell Phoebe, Mrs Rowlands, that Alex is perfectly free to marry her. The divorce is through.'

'That's not what my son says.'

So Alex was at his games again; he was an expert in half-truths which blossomed richly in their own season into the downright lies which he himself believed.

'Get on to his solicitor and check.'

And I, thought Emma grimly, replacing the receiver, will change my name back to Forden. As if Alex had never happened. Glancing down at her left hand, she eased off her wedding ring and left it by the telephone.

Across London, in her two-bedroomed flat in a modern block near Hammersmith Bridge, Adela contemplated the salmon steaks she was wrapping in foil. A little butter, a little lemon juice? Had she time to go out and buy some decent brie and a bottle of wine?

It was a pleasure to cook for two. Even after nearly three years Adela had never learned to enjoy eating alone. It seemed like clapping with one hand, to prepare a meal and sit down before it with only a book or the radio for company. Some of her friends gobbled their food in front of the television, which seemed to her a regrettable habit. She and Hugo had kept the television firmly in its place, although during those last months of his illness concentration on the screen had dulled his pain. The world snooker championship had been on BBC2 and the hypnotic click of cue on ball; the accurate potting of blue, yellow, red, brown, green, pink and black had eased him. He appreciated ceremony in all games. Together they had watched for his favourites to win. Steve Davis he couldn't stand; the mechanical brilliance of his shots, the impeccable

115

stance, the immobile face, irritated him beyond endurance. He had been delighted when the odd-looking man with the huge glasses had beaten him by one point. Pot the black. The game had finished well past midnight and even Adela had been enthralled. But watching a dying man take such pleasure in another's triumph was unbearably moving. It humbled Adela, made her grateful that there were still things they could share, kept terror at bay.

So snooker was one of those taboo things: not to be watched. In shops there were certain things not to be bought: marzipan-covered church-window cake, prawns, Tiptree strawberry jam. Bargains in men's shirts. They had never lived by a river, that was why she had chosen this flat.

From her windows she could see the calm grey curve of it and the bridge beyond. Within ten months of his death she had sold their Islington house at a good price, just before the market started to fall, and bought a short lease on this flat. High up, impersonal. Neither she nor Hugo had ever driven a car, so that was no problem. She had settled in quite quickly, almost before she was aware of what she was doing. The pain of loss was so great that she perversely felt the need to add to it, to increase the distance between life then and life now. Each night, sitting creaming her face at her dressing-table, she realized that Hugo might not recognize the woman sitting there; with hair cut short, quite grey now, in a high room overlooking a river. She wondered whether he would know where to find her, should he ever feel the need to come back and see how she was getting on. She missed his touch. Being held close against the dark. Being held.

But you could rebuild your life within new limits, she found. Create a careful framework of daily habit, a necessary precaution. For when the responsibilities of a shared life vanished, breakwaters went as well. After the move there were odd moments when peace or pleasure crept up and took her by surprise. Not happiness, that no longer mattered. After all, the universe wasn't a happiness machine just made for *you*.

Yet she missed their house; friends had advised her not to move in such a hurry, but she had ignored their advice. The smoke from Hugo's pipe had clung to the curtains, his chair was comfortable from the contours of his body. The first thing she sold was their bed. His clothes still hung in a cupboard; only shoes and underwear had gone to the Salvation Army. Other men's tobacco smoke tormented yet comforted her, although today fewer men smoked. While allowing for the sense this made, Adela found it lessened the pleasure of social intercourse, for people were less relaxed. It made watching old movies an amusing recognition of forgotten courtship manoeuvres; a lover lighting two cigarettes and passing one across. The vamp's slow withdrawal of a cigarette from a proffered case or packet, eyes half closed, long-nailed fingers lightly touching the man's hand as he lit it for her. Had he used a silver or gold lighter or a match? All these things were shorthand to a character build-up Hollywood style. Hero or villain designated by what – and how – he smoked.

When Emma arrived Adela was sitting by the window with a glass of sherry, enjoying her first cigarette of the day. It was also maybe her last. That depended on how the evening went; her daughter could be judgemental. Judging others seemed to be the climate of the times; every silly young man or woman or politician had an opinion to air, and aired it at length in newspaper or TV interviews. Adela was not used to criticism and resented it. But she was pleased to see her daughter; she was, after all, her own flesh and blood and there was a good deal of Hugo in her.

She thought Emma looked tired; her hair could do with some attention; it had always tended to be dry.

Had she put on weight and was the colour in her cheeks the beginning of weathering? Could she warn her about broken veins?

'Darling,' she said. 'What a frightful day you must have had. Are you worn out?'

'Yes,' said Emma. 'I've never been in a police station before.'

'Sherry or whisky?'

'Whisky, please. Madge sends her love. She's in a high state of excitement.'

'Nobody will prise her away from that window now. It's her own private box on to the world. But what presence of mind, and how lucky she was!'

Emma realized that Madge must have been on the telephone to her mother.

'The sooner you're out of there for good, the better,' said Adela. 'Just relax now. I'll see to the dinner. We're having salmon, I thought it would be a treat for us.'

Feet up, shoes off, Emma felt the long hard day drain away. As always, her mother had everything under control. The flat was welcoming and tidy, although unfamiliar; it was still strange to see her in these new surroundings, as if they were both on a visit, ready to take off again. She was comforted to recognize chairs and pictures and bookcases from the old house and noticed that several books lay about, with markers in them. Too lazy to get up and look at them, she knew one from its green leather cover. Hazlitt's *Selected Essays*, her father's copy.

They had a creamy mushroom soup, then the salmon with small tinned potatoes done up in butter and parsley, and green peas. Emma was ravenous, and ate two buttered rolls as well.

'There's fruit and cheese, is that enough for you?' asked Adela, watching her daughter with some amusement. At least she had a healthy country appetite. For herself, she refused to indulge in the comfort eating to which some women of her age were addicted, which put inches on stomach and hips. She had always had a trim figure and intended to keep it. She hoped that Emma was not letting herself go; at her age she could surely marry again. As she went out into the tiny kitchen to make coffee she felt a stab of pity. They were both on their own, she and Emma, but Emma had been left, abandoned, whereas she had been lucky enough to be cherished to the last. It was the first time she had acknowledged this.

As they settled to their coffee, she said, 'Now tell me the worst. Was it awful?'

'Yes,' said Emma. 'The kitchen was filthy. I've got to clear it up tomorrow. But thank God they didn't get into Charlotte's room. I rang South Africa, by the way—'

'You rang South Africa? Did you get Alex?'

Emma suddenly burst out laughing.

'No. But I got his next wife. You'll never believe it, but she came on hot and strong – Phoebe's her name – she's pregnant, poor girl, and didn't even know that Alex was free to marry her.'

'What a . . . a trickster that man is—'

'His mother didn't believe me when I told her the divorce was through. He's playing some sort of game. I bet he's livid she's pregnant. He was never keen to have children anyway. I do feel sorry for her.'

'What about his things that were stolen?'

'Oh,' said Emma, yawning. She was deathly tired of the whole thing. 'I'll ring his solicitor tomorrow.'

'Why don't you have a nice long bath and an early night? You'll feel better in the morning. And, Emma – where's your wedding ring?'

Adela had only just noticed her daughter's bare hand. She had been biting her nails again, too, a habit from childhood.

'I left it by the telephone in the flat. I'll chuck it in one of the black plastic bags when I'm clearing up tomorrow.'

Adela shook her head, compressing her mouth in a gesture Emma remembered.

'It might be better to sell it. It's platinum, isn't it? You could buy some new clothes, or something you want.'

Only her mother could have thought up an idea in such joyously bad taste, and it made Emma laugh again.

'I could put the money towards central heating,' she said. 'Warm my bones on the ashes of my marriage. I wonder what I'll get for it.'

'We'll have to see. Now, I'll run your bath and put on the electric blanket in your room.'

It gave her pleasure to do these things for her daughter; it was so seldom she had the opportunity. Their lives had veered apart since Hugo's death; she had had no thought for anyone other than herself. While Emma was in the bathroom she went into her bedroom and looked in her jewellery box. Apart from her own mother's pearls which she always wore she did not have much, for Hugo had thought it primitive for women to deck themselves, and so had never given her any. With one exception. One day, before they were married, they had been sheltering from the rain in the doorway of a little antique shop in Church Street. In the window she had seen a pretty ring with a band of amber set between two bands of silver and had longed for it. He had relented and bought it for her. She had worn it until they were married, and then replaced it by her wedding ring. Hugo had shown some imagination over that: together they had chosen a plain gold band, but he had asked for the entwined initials to be incised inside. H and A. This was because they had just been to Hampton Court where, high up on a stone boss in an archway, they had spotted the only intertwined carving that had escaped the destruction Henry had ordered after Anne Boleyn's execution.

She always remembered that day.

'H and A,' Hugo had exclaimed. 'Look, up there!

There we are, H and A. Writ large in stone.' She had shivered and Hugo had put his arm round her. 'I promise never to behead you, my darling, if you promise never to betray me.'

They had laughed, then disagreed as to whether the wretched Anne had really been as bad as history made her out, or whether – more likely – it was one of those devious Tudor plots.

'It was so unfair,' Adela had said. 'First she had a girl when Henry wanted a boy, then a miscarriage. Fancy condemning a woman for that.'

Odd, really. Much later she was to remember that remark. First a girl, then a miscarriage, if you could call it that. But no-one had condemned her for it.

Now she found the silver-and-amber ring in its little red leather box and took it back into the sitting-room. She would give it to Emma as a present from them both, so that her finger would feel less bare. Slipping it on her own finger, Adela realized it was loose and would therefore fit Emma, whose hands were larger than her own. Glancing down, she acknowledged that since Hugo's death she had felt thinned down in her very being, her identity pared away. Even her fingers were thinner. As she slipped it off the telephone rang.

In the bathroom Emma was drying herself on one of her mother's fluffy pink towels. She had used some bath salts from the Dead Sea which promised miracles, but made the water a dirty colour. Body lotions, cream for the feet, for the neck, for the face, were arrayed on glass shelves. Her mother evidently still took good care of herself. It was second nature, thought Emma, when you had always been regarded as somewhat of a beauty. For in her younger days Adela had been striking, with her pale skin and chestnut hair. No wonder Bryntanat still remembered her. Maybe Emma should take some care of herself; she wasn't so bad, her breasts still firm and large, her waist slim. Good legs, good strong face with her father's dark eyes and her mother's hair.

Her mother was calling now. Charlotte was on the phone, but she was talking to her. Don't hurry or you'll break a leg . . . But Emma did hurry. Hair done up in a turban, her mother's heavy white towelling bathrobe tied tightly round her waist, she ran into the sitting-room. Charlotte at last.

Adela was lying back on the chintzy sofa by the simulated coal fire, talking into the telephone, the light from the table lamp on her shining cap of grey hair. She had been lucky, turning from her rich tawny colour to metal grey, with no intermediate step. Or rather, it struck Emma, she had been lucky – or discerning – in finding a good hairdresser. It changed her, that short hair; set off her cheek-bones yet gave her a vulnerable look. Emma thought of her father brushing that hair when it had been below her shoulders—

'Come along, Emma. It's costing this child a fortune—' and Emma took the telephone and listened to her daughter.

Such a long way away, and yet Charlotte's voice was clear, if small. Like most girls of her age, she tended to talk too quickly, as if her thoughts would escape before she could find words for them. She was in Udiapore. She rang Gran because there was no reply from that Welsh number, and what was happening?

'Udiapore?'

'We're in a posh hotel for a change and stay in the pool all day and watch Indian dancing at night, swathed in shawls because of the mosquitoes . . .'

'Are you coming home for Christmas?'

'Well, no. Dirk and I might go on to Thailand after all. We're planning to go north first. We're fine. Don't worry. The others may go back to Varanase. Beth's gone home.'

'Yes, she sounded upset. Who are these film people?'

'Just a small company roaming around, you know.

It'll be fun to make a film. I'll be interviewing people. They're paying us as well. Look, Mum, I'm sending you and Gran some gorgeous stuff. It's fabulous here. The Rajasthani women are so beautiful in their jewels and saris.'

'Just a minute, darling. Did you get my letter? I expect you're surprised, but it'll be all right, I promise—'

'Yes. Yes, thanks. It sounds weird, but it'll get us out of a rut, won't it? That's what Dirk says. Go with the flow.'

Evidently Emma's move, exhausting and traumatic to her, meant little to her daughter, caught up as she was with exhilarating new experiences: jewels and saris, camels and film people and a whole dazzling continent to discover. She gave up.

'Did your grandmother tell you we've been burgled? She did? Well, nothing of yours has been touched. Listen, please. Shall I take your things to Wales or do you want to come back to the flat? I'll have to sell it eventually—'

Adela broke in. 'If she wants a London base she can come to me. Take her things to Wales, that's best. There's no room for them here.'

'Things aren't important, Mum. I've learnt that. I don't care really. I'll ring you again. Don't worry, I'm OK now. Everything's cleared up. Give a big kiss to Gran.'

'Take care . . .'

'I will. Go with the flow, Mum. Bye now.'

The telephone was silent and Emma found she was crying.

'What's cleared up?' she asked her mother, wiping away tears with the back of her hand. 'I know she had a gash on her leg, Beth's mother told me, but—'

'Well, if it's cleared up, darling, why worry? It's past.'

There were a hundred things Emma had wanted to

say to Charlotte, not stupid things like whether she should— Greedily she asked her mother what she had told her.

'She got a sore bottom while they were camel trekking, that's all. And how hot it was, and how she loved India and wouldn't have missed it for the world, and wouldn't I like to go to India now I've started to travel.' Adela poured a little whisky for them both and said, 'Let's celebrate. Come on, let me dry your hair. Sit here by the fire.'

Obediently Emma sat on the floor by her mother's legs and felt her remove the turban and start gently rubbing her hair. She sipped her drink. Such a strange feeling to be cared for. Go with the flow indeed, well, she was, wasn't she?

'Bend over to the fire. I'll fetch my hairbrush and we'll have some Vivaldi. I've bought a cassette of one of his concertos for flutes and piccolo.'

As Adela brushed Emma's hair the music filled the room. It was a light-hearted piece, both stimulating and orderly; the flutes and piccolos were like birds piping in a greening garden. The music was both spare and cool; at times it sounded as if someone with a sweet whistle joined in, which made Emma think of her father. He had had a tuneful whistle and, as a child, looking for him, she would hear it from a distance and locate him – sometimes in the garden or perhaps in the house. She would fling her arms round him over-whelmed by an emotion she could not express, but knowing that she was safe, her world complete. If children could choose their parents, she would have chosen him. She was not so sure about her mother. But now, feeling the soft sweep of the brush as it crackled through her hair, she felt compunction. Wryly it occurred to her that Adela was the only mother she would have, so she had better make the most of her.

'Do you remember how my father used to brush your hair in Wales? I loved to watch.' She sometimes referred to Hugo like that, formally. Why? Adela wondered. As if Hugo belonged to her alone. 'It was so peaceful in those days. You never quarrelled.'

'No. Hugo was a peaceful man.' Emma flung back her head so that her mother could draw the brush from the forehead to the nape. 'Your hair's nearly dry. It's still a lovely colour and wavy, too, but I think you've got some split ends. You should use a conditioner.'

Emma twisted away, suddenly irritated. There was always something not quite right about her, she knew, and her mother unerringly homed in on it.

'By the way,' she said, gathering up her hair and twisting the length of it into a coil, 'Archie told me you'd given him some of Father's notebooks. I wondered whether you had any more – you know that anthology he was putting together years ago—'

'I've got that somewhere. Oh dear, I promised to help him with it . . . wasn't there some idea for you to illustrate it?'

'Yes. I feel guilty about it. I simply didn't have time – or make time, I suppose.'

'Well, it was really up to your father. He gave up as well, so we needn't feel guilty. Guilt can be . . . so corrosive.'

Adela spoke quite sharply. She had been over this in her own mind and decided that the failure was Hugo's. She felt the need for another cigarette and lit up. 'As for the other notebooks, they were to do with the history of the parish. I thought Archie would appreciate them. Has he shown them to you?'

'Not yet. He told us something about them the other evening when they all came to dinner. They're looking forward to seeing you at Christmas, by the way. Unless you'd like to come back with me. Would you? There's only a week or two to go.'

Adela considered. She had planned nothing until after Christmas. Perhaps she might enjoy some time with her daughter, although living in Rhys's house would be strange. And cold. Wales was always cold in December.

'That's nice of you, Emma. How long do you plan on staying in London?'

'Well, I've got to see Mark Ingrams. I've brought up some layouts for a children's book for him to see. Then there's this boring business of the flat . . . say a couple more days? I could ring through and ask Mrs Hughes to get everything ready. There's a fire in your bedroom.'

She knew how her mother hated discomfort. And would she be bored?

'We'll think about it in the morning. You get off to bed now.'

When Emma had gone Adela saw the little box with the ring in it. Well, she'd wait for the right time to give it to her.

It took Emma three days, after all, to clear up her affairs in London. On the first day Adela came with her to the flat but stayed only briefly, picking up the wedding ring by the telephone and then going on to look in on Madge.

It was odd about Madge, how she had become more or less a friend. She was a tiny woman, plump as a Russian doll. Unmarried, independent, chronically cheerful, and, until arthritis slowed her up, an efficient social worker. Now she did all sorts of voluntary jobs for the local council; visiting the housebound and giving two days a week to the Citizen's Advice Bureau. She had telephoned Adela once a week since Hugo's death and Emma's marriage break-up. Guiltily Adela caught herself thinking in an irritated way that Madge regarded her as a client and in need of counselling, the biggest growth industry of recent times. She had come to dread her brisk adjurations.

'But, my dear, I've been alone all my life. It's a great boon. Do what you want, when you want. Eat when you want – go where you want . . .'

Ah, but all those things, the wanting things, Adela no longer wanted. She had never been alone. In the large family now scattered or dead, of which she was the youngest, all activities had been shared. She had shared a bedroom with her sister. Then with Hugo. She had never slept alone. But how to explain this to Madge, or other friends who spoke bracingly of women's independence? Good works were mentioned, thinking of others was a great healer; and these sentiments carried reproach. As well they might, Adela conceded. Good works sopped up both time and grief. Yes, maybe later, she told them. She did not bother to mention that within her family help and sustenance had always been given to old aunts, widowers, grandmothers. She sensed that people tried to talk her out of grief because they feared it might rub off on them. Like a contagion.

But it was Madge who started her off on her travels. Travelling had never been Hugo's choice. He lived retrospectively, had done so ever since childhood; his mother had told her it was agony to get him to a pantomime. He was terrified he'd never find a lavatory in time to have a pee before the curtain went up. But afterwards! Days of turning that pantomime into a film; drawing the scenes, the characters on long rolls of transparent paper, so that he could pull it through the crude magic lantern an uncle had made for him. He had relived their time in Wales in the same way, not wanting to go back, but writing his books, retreading old paths in imagination ... '"Travelling" in its real sense was finished before the war,' he'd say. 'It's only tourism now.'

Well, Adela decided to be a tourist when Madge rang up one day with a suggestion.

'I'm going on a week's coach tour of gardens in France, Belgium and Holland. Why don't you come?' Madge loved gardens, stuffed up in her top flat with only a pot or two of African violets and a spotted-leaved trailing plant to feed her passion.

It was in at the deep end with a vengeance. She had to share a bedroom with Madge; she didn't know then that she could have had a single room on payment of a supplement. After the first shock of seeing Madge without her teeth and her grey plait down her back instead of coiled around her little nutlike head, Adela had accepted this calmly. But the coach was full of the kind of people she never normally met. Mostly women, whose asexual joviality sometimes set them rocking in their seats; they came in pairs, like nuns or Jehovah's Witnesses. Looking along the lines of heads she noted identical meringue hairdos, ranging in colour from tinted lavender through pinkish mauve and grey to whipped eggwhite. She could have lifted off each crisp confection to reveal a scalp as pinkly innocent as a babe's.

The seats were too high for eavesdropping. Otherwise, thought Adela, Hugo would have been in heaven in spite of his strictures. Listening to women's talk in the weekly bus from Bryntanat to Oswestry had been one of his great joys. He relished women; he felt they held the secret of real life and from them flowed stability and wisdom. Their fragmented retailing of domestic scandals highlighted by sage nods and winks, the robust lilt of Welsh voices, had held for him all the high drama of a Greek chorus; touched a deep chord. Teasingly, his friends put it down to his mother; solid, practical. A cornucopia pouring forth comfort and goodies.

They swept across three countries, calling in at formal French gardens which spread like stage sets around austere grey châteaux. Very knowledgeable her companions were, tossing about the Latin names of the perfectly drilled shrubs and flowers. In Belgium, a short stop at Bruges with its calm contained waters and ancient stone churches and the sound of bells. Madge was a provider. She had a troublesome digestion and distrusted nasty foreign food, so she travelled with packets of digestive biscuits, triangles of foil-wrapped cheese that tasted of condensed milk, and English apples. She drank nothing but Perrier water and looked askance when Adela ordered a bottle of wine with their dinner.

The party munched its way across a flat Dutch landscape. Cyclists, in ones and twos, pedalled off on to the small roads on either side of the motorway to vanish among neat lines of trees and clean-looking strolling cows. Adela wanted a sixteenth-century sky, full of cloudy drama, to wake up these hill-less expanses. But the temperature soared into the nineties. A hard blue sky outside the air-conditioned coach was as bland as a postcard.

In Amsterdam, their courier, a spiky young woman with a flat Midlands voice, carried on a subdued argument with the driver as he swept past the Rijksmuseum for the third time, unable to park. The city was packed. Coaches and cars nose to tail and pavements awash with processions of men and women of all ages carrying banners. The Jesus people had come to town and stopped the traffic.

All Adela wanted was to see the Rembrandts, maybe take a canal boat. She was able to do neither. The coach came to rest at last near the railway station.

'We'll meet here in an hour's time, OK?' said the courier. 'You can explore a bit.'

When Adela asked where she could find a taxi to take her to the Rijksmuseum, she was told they were all on strike. So she saw neither the Rembrandts nor the Van Goghs. Still, she was grateful to Madge. That trip had broken the spiralling despondency of those first months and given her a taste for travel. 'Out of my country and myself I go,' she told herself and booked up for more excursions abroad, but alone and more comfortably and not by coach. Out of my country, yes. But there was no guaranteed free entry into another country of the self. That you were stuck with. In fact,

129

the more she travelled, the further into herself she retreated. The world became more alien as she nodded to strangers across foreign breakfast tables trying, out of her own innate courtesy and girlhood training, to interest herself in them.

Now, joining Madge for coffee in her overcrowded flat, she made a similar effort as Madge reminisced over that first coach tour.

'Do you remember that tall old man, Adela, whose wife was always keeping the coach waiting?'

He had stood on the pavement like a tortoise anxiously in search of a lettuce leaf, Adela recalled.

'She always sped off with a dinner fork and a plastic bag, collecting specimens. Yes, and then he'd grumble when she came back that she'd catch it from the courier and wasn't it against some law, to collect plants in a foreign country?'

'You should have come with me to the Floriade,' said Madge, nibbling at her biscuit. 'They were on that, too. Only this time she was always going off to find ice-cream. Then she'd say "Off we go, driver" and slip in beside her husband.'

In fact, Adela had grown quite fond of this pair; envying them sitting together, walking hand in hand. Where would he be, this ancient husband, without his small nimble wife to prod him into indignation? Where would she be, without him to shuffle up to like a hen on a perch? All her journeys, successful or not, had taught her something about the contradictions of human nature. She discovered that she had enough adventure in herself to enjoy adventuring abroad; brief friendships with fellow travellers sharing an interest in old churches and pictures made no lasting claim; no confidences had to be exchanged. Over-whelmingly, she wished Hugo with her to share a sudden joke, to be excited by the Tintorettos in Venice. In Venice she missed him painfully, for it was a city that would have enfolded them both. The quiet, almost medieval domesticity of the stone-paved squares behind the furious buzz of the Piazza San Marco would have pleased him. The tall windows with their iron grilles and spillage of geraniums, the lines of washing strung between balconies, boys playing football: a sort of backstage muddle to the theatrical curtain-raiser of the Palazzos. As she ate her lunch with a woman friend – peaches, tomatoes, rolls and cheese under a plane tree in the Campo Margherita, watching the stallholders hose down their fish counters – she could scarcely believe that Hugo was not about to lean out of a window above them and call down. In imagination they were both teenage students. Venice was a city for lovers.

'Adela, you're dreaming!'

Adela had been gazing, without seeing, at one of Madge's pot plants and had quite forgotten where she was. It happened from time to time when she was thinking about Hugo, as if she could turn quickly and catch his eye. Now she stared at Madge's round worried face, noted the thin grey coronet of plaited hair, the fleshy pink ear lobes, and frowned.

'I asked you whether Emma will be selling the flat after this nasty business. You're not getting deaf, are you?'

'Deaf? Oh no. No, I don't think so. Yes, well. I think it would be best, don't you? Then you'll have people there, in it, I mean . . .'

'It all depends who they are. Now, are you going away for Christmas? You could always come here.'

Adela only just suppressed a shudder. So Madge would be on her own, unless she found some good works to do, like feeding the homeless or dishing out turkey and pudding to a local old people's home. Single women had to plan their lives so that not too many empty spaces proved their inconsequence.

'I'm going to Wales with Emma. We've friends in Bryntanat. But thank you, Madge.'

She got up, duty done. Now to find a jeweller and sell Emma's ring. That would put an end to the past – for Emma at any rate.

Meanwhile Emma, full of rage, had decided not to wash up after her intruders. Instead, wearing a pair of her mother's rubber gloves, she flung all the dirty dishes and plates and saucepans into large plastic bags with the takeaway containers and milk cartons. The water drained away, leaving wide grease marks and these she scrubbed out until the sink was clean. Then she scrubbed the floor. The curtains from the dining-room went into another bag. Anything they had handled she threw out.

She had cleaned the bath twice when she heard the door open downstairs and Madge came in with a Thermos of tea and helped her haul the bags into the front garden.

'I'll make sure the dustmen take them,' she said. 'You couldn't tell anyone'd been in now, dear. Your mother's just gone.'

Emma leaned against the wall, giving the only chair left in the house to Madge. They drank tea out of the mugs Madge had brought with her.

'It's the times,' said Madge. 'What can you do?' She sighed. 'If only they'd put a policeman in the garden they'd have caught them. I could have talked to them. I used to be good with children.'

'They might not have been children. There were syringes, Madge! Heroin or something. Not children.'

Madge did not argue.

'I hate this place,' said Emma. 'I'll ring up those removal people and get them to send Charlotte's chest of drawers on. I must pack her clothes. Or I could leave them in the wardrobe and they could just put it on the van or whatever. What do you think?'

'We could tie up the wardrobe with the clothes inside. Unless Adela has a big suitcase and you could

132

take them with you. It would be heavy, mind.'

'God, can you trust anybody? I wish now I'd brought the car.' Emma knew she sounded paranoid. 'Do you know what Charlotte said last night when she telephoned? Things don't matter. Go with the flow. When all that wears off she'll be furious if anything at all of hers is missing. I threw away one of her tattered old rag dolls once and she's never forgotten.'

'Nothing was missing the last time you used the removal firm, was there?' asked Madge reasonably. 'When are you going back to Wales? I can see the men for you, you know that.'

'Couple of days. Mother's coming with me, I hope. I've a few things to do, but I can't wait to get home.'

Home. She had said it. The kitchen at Domengastell invaded her mind, with the Aga and the kittens playing on the rag rug Mrs Hughes had given her. Her mood lifted.

'It's so good of you, Madge. You do such a lot for me. I hope you'll come and stay in the summer, you'll like it.'

That afternoon she rang the removal people and Alex's solicitor. The police, she told him, had a list of what was missing if he wanted to deal with the Insurance claim. Also, she added crisply, it was time the flat was sold and the proceeds divided. Wasn't that the law? Well then. She'd be willing to put it in the hands of a house agent herself.

She was in the bath when her mother returned in high feather. She heard her calling as she scrubbed away all contact with the filth of the flat. Then, feeling clean, stepped out and dried herself, used a generous amount of Adela's body cream and dressed.

'You'll never guess, just look at this.'

Adela waved a cheque at her. 'Alex was more generous than we thought. You've got £150 for the ring. I went to two jewellery shops I know, both reputable. One offered me £100 but the other £150. There!'

Emma looked down at her bare hand. £150 – for how many years of marriage, of bondage? She would rather have thrown the ring away.

'Good,' she said, hating to cloud her mother's bright face. 'It can go towards heating at least one bedroom, and that can be yours. Thank you, Mother.' She moved towards her and gave her a hug.

'I've something else for you. Hold out your hand.' Adela took out the amber-and-silver ring from its box, slipped it on Emma's marriage finger. But at once Emma took it off, looked closely at it, puzzled. It was pretty, but no ring was going on that finger. She put it on the third finger of her right hand, spread it out and looked again. It would look better if she stopped biting her nails.

'I'll tell you the story of that ring while we eat. Aren't you starving?'

The following day, while Adela packed and bought Christmas presents, Emma took her layouts along to Mark Ingrams. Like most small – and large – publishers he had moved out of the centre of London. His pleasant house in Wimbledon was big enough for him to have an office on the ground floor and live above.

He was a tall man in his forties with thinning hair and of indeterminate sex, which made him easy to get on with. His assistant combined the duties of editor and secretary, mastering the computer with furious efficiency. Tess was a young woman just down from Oxford and gave the impression that she was well aware that she was over-qualified for the job.

'All the same,' said Mark, over lunch, 'she's damn lucky to have one at all, poor lass.'

'I hope you don't exploit her, Mark.'

'Come now, Emma. You know me better than that. The milk of human kindness fairly bubbles in my veins. Anyway, I'm far too frightened of her and she knows it.'

They had met at art school, and Emma had never imagined Mark going in for publishing. Over the years their easy relationship had been a source of comfort in difficult times and he was the only friend to whom she had confided the truth when he noticed a bruise on her cheek one day. He had winced as if he himself had been hit. Then he had become thoughtful, asked her several pertinent questions and remarked that in his opinion Alex wasn't trying to drive her away, but dominate her. He probably needed her to bolster up his own sense of insecurity. 'So watch out,' he'd told her. 'And get out. The irony is that the longer you let it go on the harder it'll be to leave. Have you told his parents?'

'Good God no! In their book domestic violence calls for net curtains and dark glasses, not a solicitor. What would the bridge club say?'

Now, free of all that, she looked at him with affection. They talked about Wales. About his latest brainwave of publishing small pocket books of shortened biographies of writers and poets, with extracts from their work and a few inexpensive black-and-white illustrations.

'They sell like hot cakes to the people who go – say, to Wordsworth's cottage, Shaw's place, Keats's house. Literary pilgrimages, that sort of thing. Blue-plaque country, Tess calls it. She thinks it's down-market, but it helps to pay the mortgage and lets me publish promising unknowns.'

'Children's stories are a new departure for you,' said Emma. 'I thought the ones you gave me were original and somehow magical.'

'I think the tide's on the turn with children's stories. After all, poetry and the fairy-tale are the two most accessible forms of literature because they're the simplest, most direct. Primitive and universal. They slip past the defences.'

'I do hope you'll like what I've done with them.'

135

'Let's go back and see, then. My whizzkid ought to be let out for her fodder.'

In his office, standing over his large Regency desk – for Mark liked only the best – on which the drawings were spread, he concentrated entirely.

'Yes,' he said at last. 'We'll do them your way. It'll give an air of the old illustrated monks' books, if you see what I mean. I think children like this sort of traditional thing. A few scratches and that's a cat is an insult to the eye. We don't want to brutalize them before the telly has a go, do we?' He picked one up and put it aside. 'Not that. The story's about a mouse that runs up a flagpole and says he's the king because he's higher than anyone else, isn't it—'

'And falls,' Emma mavelled that he knew the stories so well. 'And the king buries him in the market-place with a column over him, and he has a small white mouse embroidered on the flag and the badges of his men-at-arms to remind people not to get above themselves . . .'

'Could you think about this some more? It's not quite right. The others are lovely. Wales is loosening you up, you know. There's more freedom in your line. I've had an idea. How about you illustrating the *Kilvert* for us? I've got a chap writing it now. Small black-and-white chapter heads and endpieces and the jacket. I'll send you the text sometime in January. Here.'

He gave her several small paperback booklets and she looked through them.

'You could do Europe as well,' she said. 'How about translations? French and German and English? My mother picked up something of the sort in Padua, about the pictures. They were in Japanese as well. You'll always find a Japanese at these places.'

'Worth a thought, my love. But they all understand English as well as we do. Probably better.'

As she sat in the train on the way back to Hammersmith, Emma had yet another idea. Would Mark be

136

interested in her father's Welsh anthology? Places and people, poetry and prose, with her illustrations. It could keep for the future.

In the evening she rang Debby.

'We'll be coming back the day after tomorrow. Thursday,' she said. 'Mother's coming with me. Should be at Gobowen at about two-thirty. Are you sure it's no trouble to meet us?'

'No. That's fine. You've checked the train times? Are you all right?'

'I've checked,' said Emma, knowing that Debby would check as well. 'Yes, I'm OK. Tired. Tell you all about it when I see you. I must ring Mrs Hughes to get her to see about beds and so on.'

'Right. Super to have your mother here, and good for you, too, don't you think?'

Why? Emma supposed it would be good for her. She agreed and rang off. Mrs Hughes was gratified as well.

'There's lovely for you to have your mam,' she said, enunciating her words like an automaton. She wasn't telephone friendly, as she had told Emma in the new jargon. 'I'll light the fires and make the guest-room nice. That Ivor and his friend have done the floors. The mess! Shall I leave you a chicken pie to heat up? You'll want milk and vegetables and bread getting in—'

'How are the cats?'

'Wicked, that's what they are, everywhere and under my feet. Your Miss Matty sits in your old chair. Missing you, I'd say.'

'Well, I'll be glad to be home, Mrs Hughes. Thanks very much, it's good of you.'

She took her mother to an Indian restaurant in Camden Town on their last night. She thought she owed it to Charlotte to go Indian.

'Will you go to India, d'you think?' she asked as they ate their way through a hot curry and all the delicious little dishes surrounding it.

'Darling, I'm only just back from Jordan.'

'Of course. From your card you sounded disappointed in Petra. I thought it was supposed to be *the* most romantic place.'

'It was. But it's crumbling away. Little Arab children sell you pieces of lovely striated pink rock they pick out of the tombs. They used to make fires in them, so that the roofs are black with smoke – not that there's much decoration left. But it is magical.' She fell silent, thinking of how she had walked in the fine red dust of once-marvellous carvings, of the shepherd boy coming over a low hill in little Petra, driving flocks of white and black goats, a thin moon rising. 'It's like living in the Bible.'

'I love your Dead Sea bath salts. They leave your skin all satiny.'

'I wonder whether Prue would like some for Christmas? I've got one or two spares.'

'I think she'd disapprove. They do turn the water a funny colour.'

Adela smiled. 'That means you'd like them. All right, I'll put a jar in your stocking.' Then involuntarily, she drew up her shoulders in a shiver of distaste. 'I bought them in the shop of a brand-new hotel we were staying in, on the Dead Sea. We looked straight across to Jericho, you could see the lights of Israel all along the far shore. All round us, out of sight of course, there were soldiers, and I spotted a gun emplacement facing across the sea. They do hate each other so, it seems such a pity. And then there were the cats, families of them; tiny kittens foraging for food in the shrubberies. They were all newly planted, fully grown, those shrubs and flowers, brought in from a nursery somewhere. It gave me an odd feeling – temporary, you know – like being at the Chelsea Flower Show. There for ten minutes, then back to desert again.' She pushed her rice aside. 'I used to save food for the mother cats, they were so thin. The hotel people just ignored them or kicked them aside. That's one thing I hate about abroad, people are so horrible to animals. You never see a cat or a dog on the streets in China though. The Chinese eat everything that moves.'

'Just as well we're in an Indian restaurant, then.'

Emma watched her mother's face light up.

'Except in Venice. You'd love Venice, Emma. On the island of San Giorgio we found a colony of pure black cats with pointed faces like Siamese. People left out dishes of food and water in the bushes. And in the public gardens there was another colony – but they were pure white, imagine! I saw old men and women putting food down for them.'

'Let's hope some kind person takes the females to be spayed,' said Emma. 'Perhaps you'd better go on a cruise next time, Mother. At least there'll only be one ship's cat. If that.'

It was extraordinary to be listening to her mother talking about foreign places. It distanced her, gave her an independence she had never before claimed. In the past Emma had often felt impatient with her mother's generation, standing like sheep, waiting for doors to be opened. So she smiled now to hear her say in a matter-of-fact voice, 'Well, you know, dear, I did try to book up, but I'm afraid it was too late.'

PART 4

Mrs Hughes should have gone home an hour ago, but, as she told her husband later, she couldn't resist being the first to clap eyes on Emma's mother after all these years. She wouldn't have known her, she told him, with that short grey hair – such a glory it used to be – well, we all got old, didn't we? Young Mr Robert from the Hall had driven them from Gobowen. She'd made a jam sponge and some bara brith and they'd insisted she took a cup of tea with them all in the kitchen, although she had set a tray for them to have it nice and cosy by the sitting-room fire.

'The house is lighter than I remember,' Adela had said. 'And you're still here, Mrs Hughes.'

'Just married, I was, a young girl, when I came to work for the doctor. Forty years it's been, near enough.'

She'd left them soon after, so as not to intrude.

'It'll be all round the village now,' said Robert. 'Look, I'll get off as well. But you'll come to tea tomorrow, won't you? Debby's longing to hear all your news.'

Adela did not wish to be rushed. It took time these days to resettle herself. So she demurred and left it to Emma to make the excuse of them both being in need of a rest. She'd ring in a day or two.

'That was well managed, darling.'

Emma smiled. 'I'm not really in the mood for Debby's well-meant advice. Let's take your cases upstairs and then we can settle down and have a proper tea. You're honoured to be given Mrs Hughes's sponge cake. She's never made one for me!'

The guest-room was warm, Adela noted with relief. A fire blazed in the little Victorian grate and some rugs she recognized from the Highgate flat were spread on a shining floor. A lamp by the bed, and the bed turned down. She had brought her own hot-water bottle, not expecting an electric blanket.

'Good heavens, Mrs Hughes has been busy! Ivor and his friend hadn't sanded this floor when I came away. I thought I'd stain it—'

'You can't. She's waxed it and it looks wonderful. It's oak, Emma, it would be heresy to stain it.' She lifted her case on to a chest she remembered giving Emma when she moved. 'Oak, like this. What a pretty room. I'm longing to see the rest of the house.'

In the bathroom clean towels were hanging from the old-fashioned wooden towel horse and Emma left her there to wash her hands while she went into her own room. Maybe the floor there was oak as well. Sure to be. Evidently Mrs Hughes had not had time to wax it, but it looked a great deal better without the cracked lino. She could seal it to save work. She wondered what her mother would make of it. Then, to her surprise, she heard her mother's steps on the stairs, going down.

When Emma came into the kitchen, Adela was lifting the lid off the teapot.

'Let's make some fresh tea, shall we, and sit down? I'm suddenly terribly tired. I can't quite get the hang of this kettle – it's so heavy.'

All at once Emma saw how drained she looked and took her into the small sitting-room, settled her into an armchair and made up the fire. When she brought in the tray she said, 'This used to be Dr Lewis's snuggery; that's what Mrs Hughes called it. Archie said he kept his poisons in here. Look, it leads into the surgery.' She opened the door.

'Do close it, Emma, there's a draught! Oh, delicious bara brith—'

Adela's voice was sharp and Emma sat down in silence to pour out the tea.

'I'm just using it as a sort of storeroom while I think about where to put what.'

'You must stop calling it the surgery, that's your first step.'

How pale she looked! And instead of taking a piece of sponge she had lighted a cigarette. Emma found that she, too, was no longer hungry, but ate a piece so that Mrs Hughes would not be offended. She tried again, 'I've just stopped calling the waiting-room a waiting-room. It's just the big room now. Prudence doesn't approve, she thinks I'm wasting space, it ought to be a fully blown dining-room.'

Faintly Adela said, 'It will take time. Houses have a hold on themselves. Sometimes they resist change.'

'Look, Mother, why don't you go up and have a rest? I'll fill a bottle for you. It's been a long day. I'll call you when supper's ready.'

Upstairs, lying very still on her back with the hot-water bottle in her arms, Adela closed her eyes. Something had made her deathly tired and it didn't take three guesses to know what it was.

Drifting off to sleep, she was invaded by the rhythm of the train. She had sat with her back to the engine so that the shabby outskirts of London had receded as the train swept forward. She was drawn backwards through fields, roads, trees, houses and cattle. Past the Wrekin, past bridges and faint blue hills; seen for a second and then gone. Like old age, everything receding, curiously peaceful. Yet travelling backwards wasn't easy, it wouldn't heal anything. She had been a fool to come.

She woke up feeling much better. The fire was a glow in a room full of an alien dusk. It had been a shock, that was all, walking up those stairs, using the bathroom with nothing changed. Safe in London, she had been happy for Emma to come here and make a new life.

142

But she wanted no part of Emma's life for herself. Could she bear to stay for two whole weeks? She could decently leave after Boxing Day, surely?

A tap at her door brought Emma in to tell her that supper was ready and a glass of sherry waiting for her downstairs. Emma looked anxious, uncertain of her mother's mood.

'Lovely, darling. I'll be down at once. That sleep did wonders. Aren't you tired?'

'Not really. I'm just glad to be home. Did you smell the air when we got here? So fresh, so different from London.'

Adela was sitting on the bed feeling about with her feet for her slippers. While she put them on, she said, 'Oh, Emma, you do sound like your father! That's just what he used to say when he got off the train at Gobowen. "Take a deep breath, this is the real stuff." Do you remember?'

Emma did indeed. Her father slid in and out of their lives like a fish in a river pool, shadow to sunlight.

Downstairs they sat companionably at the kitchen table, enjoying Mrs Hughes's chicken pie.

'She's teaching me the Aga's odd little ways, but I'm sure she prefers to do the cooking herself.'

'Be careful, or she'll take you over as she did poor old Rhys. He couldn't make a move without her say so. Ask anyone.'

'He seems a bit of a legend around here. Debby and Robert were telling me some very odd stories – how he rolled his cigarettes in Izal loo paper for instance, and read the lesson in church without his teeth.'

'He had his own when we knew him – but he was young then. I can't imagine him as an old man.' Adela shivered, as if something had walked over her grave, then pulled herself together. 'I'd love another slice of that pie, Emma. What delicious pastry – so light.'

'That's why I don't mind Mrs Hughes taking over. Being taken over lets me get on with what I want to do, and can do. It's a kindness to let her do what she's so good at, don't you agree?'

Adela laughed. She seemed much better, Emma thought with relief.

'Well then,' she said, 'so long as you can afford her, that's a sound enough philosophy. How are you getting on with the Wentworths?'

'Archie's lovely. I find Prudence a bit difficult, she seems a bit wary of me. Robert's nice, isn't he? And, of course, Debby's an old friend.'

'You'll have to go slowly with Prudence, she's one of the old school, as they say. If you're going to live here you'll have to get on with everybody, it's a small place.' She looked round the kitchen, down at the cats. 'Have you thought of getting a dog? You're fairly isolated here. It would be company for you, and the cats would soon get used to it.'

Emma had already thought about that. Something big and reliable and friendly with a good deep bark. A springer spaniel or a Labrador, perhaps. So she nodded, yes, it was a good idea.

'Cheese? Coffee? Shall we take our coffee in the other room—'

'No,' said Adela quickly. 'I prefer it here. I like big kitchens, and it's so warm.'

There was something too familiar about that other room – an intimate shabbiness in spite of Emma's changes. You could step through the doors into the garden, quite privately, she remembered.

After they had washed up and listened to the news, she said she ought to unpack and have an early night. Emma could show her round tomorrow.

But she couldn't get off to sleep. Maybe because she had slept earlier in the day, or was it the house surrounding her with its silences, its darkness, its memories? She heard Emma come up, lights switching off, a cistern flushing. Her fire had died down and a chill entered the room; her hot-water bottle grew cold.

144

Getting out of bed she put on her dressing-gown. It was very dark outside; in the country the night was always solid black and creatures called through it. It took her back to those first six months after Hugo's death, when sleeplessness was a whole new country.

Waking perhaps at the zero hour of three or four in the morning, switching on to the World Service on the radio to be belaboured on one occasion by an angry play which never matched her own anger. Or to be invaded by the inane chatter of a phone-in station. Why share the early hours with morons? As she switched back to her own empty silence she had wondered at all this nocturnal energy waiting to burst out of the slim black box by her bed. Snatches of remembered music – jazz or classical – occasionally extended a healing hand only to be succeeded by a rapid flow of talk from some foreign tower of babel.

One soft summer night, leaning out of her window into the never quite dark of her north London suburb, she had thought grimly that this mighty heart was certainly not lying still; a rumble of traffic somewhere on a great road, a train whistle, a police siren. It had been a poetic fancy of Wordsworth's, a poet she had thought embroidered nature, quite unlike his sister.

On impulse she had gone downstairs and found the *Oxford Book of Verse*, taken it back to bed to find the poem about Westminster Bridge and was over-come. Once, as a schoolgirl, she had had it by heart, purely as an exercise. Later, lines escaped her as she tried to remember them, fallen into one of those black holes which swallowed memory as you grew older. Now it was as if she read it for the first time. Seeing London in that dawn – he had, hadn't he? He'd been there, in a coach driving out of London to the Lakes. He'd asked the coachman to pull up so that he could look across the river.

The sense of wonder was all there and she

responded to it. It relaxed her mind; the anxiety that fragmented her thoughts fell away as she repeated the lines to herself. They demanded a response, for who wanted to be dubbed dull of soul? That sonorous build-up of imagery – ships, towers, domes, theatres and temples came crowding into one's vision after the first positive statement, the beautiful certainty of an English poet that earth had not anything to show more fair. Then the perfect, daring juxtaposition of two words that made the poem accessible to anyone at all watching a city wake up in the dawn of a new day. 'Touching in its majesty.' Touching! Adela at that moment understood Dorothy Wordsworth's devotion to her brother.

Of all the millions of men and women who had walked across, driven in cars, sat in buses, or merely stood on Westminster Bridge, he alone had seen the fleeting yet eternal soul of a great city. 'Hold it there!' a film director might shout to his camera crew. Wordsworth held it, but in words. Shabbier London might be; fields gone, the skyline gapped, but ships, towers, domes, theatres and temples still lie there and the joke is, she thought, that the air is once again smokeless. And there goes the river, still gliding away . . . How would he have felt, she wondered light-headedly, on the verge of sleep, about Florence seen from the heights of Fiesole? Maybe it was Wordsworth who had really got her travelling, looking about the world to see whether he was right. But every man has his own cherished city.

Since then sleeplessness had ceased to worry her. Once, long ago, Hugo had nursed her through a bad bout of pneumonia. He'd said, 'This is just time passing, not day or night. I'll sit here and read to you and if you drop off, that's all right.'

She had always been a reader, but after his death had for some time lost the capacity for concentration. Books ceased to kindle her. Her mind spun uncertainly around words that had always been familiar – so familiar that they lost all meaning. Like statues whose features had been weathered into anonymity or lettering on gravestones obscured by moss. Words were like strawberries made into jam, perfect and robust in themselves yet stir them together and there was just a sweet mishmash. One should be grateful to poets who gave back their original flavour, made them shine in their own right. Like the happy juxtaposition of 'touching' and 'majesty'.

Now, once again rekindled by books, for reading teaches you that you are not alone, Adela sat up in bed in her dressing-gown and turned to Hazlitt who was always a comfort. Emma, coming in in the morning with a cup of tea, found her lying back fast asleep, spectacles awry, a hand flat on her fallen book and the bedside light still on.

'Well, what do you think of it all, Adela?' asked Prudence. 'Emma's certainly worked hard, I'll give her that. She's changed things at Domen.'

She's been longing to get me over to talk about Emma, Adela realized, glad that she had put off this promised tea party for a few days while she settled in and collected herself. Emma had dropped her off at the Lodge on the way to see Debby, and Prudence had at once taken her through to the kitchen where she was preparing the tea.

'Letty's in the sitting-room, that's why I brought you out here. We can have a private word. She came earlier than expected. Robert picked her up this morning. But—'

'You don't need to worry about Emma,' said Adela. 'She might have some ideas that you and I find a little odd – but it is her house and she's young.'

'But have you seen those terrible pictures? And that room? And having to huddle in Rhys's tiny snuggery or whatever ghastly name he gave it – you must put her right, Adela, or she'll be a laughing stock.' Prudence had overfilled the teapot, unlike her.

'Who's going to laugh? She doesn't know anybody except your family. Give her time to settle, Prue. It's all been a bit overwhelming.' Adela, for the first time in years, felt strongly protective towards her daughter. 'What terrible pictures?'

'Rats. Hundreds of rats and dogs. Horrible. On the wall in the old waiting-room. She *would* go on a rat hunt with Ivor – our cowman's boy.'

'He's the one who sanded the floor and helps in the garden, yes? He seems a nice enough young man. Rats? No, I haven't seen any. She must have put them in her studio upstairs. She's a good artist, Hugo always said so.' Disturbed in spite of herself, she took hold of the tea trolley.

'You'd better carry the teapot, Prue, or it will spill.'

'Well, it's not natural in a girl.'

'I haven't seen Letty since we left, have I? How is she?'

Prue pursed her lips and raised her eyebrows, said nothing.

As they came into the room, Letty made no attempt to rise from her nest of downy cushions in the corner of the sofa. Like a small plump bird she raised her soft disintegrating face and pecked at Adela's cheek when she came across to her.

'Isn't this nice,' she said in a little old voice. 'You do look well, Adela. But you've changed your hairstyle. What have you done with your hair?'

'Cut it off. I had a sudden impulse. But how are *you*?'

'Ancient but happy, that's what I always say. Still keeping busy—' She gestured to two large knitting needles skewering a ball of mauve mohair wool at the other end of the sofa. A heap of knitting flapped out of a canvas bag.

'What are you knitting now? You always used to knit Archie's long socks, I seem to remember.'

Prudence brought a cup of tea over to her sister-in-law and set a small table by her side.

'Hot buttered scones, Letty,' she said. 'No jam because they have sultanas in them. She's on her fifth bedjacket. Aren't you?'

'Why? Are you knitting for charity?'

'Charity? That begins at home. They're for my old age. I've been blessed, you see, with two husbands who adored me. My second had money and died before he could spend it. Lucky me but not so lucky him.' She nibbled joylessly at her jamless scone. 'I miss their little attentions, so when the time comes I'm booking myself into a really nice retirement home to be looked after properly.' And that means jam, she thought. How sharp Prue is getting, how does Archie put up with her?

The two women couldn't be more different, Adela noted, amused.

Letty seemed born to blur boundaries while Prudence defined them. Prudence's style of dressing never changed whatever the fashion. Well-fitting tailored skirts, Pringle woollens; in winter her stockings were warm and ribbed, in summer lighter but sensible. Her clothes had the same classic simplicity she herself possessed. She kept her stomach in and her shoulders back, disapproving of women who let themselves go as they grew older. Buttocks spilling over bar stools and large joggling breasts disgusted her. She suspected that under her sister-in-law's pretty multicoloured layers of silk and cashmere her hips and thighs wobbled in more layers of cellulite.

Just having Letty to stay made her brisker.

Rosie, the old golden Labrador, came in and nosed at the balls of wool on the sofa, sneezed and went over to Adela and laid its head on her lap, gazing sagely up at her. Prudence clapped her hands sharply and the dog reluctantly moved its head, flopped down in front of the fire.

'Do drink your tea, Prue,' Letty said. 'The more you rampage the more nervous I feel. The dog's doing no harm.'

Prudence said nothing and drank her tea. Letty turned to Adela.

'I heard of your sad loss, my dear. But we women learn to be brave, don't we?'

Before Adela could speak, Prudence cut in in her driest voice.

'Adela is over being brave, Letty. She's enjoying life. I hope she's brought some snaps to show us. I'm longing to see you up on a horse again, Adela.'

But Letty persisted.

'Well, I always say you've got to get out of yourself when you lose a husband. I've lost two, so I know. Life can be very inconvenient for a woman without a man to take care of the little things. I wouldn't care to travel alone, but then it takes all sorts.' She cast an eye on Prudence's famous lemon cake. 'I feel safer rolling up my little nest egg. If I'm going to go potty then I'll go potty in comfort.'

Silently Prudence cut her a slice of cake, but Letty was not finished. 'From what I've heard, the world's your oyster, Adela, and you're not short of cash.'

Adela was sorting through her photographs and stopped, looking at Prudence with raised eyebrows. Prudence had the grace to blush, and her neck seemed to take on a red dye which spread up to her jowls and cheeks. She made a futile gesture with her hands, as if to say that Letty had not changed with age, but was even more so.

'I certainly got a good price for our house in Islington,' said Adela with a forgiving laugh. 'Hugo and I bought it so cheaply all those years ago that I felt quite guilty. But it's lovely having money. Isn't that a vulgar thing to say?'

The delicate implication did not touch Letty, but Prudence acknowledged it with a small grimace.

'Don't you miss a garden?' she asked.

'Not now. I've got a few well-behaved plants on my balcony, with a view of the river thrown in. Lawns are so tyrannical, don't you find? There's always something wrong with them, like a permanent invalid.' She sighed. 'Such a relief, Prue, cutting down on *things.*'

Letty had settled down to her cake and been given a second cup of tea, so Adela handed a few photographs to Prue, with a few words for each one.

'We all rode through the Siq to Petra,' she explained. 'It was a narrow way through a sort of gorge. Arabs raced their horses past us and covered us with dust – that's why I'm wearing that scarf round my head, I had to hold it over my mouth and nose . . .'

Archie came in and looked over their shoulders.

'You look very good up there, Addy.' His lips were cold on her cheek. He had just come in from the first flurries of snow. 'How do they treat their horses?'

'Thank goodness, there's a veterinary clinic by the horse lines, founded by one of the Jordanian princesses, I believe, and there's some international funding. Water troughs and a shaded area where the horses can wait out of the sun. All free advice. I went to see it and they told me it had cut down ill-treatment and injuries by a huge amount. It was a relief after some of the things I've seen.'

Letty pursed her lips and shook her head as Prudence passed the photographs over to her. She put on her spectacles.

'Oh, I wouldn't care for all that desert,' she said. 'So nasty and hot. I've always felt sorry for Moses wandering about in it for forty years—'

'Well, I must admit I'd rather travel in those parts with the tour people I went with than with Moses. He'd never make it to the top of the travel business. People simply couldn't spare the time.'

Adela heard Archie exploding into laughter behind her while Letty looked bewildered and Prue smiled.

Maybe travel had sharpened her wits. 'It's odd,' she went on, 'Hugo used to say that a creative imagination was the best kind of traveller's ticket. But I couldn't have imagined half the things that have happened to me, or the things I've seen.' She stared into the fire pondering this secret hunger. No-one spoke. With the passing of years some friends acquired the patina of old furniture, well loved but disregarded. It was when they died the space they left was more apparent than their presence. She was glad of these two. 'For instance . . .' her face lit up into a smile. '. . . I bet Hugo couldn't have imagined that in a Chinese market you can buy bundles of chickens' legs for soup. Or be told that you smell differently from the Chinese because they don't eat dairy produce.'

'I'm with Hugo,' Archie said. 'I'd rather hear you telling me about things like that than go and see them for myself. I'm a born listener, not a doer. Bards were invented just for people like me!'

'Bards,' fluted Letty. She had lost interest in the photographs and was back at the knitting. 'We went to the crowning of a bard once at the National Eisteddfod, didn't we, Archie? Didn't understand a word, of course, but it was very exciting. There were some lovely dancers there . . . oh dear, who's tapping the window?'

'It's Emma.' Prudence went to let her in. As Archie had done, she brought the weather in with her and as she kissed Letty a melting flake dropped on to her knitting.

'You've grown up,' said Letty. 'Now that's a funny thing, my dear. We were talking about the eisteddfod and here you are! Not the big one, of course, but the one in this village. I haven't seen you since, have I?'

'I don't know, but I do remember you. Didn't you have a car with a sort of silver archer on the front – and there was a man with you, a man with a moustache?'

152

The room was very quiet. Adela looked into the fire, flicking up the dog's silky ear.

'There!' Letty was clearly delighted. Her memory was as good as anybody's. 'That was Arnold, my first husband.' She turned towards Adela. 'Adela, surely you remember that dreadful night – Arnold and I ran you to hospital with the doctor and your husband. You didn't have a car, and neither did the doctor. If we hadn't been there it would have been bicycle or horse-back, Arnold used to say. Oh dear, he made a joke of everything.'

'Debby and I won red ribbons and half a crown,' said Emma, looking at her mother. 'We had to recite in Welsh. Wait a tick – didn't Myfanwy get a prize for doing that thing about old Nod the shepherd? We used to imitate her. "*Softly* along the road at *evening* . . ." Sorry. Isn't it funny how it all comes back . . . ?'

'Yes, well, it was a long time ago,' said Prudence.

'What happened? Why were you rushed off to hospital, Mother?'

'I was taken ill. The chapel was so hot and crowded, even the window-sills had children sitting on them. It just went on and on, the singing and the noise and—'

'Such a pity to lose your baby,' said Letty.

'You came home with us, Emma. You and Deb took it in turns to ride piggy-back.' Archie spoke very fast but Emma did not look at him.

'You lost a baby? You lost a *baby*? You never told me. How? How far on were you? Tell me.'

Emma seemed beside herself. Her eyes glittered at her mother. Prudence moved to take her arm but Emma moved away to tower, it appeared to the others in the room, really tower over that slight figure sitting by the fire. The dog yelped as Adela's fingers gripped its ear tightly.

'Three months. I had a miscarriage and we were very upset. Why should we tell a child such a thing? Calm yourself, Emma, please. Sit down, darling.'

'You stayed with us for a week,' said Prudence. 'You shared Deborah's room, don't you remember that?'

'I remember an aunt looking after us at Glammon Lodge. My father and me. Yes. And I remember going for some rides in your car, Aunt Letty.' Emma had always shared Debby's relatives, as Debby had shared hers. Emma sat down on a small stool, still staring quite fiercely at her mother. 'I never knew why. But you could have told me later on, when I grew up. Why didn't you?'

'Why should I? What was the point?'

Archie appeared with a tray of glasses.

'I think a spot of whisky would be just the job, don't you?'

Prudence shot him a look of commendation. His flashes of near-competence never failed to disconcert her.

Letty had been watching them all with a comfortable smile on her face, her little fat hands knitting away, loopy stitches galloping along the needles as if under their own volition. Yes, there was nothing wrong with *her* memory. Maybe, like eyesight, it lengthened as you got older.

'I don't see why you had to make such a scene, Emma,' said Adela as they drove home. 'I was going to ask Prudence about getting you a dog, but not unnaturally I quite forgot.'

Emma's face was set. Her wet boot drove hard down on the clutch as she changed gear and slipped off it, making the gears clash and the car swerve dangerously into the hedge at a narrow corner of the lane.

'I hate secrets,' she said harshly. 'I hate having things hidden from me. Why did you let me go on talking about having a brother or a sister without telling me?' She backed the car away from the hedge, then drove slowly on.

'Has it occurred to you that your father and I had to

154

deal with our own grief and loss? Why bring a child in on it at all? Would you tell Charlotte everything that happened between you and Alex?'

That was a poser and for the rest of the short drive Emma said nothing, concentrating on her trembling hands on the wheel. Her flare of rage had shocked her, springing up so uncontrollably, as if it had been lying in wait. With a sort of horror she thought of the empty house ahead and the two of them alone in it, bitterly at odds. It wouldn't do. So, as she opened the front door for her mother, she said, in a mumble, 'I'm sorry,' and went to put the car away. For once again, implacably, silently, curtains of snow were being drawn against the night.

When she came back her mother had gone upstairs to put on her warm bedroom slippers and another cardigan, for the house struck cold. Emma went up to change out of her jeans into a long warm skirt, her habit in the evenings. There was a knock on the door as she was making up her fire and Adela came in.

'I've made up my fire, I was going to do yours,' she said, and bent to put her arms round her kneeling daughter. It was a brief caress, and as she straightened she noticed the shell house on the shelf above the fire.

'So there it is, the start of it all!' she exclaimed. 'It does look pretty. May I look inside?'

She handled it with the same care she handled books, and as Emma's father had handled books, and Emma warmed to her in spite of herself. She looked at the King and Queen on their thrones and their courtiers standing by. The tiny celluloid baby sat on the floor by the big conch shell.

'I'd forgotten I'd put it there when I found the shell house in the attic. I suppose I imagined they'd like to have a baby—'

Oh dear, Adela thought in consternation, I hope she's not going to cry, Emma had always been emotional and all this fuss over what's long done with! Trust Letty to bring it all up again.

'You would have been so disappointed, Emma,' she said bracingly, feeling that in spite of herself she had to broach the unfortunate subject. 'I know you wanted us to have another child, there always seemed to be a new baby arriving in the village—'

'It's all right, Mother. It was a bit of a shock, that's all. I haven't done any better myself, have I?' She got to her feet. 'And to think that Phoebe's having one – that got to me, I suppose. Alex must be furious.' But was he? The unfairness of it filled her with bitter rage. 'Anyway, let's go down and find something to eat. Sorry about all that at Prue's.'

So that was the trouble. Adela felt nothing but detached pity for her daughter, marrying a man who never wanted children. For herself, one had been enough, she was not a maternal woman and had found a nine-month pregnancy incredibly boring. Time had always bothered her. Her candle, she had always felt, would never last the night – not because she burned it at both ends but she might want to blow it out herself, halfway through. Emma's birth had been tricky enough; she had to have a Caesarean and had been determined never to go through all that trauma again. She didn't want to remember that summer; her dismay at finding herself pregnant and wondering what to do about it. She had been learning to ride – and it was Hugo who suggested she should. He had sensed a restlessness in her and knew that boredom, which had always been her trouble – her attention span for anything undertaken was short – could descend on her blackly, like accidie on medieval monks (the ultimate sin) and sit like despair and horror over a frightening void. Cantering over the hills with Prue, who had lent her a horse, enlivened her. As did the chance meetings with Dr Lewis, out on his rounds on his roan mare.

In the kitchen, over scrambled eggs and coffee,

mother and daughter made plans for Christmas. When to make mince pies and what to give the Wentworths when they came over on Christmas Eve. They went to bed warily with their separate thoughts. Emma, lying awake, knew that her mother had somehow got away with it again. But if you asked questions you had to be sure you could cope with the answers. For sanity's sake, she decided, you couldn't stone the past to death. Best let it go.

The next day Adela sat with Mrs Hughes in the kitchen drinking coffee while Emma was upstairs in her studio.

'I hope Emma won't be lonely here,' she said.

'Lonely?' Mrs Hughes bit at the word as if a piece of grit had lodged in her mouth. 'You're only lonely if you shut your eyes to the world. Your Emma's not like that. She'll do, I'd say.'

'Well, that's all right then. I think I'll stroll down to the shop and buy a paper, it's not snowing.'

She had no intention of walking to the village but felt the need to get out of the house. Borrowing Emma's wellingtons and wrapping up warmly, she set out from the back door, crunching through snow flawless from the overnight fall. She could still smell it in the icy air; the keenness of it sharpened her senses. She made her way out along the path towards the kitchen garden, and in memory scented roses lolled and over-grown shrubs vibrated with bees. On she went, as if sleepwalking, over the short winter grass to the curved stone seat near the half-frozen stream. Lavender bushes she remembered there and for a moment could not make out what those crusty white cannon balls were doing at either end of it. Snowbound cannon balls? In that lost summer she had pinched the luxuriant sprawl of the flowers and leaves, smelt the sweet blue tips, all the time looking across to the far hills, wanting to finish it and not sure how. As if from habit she touched the spiky roundness and found that it was indeed a lavender bush which even on this bitter day yielded a faint fragrance when crushed between her fingers.

As she sat there the garden seemed suddenly full of past anger, buried fury – but so long ago and both men dead. What a nonsense that made of life! The stream, despite the freezing cold, still ran chidingly past her as if to emphasize its immortality. What was it Rhys had said to her once, standing here after a hurried love-making. 'Only a half-dead salmon swims with the current.' She had laughed, feeling liberated. And yet, later – hadn't he after all swum with the current? Refusing her help to get rid of the threatened baby? Hippocratic oath be damned! As usual it was the woman who had to take action. 'Welsh washout, you, Rhys Lewis,' she said aloud, watching her breath thicken and drift away on the bitter air.

'Girls in this village must know what to do,' she had said. 'There's surely some old woman who cures warts and so on, up in the hills?'

'You'd not disgrace your husband by causing gossip, I know,' he'd replied. 'He's a good man, respected as I am and you love him.'

That was true. That she couldn't deny. That was when it ended.

Now she stamped her feet against the cold – no socks in these chilly wellingtons – remembering how she had walked away in tears, wondering how she could live with this lie, waiting for it to be born, to be endured, and never to be sure. Why had she come back to be reminded of all this when for years she had put it behind her, made a good and loving wife with Hugo who knew nothing?

What hypocrites men are, she had thought then and still did. Blackmailing hypocrites, with their fear of losing position, losing respect. There was a beautiful irony to it though, and at the thought of it her anger turned to laughter as cold as she was in this remembered winter garden. For she had managed it herself, telling no-one what the hospital check-up revealed, that riding would endanger the child, her first birth having been so difficult. 'It's as if your body isn't made for children,' the gynaecologist had told her gently. (He wrote poetry which was sometimes published.) 'I'm so sorry. But with care—'

She had determined to ride well enough by the hunting season to follow the hounds on Boxing Day. So she rode hard over the hills, set up jumps in the home paddock, practising until she earned Prue's approval. At the village eisteddfod, then, in that sweating chapel brimmed up to the window-sills with excited children and their families, Rhys had had to take care of her, deal with the miscarriage, drive with her to the nearest hospital. He knew, of course he did, but said nothing. Of course not. That Welsh puritan streak, self-preservation, stared out at her like a yellow streak. Eccentricity worn like a cloak.

So she had ridden to hounds on Boxing Day and everyone remarked on her good seat and wasn't she plucky so soon after her trouble? It was my right, she thought, watching the water pulsate slowly, like a living embryo, white under the slabby ice. I have a right to my own decisions and I feel no guilt. But damn Letty for bringing it all up.

She had a great reluctance to go back into Rhys's house, but when she heard her daughter's voice calling, became aware that she was beginning to shake with cold and her fingertips were quite numb.

Emma was flushed as she stood at the kitchen door. She was holding two parcels done up in brown paper, crisscrossed with special tapes and covered with labels and brightly coloured stamps.

'They've come, look! They're from Charlotte. One's for you!'

Still under the spell of the cold seat, the frozen stream, the waiting unchanging hills as witnesses,

Adela had difficulty in placing the woman standing there; bonny, blooming with excitement. She felt suddenly outmoded and frail, the years behind her dry and crumbled as fairy gold at break of day.

'Mother, do hurry. Oh, you look frozen, I'll make you some coffee.'

Together they put the parcels on the kitchen table, scrubbed clean by Mrs Hughes who had just gone. With kitchen scissors they cut the parcels open and out sprayed silk and cotton in a riot of reds and greens and yellows, blues and purple.

'They're elephants . . .' and Emma spread the silk over the whole length and width of the wooden table '. . . walking through a landscape of temples and trees and lakes . . .'

'Rather gaudy, darling, don't you think?' Looking at the sequins and tiny pieces of mirrorglass winking and glittering up through the embroidery, Adela made a moue. She was too cold, too lost for all this colour. She eased off the wellingtons, sat down and rubbed her cramped toes. A fleeting thought: Hugo would have taken her feet warmly in his hands, caressing each one, kneading the toes back to normal circulation. What big warm loving hands he had! She pushed her feet into her slippers and sat silent, listening to Emma enthusing.

'No. Beautiful! I think it's beautiful. Full of colour and movement. This other one is cotton. Appliqué. Look, flowers and trees and people walking and animals and a lake and birds flying . . .'

'I like that dark green background, yes—'

'Let's open yours.'

Adela was relieved that the elephants were not for her. She had always been sure of what she liked and as she grew older had grown even more discriminating. A difficult woman for whom to buy presents.

Emma, slitting open her mother's parcel, felt dashed. Would Charlotte come up to scratch or not?

There was a letter and a shimmering cashmere square with a deep fringe.

'Oh!' Adela picked up the square, folded it into a triangle and flung it round her shoulders. She glowed in the subtle patterns of rose and green and blue. She read the letter aloud. 'Dear Gran, thought this looked like you. It's from Kashmir and creaseless. Try pulling it through a wedding ring! and wear it for Christmas. I don't know where we will be, but at the moment we're in Varanase. Wonderful with narrow streets and cows walking about and brilliant saris for sale and coloured cycle rickshaws and wedding processions met in the cobbled alleys. It's a very sacred place – and the Theosophical Society have a centre here. Eighty or so ghats on the river Ganges where the dead are burned and everyone washes away their sins. The water's pea-green, so although it's boiling hot I'm not tempted in. Tons of love, Charlotte.'

A little drawing of a laughing buddha wearing a shawl round his head accompanied it.

'Here's some incense for us to burn and a little brass holder. You look wonderful, Mother! Wait a minute, here's a letter for me. She says I can choose one of these – they're wall-hangings or bedcovers – whichever I like. Which one shall I have?'

Adela didn't care which one her daughter chose. She was on her way to look at herself in the bedroom mirror, entirely restored. Emma sat down at the table, listening with an indulgent smile to the sound of her mother's hurried footsteps on the stairs. She found a card in the envelope with a picture of a tortoise being carried through the air on poles supported by two ducks. Villagers looked up in wonder.

We shall be flying to Bangkok soon. Isn't this nice? The ducks can't bear to be parted from their friend. That's how we feel! Don't forget, Mum, 'existence sings with you.' We're having a Zen Christmas.

What on earth was that? A non-existent Christmas, at a bet. There was something else, caught up under the silk. A small box of carved cedarwood. It smelt sweet. Inside were tubes of paint, yellow and red and blue. And a note: 'This special Indian yellow is made from the urine of local cows fed on a diet of lotus leaves. Isn't it just wonderful?'

Wonderful indeed if it were true. Amazing, in fact. And why not? If emerald green was arsenic and smelt of bitter almonds and had killed Napoleon, and ivory black was made from burnt ivory chippings, why not this vivid yellow from the urine of gentle-eyed Indian cows chewing lotus leaves? It made her want to paint a glowing, cheerful picture. Her daughter's thoughtfulness and generosity healed a wound. Be thankful for what you have, she told herself. Suppose I had had a son like Alex. But, of course, she wouldn't let him grow up like Alex; he would be her son—

'You're dreaming, Emma.' Adela came into the kitchen without the shawl; she had folded it away carefully. 'I think the child has excellent taste. How kind of her to spend her money on us. *Is* she all right for money, do you think?'

'Well, this film company are paying her something. I think she can manage. Look, she's sent me some paints. Let's take this into the big front room. I'd like to try it over the fireplace.'

Each holding a folded end, they walked along the hall and into the white empty room. Their feet went smoothly over the newly sanded floor and they did not hear footsteps behind them. Only when they stood before the fireplace did they hear Archie's voice.

'I barged in through the back door, hope you don't mind. Hullo, what have you got there?'

He had come to see that all was well, Emma realized. Sent by Prue?

'We're trying out our Christmas presents from Charlotte,' said Adela, sending him a quick reassuring

162

look. 'Emma thought these elephants would look rather splendid up on the wall here, but we can't heave them up. How lucky you've come, Archie!'

'I'll fetch the stepladder,' he said at once.

'Archie did these walls,' said Emma. 'How do you like them?'

'Well, they're certainly clean and bright.' Adela thought that it would have been better if they had been a putty colour, not so glaring, but she wanted to keep Emma happy. 'A good background for your pictures.'

When Archie came back with the stepladder, Emma fetched a kitchen chair and they sood up on either side, holding up the hanging.

'Tell you what,' said Archie, 'I'll make a sort of frame, it'll hang better. It's gorgeous, Emma.'

'D'you remember the picture that used to hang there in the old days?' Emma asked her mother, watching her face.

'Picture? No. There was this awful wallpaper and a round table and lots of chairs . . .' As they climbed down, Adela looked critically at the dangling centre light while Archie helped Emma fold up the hanging. 'I'll buy you some lamps. How about that? One on either side, we'll choose some pretty shades. That dreadful light makes the room look like a hospital. Let's go into Shrewsbury and see what we can find.' The prospect excited her: anything to make something of this austere room. Change it completely. 'Have you still got my old sewing-machine? We could get some material and I'll make some curtains and cushions – this room used to look so dingy and smelt of sickly bodies! I'd love to help you, if you'd let me.'

'I was going to get some benches and maybe a long table – I sold your sideboard, d'you mind? We won't have time for making cushion covers and curtains, Mother . . .'

She knew her mother of old. The things would be left half done, when her enthusiasm suddenly cooled.

'There's a sale coming up at one of the old chapels,' said Archie. 'Not till after Christmas, though. Oak benches, Emma, not pine. We could drive out and see what there was – anyway, I'll be off. I'll take this with me – I've got the car. See you on Christmas Eve, then?'

Emma put the other appliqué hanging in her daughter's room, laid it over the bed. She'd let Charlotte choose her own decoration. The wardrobe and chest of drawers from Highgate should arrive in the next few days and that would make it look homelike and familiar.

That afternoon they drove to Shrewsbury and found two standing lamps, tall plain wooden ones. Emma chose pinkish yellow shades, unpatterned, which would soften the light. She didn't want to create a cosy image. Later on she'd have to find wall lights for her pictures. To please her mother she picked up a big round paper Chinese shade for the centre light, cream, and bought another for the hall and an orange one for Charlotte's room, and another for herself. She liked the idea of light being enclosed and unfocused. To her relief her mother said no more about material for curtains – after all, she had some up and they would do. Adela was tired; they had tea in an hotel she remembered from years ago. That it was still there, with its comfortable lounges, was an added pleasure.

One curious incident disturbed the new harmony between mother and daughter. One tea-time, when they were sitting in the small room that gave on to the garden – for Adela had conquered her first aversion to it – they heard a kind of scratching noise outside by the French windows. A crunch of gravel, as if someone approached, then stopped. It was dusk, but they had not yet pulled the curtains completely to and Adela, glancing across, saw a dark figure, a shadow in the darkness, looking in. Then it vanished, but no footsteps went away and she grasped Emma's arm, her face white.

Emma was sketching her mother, out of sight of the window and saw nothing. But she had heard something and at once got up and called out, 'Hullo? That you, Ivor?' to reassure Adela as well as herself. She made no attempt to unbolt the windows but pulling back the curtains, peered out into the garden. At once there was a swift shuffle, as if someone had made off round the corner of the house. Emma ran out into the hall, round to the front door and opened it.

'Ivor, is that you?'

No-one answered. Shutting the door, she ran through the kichen; opened the back door and called again. This time she saw a tall figure running down to the kitchen garden. She knew that flapping coat, the way his hands splayed as he ran. But what on earth was Pudding Harry doing here? And why come up the garden that way? The hedges gave on to a small lane, he would have to have pushed his way through.

Slowly she went back to the sitting-room, poured two glasses of whisky and water.

'You can't tell me there was no-one there!'

'No, I'm not going to. It was an odd chap called Pudding Harry. He used to be fat and now he's emaciated – he talked about you, Mother – but what possessed him to creep up on us like that?'

'Pudding Harry?' Adela sipped her whisky, lit a cigarette. 'He used to hold Beauty for me when I drove up to fetch you from school. A fat boy. It's not a name you forget.'

'Well,' said Emma, determined to make light of it, although she was full of unease, 'I expect he wanted to catch a glimpse of you. We should have gone to the churchyard, he's a gravedigger.'

Adela gave a shudder.

'Please, Emma. That makes it worse. But this decides it. You must get a dog. A big one with a bark. We'll ask Prue.'

On Christmas Eve, after their mince pies and hot

punch, the party walked to church, accompanied by a sporadic snowfall and a quiet ring of bells. Archie had brought the Indian hanging and put it up over the fireplace, and it gave Emma a perverse pleasure to fling open the door into the room that had so horrified Prudence a few weeks before, and show her guests its transformation. The two lamps glowed on either side of the bright stepping elephants, in the centre the paper globe gave an added exotic air and a few pictures Adela had persuaded Emma to put up showed to advantage: the bonfire, the hogweed, some charcoal sketches of the barn and the figures inside. Ivor brandishing his rats. She had done another one for herself, and given one to Ivor, who had taken it with a child's pleasure.

Prudence did not entirely approve but did not show it. Letty, holding on to her arm, shook her head in amazement and said that it would look very nice when it was properly furnished, but these things took time.

Heads turned when they went into church. The older men and women smiled in recognition. Adela, gazing round at the simple nativity scene, the holly and the flowers that glowed against the old grey stone, sang the carols and hymns, listened to the well-worn familiar readings and felt disembodied, as if she could at any moment fly off through the shadowed roof and away round the belfry . . .

Debby and Robert walked them home. They left the older Wentworths at the church porch to be picked up later in the car. Adela lagged behind. Her shoe was hurting for some reason, and she stopped and bent down to look at it.

Then there was warm breath on her neck and a hand on her arm.

'Happy Christmas, missis. I've been on the lookout for you.'

That cadaverous face, those loose hanging shreds of

166

hair. She stared at him, silent with fear. The others were laughing, they had gone on well ahead.

'You won't remember me. Neither did your Emma, first go. And I wouldn't really know you without your hair. Pity. Like fire it was.'

'You're the little boy they called Pudding Harry,' said Adela evenly, taking hold of her courage. 'Why did you come up to the window and scare us the other evening? Why didn't you knock on the front door and come in?'

'*You* ask *me* that? I never came in. Come through the garden, didn't I? When you and the doctor was there.' He laughed and his face was too close to hers. His breathy whisper grazed her ear. 'When I was a little chap, you'd give me pennies.'

'Well,' she said, 'that was long ago, Harry. Happy Christmas to you. Perhaps we'll meet again before I go back to London. But if you want to call again, come to the front door.'

'Real sweet on you he was. He'd be glad you came to church.'

Like a shadow he was gone.

'Come over about noon,' Debby had said. 'Robert's parents and his brother's family will be dropping in for drinks.'

Arriving at Talycoed with a box of presents, it struck Emma that the old house was made for celebrations like Christmas. They drove through a white landscape chiming with church bells and the sight of the tall resin-smelling tree in the great hall, shining with the gilt angels and transparent balls that Prudence had kept over the years was an affirmation of stability.

'But of course I remember you,' said Robert's mother to Adela. 'Your husband was so good to Robert – all those years ago!' Ruefully she indicated her stick. 'Dodgy knees,' she confided. 'Let's go and sit down. I was so sorry to hear . . .'

Emma was handed sherry and delicious hot cheesy triangles of filo pastry. As she was introduced to Robert's family she wondered whether Charlotte would ever fit into this polite society, with their talk of horses and hunting – the Boxing Day Meet which the twin daughters were joining. She thought not – the culture shock would be too great on both sides – until she heard a fierce argument carried on in undertones between Davie and one of the dark-haired teenage girls. Neither he nor Robbie cared for hunting, apparently she did.

'Gran's furious,' Emma heard him say lightheartedly. 'But we're not supposed to argue on Christmas Day. Let's go and put on some of Dad's old records in the library. They're a howl, some of them.'

Minutes later, as she was talking to Angela, the twins' mother, the strangled tones of Bluebottle came loud and clear through the library door which opened out of the drawing-room.

'They've found the Goons, then!' she said, laughing.

Sure enough, after some prancing notes of music, came the nasal strains of Spike Milligan's 'I'm walking backwards for Christmas.'

'I never did like those silly voices,' she heard Prudence saying behind her. 'Archie always found them terribly amusing, for some reason.'

'Yes, so did Hugo. He thought them clever, he . . .'

Then Emma turned to see her mother walking rapidly out of the room. Better to let her go.

Outside in the hall, Adela subsided on to the blackened oak settle by the log fire and stared at the flames, her heart pounding. The world was full of tripwires. Marzipan cake and snooker on television she could avoid but old tunes sneaked up on you and there was the past having the last laugh. Hugo turning from the old radiogram, his face open with laughter, doing a silly walk to match the words. 'I really hate Christmas,' she told the burning logs. 'I don't belong to it any more and isn't that ungrateful? But the loss is mine alone. Grief has no place in anyone's drawing-room.'

What would it have been like, she wondered, if Hugo had died in his fifties? Women still had a lot of go in middle age. Enough to make a new life? It was unfair, really, to be allowed a long life so intertwined that it could never be unravelled, like an old and complicated knitted sweater. Adela felt unravelled now, but only in part, and not ready to be knitted up into a different pattern.

Hearing a stir from the drawing-room – people were moving off, no doubt – she walked quickly along the corridor towards the kitchen, where she could be pretending to help. But she couldn't resist taking a peek into the dining-room, and the sight of that beautiful polished furniture, the panelled walls, the table set off by Prue's famous silver epergne full of fruit and flowers, the shining crackers, crystal glasses, white damask napkins with sprigs of holly made her catch her breath. I am ungrateful, yes. So, chiding herself, she turned to say goodbye to the departing family who might, in time, become part of Emma's life, if not hers.

Much later, then, here they all were, sitting round that splendid table, at the port and nuts, Stilton and crystallized fruit stage of the traditional Christmas meal, replete. And there was Davie – irrepressible boy that he was – jumping up with his new instant camera, 'Smile, please, adjust your hats,' and the flash came before Adela could snatch off her ridiculous paper crown.

As he peeled off the photograph, Letty said, 'Well, at least we're all alive in it. I scarcely like to open my old photograph album nowadays. Everybody's dead. Old Aunt Gwen died this time last year, Archie. She was nearly a hundred.'

'Have this, then. Hot from the press.' Davie passed her the damp photograph, now crystallizing into colour, into faces around a festive table. 'All aboard and correct. I'll take another from a different angle, just for luck. We'll hang on to it for posterity.'

'Yes.' Robbie was flushed with wine. 'We'll need to. All this sort of thing will be banned by the time we're your age, Ma. A Labour government and the EEC will put a stop to this sort of feast. Unhealthy eating and so on. Government inspectors will be around checking up. It'll be one glass of sangria and a handful of organic peanuts and that's your lot.'

Letty sat bemused, looking at her drying photograph.

'You've given your father red eyes,' she said, 'and my hat's crooked.'

'Never mind, Letty.' Prudence's moralist's eye homed in on her grandson. 'And you've had more than enough of your grandfather's vintage port, Robbie. It's wasted on the young. Just pass it on, please.'

She cracked a brazil nut with practised ease. It came out whole and she dipped it in a little salt and crunched it between her strong teeth with the enjoyment of a pony with an apple. How like one of her own good linen sheets she is, thought Adela. Flap, flap in a punishing Welsh wind and none the worse for it! Prudence would never wear out. Sides to middle, perhaps, that came to us all. It was sides-to-middle time for herself and the idea struck her as so comical that her face relaxed and smoothed into a smile. Archie, seeing this, raised his glass to her.

'You're looking very well in that cashmere shawl, Adela.'

'Isn't it pretty? Charlotte sent it from India.'

Over a certain age looking well was the greatest compliment a woman could expect from a man. For beauty belonged to the dewy years, beckoning sex. All the same, the compliment revived her. Prudence said sharply, suddenly, in her overseer's manner, 'No, don't smoke in here, please, Archie' – he had taken out a cigar and was turning it between finger and thumb – 'the children have made over the billiard room into a smoking-room.'

'They've what? Smoking-jackets required too, I suppose.' He did not say, 'This is still my house.' For it was and it wasn't. His family had lived in it for over a hundred years, father to son. Father to daughter. But it was plain on his face, and Debby was quick to see it.

'It's all right, Da. Of course it doesn't apply to you, or our own guests. But Robert and I have made it a rule with the shooting parties. We found some burns on the furniture and matches and ash trodden into the carpet, and the smell was awful—'

'The curtains had to be cleaned,' added Prudence. 'Well, if you're sure, Debby, find your father an ashtray.'

Robert looked embarrassed. 'Oh, please, Archie, do carry on.'

'Never thought I'd have a son-in-law who didn't enjoy a good cigar,' Archie sighed, lighting up.

'Actually, smoking-jackets might be a good idea,' said Robert. 'Add to the English image.'

'And caps with tassels. I'll join you in that case, Archie. I'll have a cigarette as it's Christmas.'

There was a rush to bring Adela an ashtray and Davie took another flash picture as evidence.

'Shall we have the Queen with coffee?' asked Debby, and flushed as both boys spluttered with laughter. 'You know what I mean, shall we—'

'We're all anti-TV at school, Ma. We had a debate and won the motion to ban it except for sports coverage.'

'But hadn't you better make the most of her while you can?' asked Robbie solemnly. 'It'll be the Ayatollah making a speech by the time Davie and I inherit.

In fact, Christmas may be banned totally. No more midnight mass or nativity plays or—'

'That's enough, you two,' said Robert. 'You may leave the table.'

'You could start loading the dishwasher, please. Plates and cutlery only. And be careful.'

'All right if we cycle over to the Johnsons' later? They asked us to tea. We'll probably stay on for the evening.'

'Well, bully for the Johnsons,' Debby said as they left the room. 'These lads are getting above themselves. We can open our presents in peace, they had theirs after breakfast.'

'They're dear boys,' Letty's crooked crown gave her a maudlin air. 'I would like to have had children. Hostages to fortune, someone said they were, but how comforting for one's old age.'

Prudence shot a look across to Archie and he took the hint.

'Come on, old girl, let's move into the drawing-room.' Deftly he whisked off Letty's paper hat.

'And I'll make coffee.' Robert escaped into the kitchen.

'Robbie got his computer,' Archie said, when they were all settled. 'Beats me. People have computers these days as they once kept parrots. Ask it "What is morality?" and it will reply as it's been programmed. My father's old parrot – over fifty years old, he told me – used to lift a claw and say, "A peanut for Polly. Parsley poisons parrots."'

'You know the old story about the man who asked his computer whether there was a God?' Robert, coming in with the coffee, caught his father-in-law's eye.

'Probably not.'

'Well, he'd fed all sorts of information into the thing and when he pressed the right key, all that came up on the screen was, "There is now."'

'Go on with you,' said Prudence, missing the joke.

172

'Here's a box for the wrapping-paper. Give me a hand with the presents, will you, Emma?'

Emma had bought the paperback edition of C. Day Lewis's translation of Virgil's *Eclogues and Georgics* for Robert, and relished his amazed pleasure as he opened the parcel. 'I thought your old crib might be disintegrating,' she said, laughing.

Giving and receiving, thanks tossed across the room for velvet slippers, chocolates, expensive soaps, scarves, pipe tobacco. A travel Scrabble set for Adela from Archie, a branched candle holder for Emma from Debby. A book on the Welsh Marches from Robert drew from Prudence the remark that there was nothing books could tell her that she couldn't work out for herself. To which Letty demurred, saying she'd be lost without her knitting patterns. This year's long socks for Archie came in mauve. 'Thought you'd like a change, dear.'

The party broke up, Letty and Prudence to take a nap, Emma and Debby to wash the delicate old coffee cups and put china back in cupboards. Adela elected to go for a walk with Robert and Archie and bundled into her coat and the new woollen scarf from Letty and joined them at the front door. The east wind met them, budded with snow.

'The Welsh call this *gywent o traed y meirw*, the wind from the feet of the dead.' Archie gasped with a mouthful of ice-particled air. 'Are you sure you want to brave it, Adela?'

Adela wound the scarf around her mouth, pulled the borrowed balaclava further down over her ears and thought what a fool she was. But she needed to scour out the warmth and oppressive cosiness of indoors, so she nodded, her eyes already fringed with snow.

'Your husband used to put his head out of the door when it was snowing really hard,' said Robert. 'He'd say it was as thick as Rhitta's beard.'

Adela remembered: Hugo had loved the old Welsh

stories of giants and warriors. Rhitta's beard was thick and black and speckled with white. Legend had it that he lived on Snowdon, top chief of the northern tribes, and cut off his enemies' beards to make himself a cloak.

She looked up. Dark birds dwindled across the heavy sky, as if driven by the wind. Robert opened a field gate.

'I thought we might go through the spinney to the Saint's well,' he said. 'We'll have a sheltered walk, and the hollies there have grown enormous.' In the distance two figures on bicycles sped out of sight down the long drive. 'Adela might be interested.'

He didn't quite know what to make of Emma's mother and only tentatively called her by name as he had been bidden. He still had schoolboy memories of her at Glammon Lodge, down on her knees among patchwork pieces in the sun. On impulse he said, tucking her arm under his, as his father-in-law had done on her other side, 'Do you still make patchwork quilts?' As if to iron out her loss, her change of circumstance.

'Patchwork quilts? No. Why do you ask?'

They were treading along a ride in the spinney, bordered by larch and fir. Frozen cones crunched underfoot, snow dropped from the branches, but the wind raged outside the trees.

'I remember you were making one when I came over for extra tuition with Mr Forden.' He laughed awkwardly. 'I'd never seen a woman with such long tawny hair – the sun caught in it as I passed the open door. You were kneeling in a great puddle of sunlight and all those squares of colour were like flower-beds . . .'

'Why, Robert, you're a poet!' Adela was touched. 'You mean you didn't expect a schoolmaster's wife to be sitting on the floor with her hair down. I must have been drying it. I've always like to do two things at once . . .' And Hugo had loved to brush her hair, bending to the electric crackle as it flowed through the bristles of the hairbrush. He would take up a swathe in his hands and marvel—

'The well, St Garmon's, wasn't it?' she said now, breathlessly. 'Or was it some other saint? We used to come and throw pennies in and wish . . .'

She stopped, disentangling her arms from her companions, and held her left side as if in pain.

'Are you tired? Would you like to go back?'

'No, of course not. I must throw another penny in – but I haven't one on me—'

'I have,' said Robert. 'You shall have one of mine for your wish.'

As they went on through a stand of beeches towards a grove of huge holly bushes surrounding the old well, she thought how lucky Debby and Prudence were to have such sensitive men. Emma had thought the same. Did such men deliberately choose dominating wives? Why? She hoped she had never dominated Hugo.

The well had been repaired since she and Hugo had stood gravely beside it, the broken stone coping had been raised. It was said to possess healing properties and women sometimes dipped their hands in to scoop up the water to drink. He had brought her here, she remembered, in the spring after she had lost the child. All he had said, facing her across the ring of water, was, 'It's time for a move. I've given a term's notice. That gives us all summer to find a place in London. It will keep you busy.'

'London, why?'

'I've accepted that offer Yates made when he came to stay last year. A big school, one of the new comprehensives in north London. I start in September. It will be a challenge.'

He hadn't discussed it with her which was unlike him, for he was by nature indecisive, letting life carry him along. But when he made a decision he moved fast. So she had looked for and found a flat which had to do until they were able to buy their house.

'Here's a five-pence piece,' Robert was saying now. 'One big wish or five little ones!'

'No. Let's all share it. I can't think of any great wish – except that Emma will be happy and marry again—'

'Hush! Don't tell it, Adela. You know you mustn't tell it or it won't come true – wish something else quickly.' Archie looked positively alarmed. He produced another coin. 'Now take this and shut your eyes and concentrate and keep quiet. Then throw it in. No-one knows how deep this well is. Ready, Robert?'

The wind seemed to have dropped, so the snow merely dawdled down on to the three of them standing ringed and dwarfed by golden and silver holly bushes, some still not stripped of their red and white berries. The coins flipped into the still, unfrozen water and Adela watched hers drift slowly down, received and accepted by the saint. As with Hugo all those years ago, they did not tell their wishes, but walked soberly home in the darkening afternoon to tea round a log fire.

Back in the house, feet up in the library, Debby and Emma peacefully watched the fire brighten as the light faded from the oblongs of the windows.

'Lovely time of day, this. Especially at Christmas,' murmured Debby. 'That huge meal behind you for another year.'

'You do things so well,' Emma responded. 'Nature's chatelaine!'

'And you're a tease. Your mother wears well, doesn't she? What energy at her age—'

'I think she's thinner and looks tired. I don't know whether all this dashing about is good for her – she needs a rest, I'd say, but of course she won't stay with me. I think she's got some plan for a cruise in the new year – she's waiting for a call in case there's a late cancellation.'

'That'll be restful. A cruise! Bliss, that would be,

doing nothing and being waited on, but Robert and I could never get away. I suppose leisure is one good thing about getting older. You can do what you want.'

'If it isn't too late.'

The kitten Debby had chosen from Miss Matty's litter had found its way into the room from the kitchen and walked straight up to the fire, stretched out in front of it, purring loudly. Emma had brought it over a few days before. It was a pretty cat, black and ginger, strong and bossy enough to leave home. She called it Joe because it boxed like a kangaroo. Debby, because it was so near Christmas, had wanted to call it Noel.

Now she watched the little cat, thought about the black-and-white one – they were a multicoloured litter – she had taken over to Myfanwy at the Lion and felt guilty at breaking up a family, which was of course absurd.

'You won't banish Joe to the stables, will you, Deb? You'll let him be a house cat?'

'We'll see if he gets on with Rosie.'

'You can see now.'

Rosie's old golden head came round the door, nosing it open. She made for the fire and stopped at the sight of this new tenant of the hearthrug. The kitten looked up, still purring, and stretched out a lazy paw. The old dog walked over, sniffed at the paw, fended it off and gave the kitten a push, then settled down in the middle of the rug, pretending to close her eyes. When she heard the tiny hiss, saw the arched back, she merely twitched an ear, opened her mouth and yawned. After prancing round for a while, tail held high and fluffed out, the little cat came over to the sofa and jumped up beside Emma. Soon it folded its paws neatly under its chest, keeping a green unwavering gaze on Rosie.

'He'll do,' said Debby, laughing. 'Rosie's not bothered. Mind you, Joe will have to prove himself a first-rate mouser . . .'

Two points gained. Emma couldn't envisage a cat called Noel catching anything but a cold.

'By the way, Angela thinks she can get you a puppy. I asked her this morning. Have you ever kept dogs?'

'Well, no, but I expect I can manage. What sort of puppy?'

'Either a Labrador from a woman in Borth who breeds them – that's where we got Rosie – or one from her own redsetter bitch.'

'I'd rather have a Labrador like Rosie. She's such a kind dog.'

'That's what I thought. We could go over one day. Angela's bitch is too highly-strung. You don't want a highly-strung or nervous dog.' Debby hesitated. 'My mother's funny about dogs. She said that the awful thing about life is the number of horses and dogs you outlive.'

'Very philosophical for Prue.'

'Isn't it? She thinks a dog should interview its prospective owner to see if they're compatible.'

'Well, lead on. I'll just have to learn to bark to communicate.'

'Oh God, here they are back from their walk. Time for tea.'

Christmas evening burned down to a comfortable glow. A memorable start to the last decade of the century. Chestnuts gently popped in the ashes, mulled wine breathed its incense over comatose figures. People told stories.

'Did I ever tell you—' Archie started to say.

'I'm sure you did, dear,' interrupted Prue. 'If it's that one about the scarecrow—'

'No, it isn't, and Adela hasn't heard it, because it happened after they'd left. It was that Christmas Rhys was called out to Lloyd's farm. One of his boys had put his tongue on the flywheel of a threshing machine for a bet. Frosty morning it was. Anyway his tongue froze there and Rhys had to scrape it off with a heated penknife.'

'I hope the poor lad managed to eat his Christmas dinner,' giggled Letty. She sat where a pink lampshade cast a glow over her plump fallen cheeks; not unlike the false health given to tomatoes by supermarket shelf lights. 'How can the young be so stupid?'

'He's still got some sort of impediment in his speech, although Rhys did his best.'

'What a beastly story, Archie!'

'Well, it's no worse than the one Prue always tells about that cat we had – Bossy – which went missing for a month and had to have his collar cut out because it got embedded when he tried to scratch it off—'

'I told that silly woman we had working here not to put a collar on him and she wouldn't listen. Best stable cat we ever had, caught rats the same size as himself.'

'Well, Joe won't have a collar, I hope,' said Emma. Country life was certainly not idyllic, maybe they were trying to tell her something.

'Rules,' said Prue strongly. 'We all have to live by rules. No tongues on frozen metal, no collars on cats.'

Letty nodded sagely, then protested. 'But at our age, Prue, we've done with rules. That's one blessing'

'Oh, I don't know.' Adela was eating a minty chocolate, her hand on Rosie's head. 'We mustn't think of ourselves as a sort of ethnic minority, Letty, and demand special rights. I've seen dreadful old women shove people out of the way with their rubber-tipped sticks. Good manners are for everyone, young and old.'

'How about a game of mah-jong?'

Debby to the rescue. Mah-jong, so exotic, so pretty, building walls of the four winds. Ivory pieces clicking together.

'Yes, let's play mah-jong.' So mah-jong it was.

*   *   *

Emma woke late on Boxing Day morning, muzzy with a hangover. A loud knocking filled her head and it didn't seem fair that champagne and brandy could do such things to her. Swinging her legs out of bed she lurched dizzily towards the window, squinting away from the morning sunlight which shafted off snow straight into her eyes. Down below the knocking started again. She could imagine some imperative hand heaving up the knocker on the oversized lion's head and cursed it.

Raising the sash window the cold hit her in the face. Unlike the old doctor, she kept it closed against the bitter night air. On the porch a tall figure with something in its arms looked up at her. Ivor.

She called to him and he shouted something up.

'All right, I'm coming. For God's sake . . .'

Tying her dressing-gown tightly round her waist, she took a deep breath and went at a staggering run to the door. Steadying herself on the banisters, she made it downstairs successfully and managed to walk towards the front door, unbolted it and held it half open. Ivor at once slipped in. Was this an old Welsh custom, she wondered, like the tradition of Mari Llywd? He led the way to the kitchen, which still held the warmth of the previous day, and at once sat down, cradling a bundle wrapped in an old piece of blanket.

'I've brought you something,' he said, and she noticed that one cheek was suffused with blood. He drew back the blanket and a narrow black-and-white head nosed up out of it, great brown eyes matching the anxiety in his. The dog's body was thin, its coat matted and there seemed to be a lump behind one of its ears.

'It's a Border collie,' was all she could say. 'Let me make up the Aga and put the kettle on. What's wrong, Ivor? Has it been run over? Shall I heat some milk?' She put out a hand to touch the dog's head but it flinched away back into its blanket.

'Da won't let me keep her.' It was then she saw that

Ivor's eyes were red and it was not the wind. 'She's not a year old and I've nabbed her like from the top farm up by the Waen. Bloody old Lloyd kicked her. No good for sheep, he reckoned. So I took her.'

'Took her?' Emma felt steadier now; she sensed a crisis. 'Just like that? What were you doing up at the Waen?'

Lloyd; she worried at the name. It sounded familiar. She'd heard it quite recently.

'Keeping an eye. Do a bit of work for him, don't I? Seen him with dogs. This one was a pup from his sheep dog but she won't make it, see? No use with sheep. Nips 'em, got no idea—'

'She's too young, surely.'

The kettle was singing and she made tea, put on a saucepan of milk, broke some bread into it.

'Old bugger locked her out of the barn, I found her curled up in a hedge, cold to death, poor little bitch, so I took her home, but Da . . .' He put a hand up to his cheek. Emma poured him a cup of tea, attended to the milk, poured it into a bowl and set it on the floor. Very gently Ivor knelt down with the dog and coaxed her to drink, but her back legs gave way and she could only squat and shiver, her head dropping low. The cats had woken up and Miss Matty was slowly arching her back ready to hiss at the intruder. Without a word Emma picked her up and took her through to the scullery beyond, then carried the big basket with the two sleepy kittens stirring indignantly and put them on the floor near her. She shut the door.

Ivor reached out for his tea and gave a great sigh. 'Aye, you're a good'un. Knew I could count on you. Need a dog, your mam was saying.'

Emma looked at the shivering heap in front of the Aga and bit back a wry smile.

'Try feeding her by hand, Ivor,' she said. 'She trusts you.' She drank her tea, hands round the mug and watched while he dipped his fingers in the milk, touched the dry muzzle and murmured softly in the ragged ears. Tentatively the little bitch responded, licking his fingers, then his hand. At last she found the bowl and her long pink tongue curled round the pieces of bread, lapped the milk, then with a sudden rapid ferocity licked the empty bowl, looked aside in fear, then up at Ivor.

'Shall I give her some more or not?'

'Yes, just a little, she's starved.'

Emma fetched the big cardboard box in which she and her mother had packed all their Christmas presents. It still had Christmas paper on the outside, but she left this, cutting away one side to within six inches of the bottom. Ivor watched as she heated more milk and crumbled bread into it.

'Blood heat,' she said, looking up, 'and we might mix in an egg for extra nourishment. They're over there.'

The blanket was damp, so she hung it over the rail in front of the Aga and lined the box with newspapers.

Adela, who had heard some commotion and found Emma's room empty, now came downstairs to investigate and found them engrossed, Ivor with the little dog, the most miserable thing she had ever seen, and Emma clearing up cardboard from the Christmas box.

'Any tea left?' she enquired cheerfully, determined not to lend the situation any further drama. This was country life, she reminded herself, and anything might happen. 'Or shall I make some fresh?' Was this young man with his poor-looking dog staying to breakfast, with them both still in their dressing-gowns?

'There's some in the pot, Mother. Look, Ivor's brought us this poor little Border collie bitch – it's been terribly ill-treated.' Surely, oh surely not – but she caught Emma's warning glance and bit back her dismay.

Ivor said protectively, 'Jessie. She comes to Jessie. Old Lloyd called her after his first wife. The one he never liked.'

182

'Jessie,' repeated Adela, looking at the little dog, now lapping her egg and milk. 'Jessie.'

To her amazement the dog looked round at her, eased itself up from its squatting position and wagged its tail. Despite herself, Adela was as pleased as if she had pulled off a clever trick.

'Well done, Mother!'

'Taken to you,' said Ivor. 'It's your voice, see? Nice and gentle. Low pitch.'

It was extraordinary. The little bitch kept on lapping up the milk, all the time cocking an eye in Adela's direction, tail slowly moving. Adela flushed, moved by such confidence. She had never kept a dog and wondered why they took to her.

'Perhaps we should dry her off, rub her gently in a towel to get her circulation going. Wait. I'll get one.'

Forgetting her tea, Adela found a towel and warmed it in front of the fire. Then she knelt down when the dog finished its meal and very gently started to rub it down. It sat under her hands quite still, looking up into her face until she tried to dry underneath its body. Then winced away with a yelp but made no attempt to bite.

'Ah, Jessie,' she breathed in its ear. 'That's enough then. Let me just dry your paws.'

'Could be a crushed rib, Ivor, if that brute kicked her. We'd best get on to Morgan Griffiths, ask him to take a look.'

'He's off visiting his auntie in Corwen. Always does at Christmas. Back tomorrow.'

'Let her rest,' said Adela. 'There you are, Jessie. Good girl then. Put her in that box, Emma, and let her sleep.'

'You put her in. Go on, you're the one she's taken to.'

'I can't remember when I last picked up a dog. Is she heavy?'

'Sparrow bones,' said Ivor, 'light as a newborn babby. Here, I'll take her, she knows me.'

'Good. Now let me put this cushion in first. I'll lay the blanket over it, it's dry now. Don't you love that frown, Emma? Those vertical lines between her eyes? It gives her such a quizzical air. Is this Morgan Griffiths a vet?'

'Yes. I liked him. He'll know what to do. I'll ring him tomorrow and we can take her over together.'

'If I'm not busy packing – I promised to ring the travel people tomorrow.'

So it was still on her mind! Emma looked at her mother as she had so often done as a child, with the same judging eyes. Accepted, as in the past, that responsibility for disagreeable jobs was hers; her mother could not be bothered.

'I'll come.' Ivor stood up eagerly, pulled on his working gloves, wet as they were. His hands were still raw from the cold. 'You'll want someone to hold her. And I'd best have a word with Mr Griffiths. Might be trouble.'

'Why is the name Lloyd so familiar? Do I know him?' Ivor shrugged.

'Farms with his two sons. One's married, wife looks after them all. Ieuan's as bad as his da. Tongue got cut about when he was a lad, given him a nasty temper. Talks funny, see?'

'Good heavens,' exclaimed Adela, at the door. 'Archie was telling us about that last night, wasn't he, Emma?'

'So he was. Look, Ivor, tell your father I'll keep Jessie until I've had a word myself with the Lloyds. If necessary I'll offer them money for her.'

As he was going Ivor said, tentatively, 'Coming to the Ratcatchers' Ball, then? We're having a bit of a do.'

But Emma shook her head, laughing.

Later that day, Debby rang up to scold.

184

'You forgot to come to the Meet. You missed them all going off! Whatever happened?'

Emma had heard distant hounds giving tongue, heard the rallying cry of the horn, but had disregarded them. As, oddly, had her mother.

'We'll just have a quiet day and keep an eye on Jessie,' Adela had said. 'I'm not in the mood for horses somehow.'

She wasn't in the mood for country things at all. And the next day, when she heard that the cancellation was firm – yes, she could have the outside cabin, but it would cost more than the original booking she had tried to make – she brushed aside the extra expense and confirmed it at once.

Time to be off. Elderly relatives should be packed off home after their Christmas airing; like Christmas tree decorations and Prue's beautiful silver epergne. Wrapped in tissue paper for another year. She was eager to get back to her own routine, such as it was. Only a couple of weeks to get ready for her cruise, and then there were the sales. She'd need some new clothes for the sun.

Letty was leaving, too. A friend from Chester was picking her up for New Year.

'Don't you mind New Year's Eve on your own?' Emma asked her mother. 'You know you're welcome to stay over.'

'I do mind New Year's Eve on my own, yes. I'd be a fool to say I didn't. What about you?'

'Yes, I do. But I shan't this year.'

The night before she left Adela dreamed of Hugo again, walking away from her down long corridors in a grey light. She could never catch him up. At breakfast she said, half laughing, 'D'you think Prue dreams? Some people don't. Do you, Emma?'

'Sometimes. The occasional nightmare. I hate them.'

'I don't suppose Prue would allow a nightmare to show its face—'

'She'd put it out to grass.'

'Darling,' said Adela. 'It has been nice. Take care of Jessie, won't you? She looks miles better already.'

From the hearthrug Jessie wagged an appreciative tail. Vitamin injections, tender care, careful feeding, Morgan Griffiths had said.

'And you wanted a sturdy watchdog with a loud bark!'

'You never know how she'll turn out. Are you all packed? We ought to make a move. I'll miss you.'

As the train left Gobowen Adela had a curious feeling of lightness. It was like taking off a heavy hat and shaking your hair loose. Unbidden, an image of her grandmother came to mind – this happened, she supposed, to old people, the past crowding in as if to compensate for the present. Anyway, there she was, her grandmother, lifting those thin deft hands to unpin a summer straw brimming over with velvet roses. Standing in the cool hall, thrusting the long pearl-topped hatpins back through the hat, laying it aside. Turning . . .

The image faded and it was her own reflection in the window superimposed on passing fields. 'We ought to make a move,' Emma had said. They both had. Did one ever stop?

PART 5

The house struck very silent as Emma let herself in after seeing her mother off from Gobowen. She had enjoyed, she realized, the sound of another person using the bathroom, of other footseps on the stairs, the closing and opening of doors, the possibility of making a comment that was answered. She had got into the habit of taking her mother a morning cup of tea, a shared pleasure. For, as Adela had remarked one day, a constant reminder of widowhood was the realization that there was no-one but yourself to boil a kettle and set out a tea-tray.

Emma did not envy her mother setting off for a cruise to the sun: she had enough to do here and each day settled her more deeply into this new life. She became aware of the weather; how it changed the colour of the hills; aware of the birds she fed, of the many tasks she set herself. Soon the year would be on the turn.

Wandering into the big bare front room on New Year's Eve she noted the pale honey of the floorboards now that Ivor had sealed them, and felt the need of some private celebration. A positive statement now that the house was hers again. Looking from the wall-hanging to the bare boards she knew at once what to do. The soft flakes of snow – for it had started again after several days of clear skies – whitened her hair like a shampoo as she ran out of the kitchen to the outhouse to fetch the clothes line, some nails and a hammer. Then, up to her studio for chalk and a metal measure.

She would design her own floor.

Two feet out from the wall, that would do it. Carefully she nailed one end of the rope to the floor, paid it out across the room, turned it and secured it two feet from the opposite wall. Then brought it down the length of the room, fixed it; turn again under the windows, two feet out, fix it. Then along and up the long side to the start. Now she had a rectangle. She drew a thick white chalk line along the rope, unnailed it. Stretched it diagonally, corner to corner. Chalked the lines. Then across the centre, side to side, and lengthwise. Now she had eight triangles. A foot and a half in from the outer edges, which gave her a border.

At last, stiff and exultant, she sat back and looked up at the sauntering green and red and yellow elephants with their glinting ruby eyes and absurd stiff tails. 'You'll like this,' she told them. 'This is an Indian room. You'll feel quite at home. And I feel the self of my former shadow.'

The sky was darkening, the afternoon drawing in. She moved to the kitchen and set out large pieces of lining paper and designed her painted floor.

The centre motif must be flowing, rounded, to offset the squares and triangles; to soften the room and echo the voluptuous procession of the wall-hanging. But not too busy, because she would be hanging her pictures and this room must be her window on the world; a private gallery where people could come and be intrigued enough to buy work. Her thoughts ran on: surely there must be a potter in the district? Ceramics would set off the whole room . . .

Several shades of green, from sharp lime to blue-green; stiff palm trees in each triangle, a yellow-and-red border in a lotus flower and leaf pattern – dark blue. On paper it began to take shape well. But would it wear, once walked on?

The next day, Archie called in, thinking she might be feeling a bit flat.

'Prue and I expected you last night to welcome in the

188

New Year,' he said. 'Debby and Robert went off to a dance across the county. What happened? Anyway, Happy New Year, my dear.'

'I forgot. I'm so sorry, Archie. I had this idea, you see, and worked quite late on it. Tell you what, let's have a drink now.'

She led the way to the kitchen to fetch a bottle of wine. At once Jessie shrank back into her box.

'Is that the little bitch? She'll never be any good, Emma.'

Of course he had heard what had happened.

'She's frightened of men. That's why she's trembling. She's made friends with the cats.'

'Prue's coming over to have a look at her. Have you fixed things with the Lloyds?'

Emma opened the bottle and handed him a glass of wine.

'Happy New Year! Morgan Griffiths is a wonder. He rang this morning and said he'd fixed it for me. All Jess needs now is loving care and vitamin injections and her ribs will heal more or less on their own.' The telephone call had made her laugh. The sound of the telephone ringing had brought out the first sharp, small bark from Jessie. 'Mr Griffiths just said that he'd had a bit of a chat with Mr Lloyd and told him we'd say no more about mistreatment to the authorities if he agreed to settle all veterinary charges.' Archie gave his curious little neigh of laughter at Emma's imitation. 'He said no money should change hands for the dog as Mr Lloyd knew where he stood in the matter.'

'All the same you don't want bad blood with the Lloyds. I had a word with Ivor's father, by the way. He's another hard man, insisted on the boy giving Lloyd five pounds out of his own money in compensation, did you know?'

'Yes. I'll pay that. But Lloyd hasn't a leg to stand on, Archie. I'm sure Mr Griffiths made that clear. What a beautiful measured voice he has—'

'Sings in a male-voice choir. Good man to have on your side.'

They sat companionably, watching the little dog. They saw Miss Matty walk up to the box, put a tentative paw over the edge, then jump in and sit against the shivering flanks. Jessie looked down at her, put a nose to her head and lay down quietly.

'They know they're both orphans of the storm. Miss Matty was a stray, did I tell you?'

'You've got an animal refuge here! Still, it wouldn't be a bad idea to think about that Labrador pup a bit later on. See what Prue says. That one's no Cerberus, Emma.'

'I'm calling her Jess from now on. Just to distance her from her wretched namesake, the first Mrs Lloyd.' She smiled. 'Until she sprouts a couple more heads, that is.'

'That's fine with me. I came over to tell you that the sale is on tomorrow. Chapel furniture up Llanfyllin way. Near Ann Griffiths's old place. You're after benches, aren't you? Would pews do? They'd be oak, not pine. That black oak settle of ours in the hall up at the house came from the church when it was renovated in the 1850s. I only found out thanks to your father's notebooks. Date 1672. My great grandfather was a churchwarden and was given the pick of the stuff the Victorian so-called restorers threw out. Along the back there's some carving. It says, "In the world ye shall have tribulation."' Emma shivered, as if a cold finger had touched her, poured them more wine. 'Several landowners paid to have that Jesse window put in, and the floor of the aisle re-paved. They found a great jumble of bones when they dug it up—'

'Bones? What bones? Whose bones?'

'Nobody knows. Maybe it was a kind of plague pit. They were all decently reburied up in the old churchyard. I go with Hugo's theory that they date from 1672 – the same year the high-backed pew was put into the church. Think of the words, "In the world ye shall have tribulation."'

'I should think twice about having it in my hall.'

'Ah,' Archie gave her a triumphant smile. 'But have you ever noticed that carved plaque over the fire-place?'

'Yes. But I could never read Latin.'

'*Ascendat oratio, descendat gratia*. Prayers rise up, Grace comes down, at a rough translation. That was on the pulpit originally. So you sat in the pew, prayed, listened to the preacher and the result was an all-round spine-strengthening exercise. Those old clerics weren't fools.'

'These benches, pews, Archie – you said near Ann Griffiths's old place. Who's Ann Griffiths?'

'She wrote hymns in the eighteenth century. She was a Methodist, lived at a hill farm, Dolwar Fach. Worshipped at Pontrobert. Died before she was thirty. Hugo used to go up there. It fascinated him.'

Emma at once saw her father cycling through the hills. He'd like her to have some old pews from one of the derelict chapels.

'He used to say that they were like extinct volcanoes and the windows were bathroom private. Remember Bethel outside the village? All that opaque glass at head level to foil the merely curious . . .'

On the way up into the hills the next day Archie warned her not to expect much. The little chapel had been built after the first wave of revivalism had swept through Wales in the 1780s and was now a wreck. Ann Griffiths had heard Benjamin Jones preach outside the Goat Inn at Llanfyllin, apparently, and had deserted the Anglican Church and worshipped here for a time. 'There's something about Calvinist Methodism that appeals to the Celtic temperament,' Archie remarked. 'Our church is too dull. They like a bit of hellfire.'

The chapel was built into the hillside, looking as if

the next big storm would bring it down, for the damp had seeped into the timbers. Outside, a small crowd of men and women, as weathered as the rocks they stood among, shuffled and laughed in the mud and slippery grass. The auctioneer, a small lively man with an eyepatch and a black balaclava, led the way inside out of the wind. A smell of damp and decay. Pews and chests and a cupboard or two, the pulpit and the big seat itself. Not much.

Emma had only once seen a *set mawr*, the 'big seat' which the elders occupied on the right side of the pulpit. This one was plain oak, with a wooden rail running along the back and curving round to form an arm on one side.

'That's what I want, Archie,' she whispered.

The auctioneer was in good voice. He took his place by the big seat and began to talk about the 1859 Revival, putting his hand on the rail.

'How do we know, my friends, that the great David Morgan himself didn't put his hand where my hand is?'

'Can't tell us, can he, Dai Jones!' one wit shouted from the door. 'Never come here, did David Morgan. Meifod, yes.'

'Don't know for sure, do we? Things lurk behind the veil, always have. But my great grandfather heard the Word from Morgan. Strata Florida way. He had old women dancing and prancing in front of the big seat. Following the Psalmist's injunction, my friends, "Praise the name of the Lord in the dance." He had drunkards falling on their knees, forswearing the devil of drink, he had—'

'Get on with it, man, there's a cold wind up my behind!'

'I'll leave you with just one word, then. My great grandfather wrote in his diary that David Morgan had a curve to his voice as delightful to the ear as the rainbow is to the eye. In this chapel the voices of

192

the ministers echo. Echo too, do the hymns of Ann Griffiths, born not a dozen miles from here, "Lo, among the myrtles standing", for one. We could sing it as a valediction if we had an organ.'

'There's no organ we're needing,' piped up an elderly woman with a sack over her head. 'We all of us know it very well indeed.'

And to Emma's amazement, first of all raggedly, then full-throatedly, the buyers, now a congregration, found their way into the hymn. By the end of it, 'O to rest me/ All my lifetime in His love!' she found her eyes wet. Archie squeezed her hand, gave her a sympathetic wink.

'Now to business. We will start the bidding for these two fine oak cupboards, just a suggestion of wood-worm, easily cured. Stand together very nicely they would, in some fine hallway—'

'Five pound.'

'Five pound I'm bid. Five-fifty. Six pound. Seven. Seven-fifty. Come on, ladies and gentlemen, seven-fifty. Simply giving them away, isn't it? Take another look now. Eight, sir, at the back. Nine—'

Knocked down to Lloyd, the Waen. Bryntanat.

'Oh my God, he's here.' Emma clutched Archie's arm. Archie glanced around, raised his old trilby hat to someone she couldn't see.

'It's Ieuan's wife. She's bidding.'

'Solid as the Christian faith, these pews. Finest oak. What am I offered? Starting at five pounds each?'

'Two pounds each, man.'

Emma raised a tentative hand.

'Three. How many you having – the lot, missis? Starting a school then, are you?'

To a roar of laughter, Emma called out, embarrassed, 'Two.'

'Any raise on three pounds? Six pound the pair.'

'Eight pound the pair.' A woman's voice.

Emma made to raise her hand again but Archie stopped her, and bid instead.

'Nine pounds.' His voice rang out strongly and they were knocked down to him. Emma turned in amazement, but couldn't catch what he whispered in her ear. He gave his name, and the auctioneer at once beamed, calling, 'Mr Wentworth, Talycoed.'

It was obvious that the big seat was the centre of interest, with the pulpit. Two black-coated ministers had slipped in and were signalling with folded-up Parish magazines. Archie urged Emma out and went back to pay and have a word about the pews. Soon after, a couple of men carrying them passed her on their way down the hillside to the truck Archie used for jobs around the farm.

'What was all that about? I wanted to stay to the end. I know I didn't have a chance with that big seat.'

'I should think not! It's Chapel. Sinners called to it to confess and all that. It's history – heavy drama – even if David Morgan didn't preach from it, or the pulpit for that matter. The deacons would never let it go to outsiders like us.'

He manoeuvred the truck down the track on to a narrow lane, drove slowly between brimming ditches. 'And Mrs Ieuan Lloyd would never have let you have those pews, that's why I chipped in.'

'OK. I get your point about bad blood. I'll call on the Lloyds. It'll be awful, but – *outsiders*, Archie? Are we?'

'Of course. Now we've gone they'll be bidding in Welsh.'

He stopped the truck on a rise in the lane. Fields and hills gleamed fitfully in the winter sun when it escaped from the rolling clouds.

'This country's a palimpsest. The past is only just under the skin of it, like Webster's skull. The 1859 Revival is like yesterday to them. It was a heath fire of faith, roaring through Wales.'

'But your family has been here for ever—'

'Makes no difference. We're not pure Welsh. We're

lucky things didn't go the way they did in Ireland. Anyway, cheer up, you've got what you wanted, so maybe you'll stay. They're a present from me.'

He started off again, and on the main road drew into the car park of the Powys Arms.

'We need a drink,' he said, and over their pints nodded gravely at her. 'Here's to you, my dear. I'm feeling melancholy, so forgive me. Always do at New Year.'

'Archie, of course I'll stay. Why do you doubt it?'

Emma felt wary of this strange mood. He wasn't teasing.

'Well, your parents left. And Adela seemed so eager to go after Christmas. Do you think she enjoyed herself?'

'Oh yes. In her way. It must be hard for her, Archie, coming back . . .'

'So she's on the move again. She's like that man in the Chinese allegory who tried to outrun his footprints, outpace his own shadow.'

'What happened to him?'

Draining his beer, Archie said, 'He died of exhaustion. The monk then blandly explains that if he had stood still there would be no footprints. If he had rested in the shade his shadow would have disappeared.'

'I don't think that will happen to Mother. She paces herself very carefully. Anyway, how boring to sit in the shade all one's life! I'd rather try to dodge my shadow and have some fun on the way.'

On the way back to Bryntanat, she said tentatively, 'I'd like to go through my father's notebooks with you some time. From what Mother said, there might be more. I've a busy year ahead. Domen will be fairly humming, you'll see.'

'I've met such an odd woman,' Adela wrote to her daughter, sitting at her dressing-table in the single

195

outside cabin which was a self-indulgence. 'I call her the Happy Medium. Her fingers are crowded with rings like a curtain rail and her eyes are extraordinary. Do you remember how Colette described Cheri's eyes? Dark, and shaped like a sole, curving above and straight below? Well, they're like that, with a fishtail flick at the outer corners. She emphasizes this with a clever touch of dark grey (not black) mascara. Her hair is drawn back with a severe centre parting and one side is white, the other black. People whisper as she processes to her table at dinner (yes, she's large enough to *process*), wondering which side is dyed, the white or the black. She strikes me as an enlargement of a much smaller woman.

'Your father's friend Humphrey – hardly a friend, but one of those people who erupt throughout one's life – is on board. I couldn't believe my eyes. You probably don't remember him, but his pomposity has run to fat and he still knows everything better than anyone else. He uses a monogrammed silver toothpick – a disgusting practice. Anyway, he insists on calling her Madame Arcati, a joke she doesn't appreciate. She has been prevailed upon to take one's hand and tell fortunes. I do not care for the touch of those large soft fingers ridged by rings, so I hover behind chairs and listen to her seductive murmurings of what is in store. She would like to hold a seance in her stateroom and I am so tempted, but I can't bring myself to go. Maybe I'm too much of a believer, darling. And what your father might say if he "came through" (how and from where?) I would not like to share with the merely curious. Especially with Humphrey. Caterina Kindersley-Bowles is her name, as phoney as her hair, for she certainly isn't English. Caterina she would like to be called. Her handsome face breaks up when she laughs, which is often, to show that although she is gifted beyond the norm she keeps the common touch, which is laughter at small things. Her lips curl back to reveal expensively filled back teeth. There is gold in them thar gums.

'I musn't go on like this and become nasty. There's such a bad side to my nature, I'm afraid, but I feel there is something she yearns to tell me that I do not – but *not* – want to hear.'

Adela stopped writing. She wouldn't send this to Emma; it would not travel well, gaining in spitefulness when read thousands of miles from this ship. She pushed it under her writing-pad and went up on deck. They were lying off the Virgin Islands, which were beautiful but unbelievable; the sun, sea and sky as yellow, blue and sparkling as the brochure had promised. Perhaps that was what gave it such a spurious air; too much looked at; a print not an original. She found a long chair and lay back to read *Cheri* once again, this time in French, which would do her good and keep her brain from atrophying. Maybe her reactions were influenced by Colette. Reading her sharpened one's perception.

After a while there was Humphrey, standing bulkily above her and blocking out the sun, his rich stomach jutting from beneath a navy blazer, white sunhat pulled down over heavy spectacles and his moustache sweating tiny pearl-like drops over thick lips.

'Enjoying yourself, are you?' he said. 'Never thought I'd see you travelling on your own. Old Hugo never cared for travel, did he? Strange chap.'

Everyone was strange who did not share Humphrey's priorities, a word he was fond of using. His credo was self-preservation. Perhaps not in itself a bad thing, but two wives had fled from him. He had no children. Adela had asked him some years before Hugo died whether he missed having them.

'We're so glad to have a daughter,' she had said.

'You never know how children will turn out,' he'd replied dismissively. 'Anyway, they'd be middle-aged by now and probably take after their mothers. No, I like pretty young things about me.'

He still did. He had the air of a portly bee rifling delicate flowers on a summer's day. He bumbled and buzzed around the youngish presentable women, light on his feet, eager for honey. And now he was saying what she dreaded to hear, with a playfulness masking determination.

'Funny thing, really, us meeting like this, Adela. Have you thought about it, eh? Both on this ship together.' He switched his gaze to a blue-and-white lifebelt on a rack by the rail. 'Both on our own.' There was no deck-chair beside her, so he could not sit down. He rocked on his heels and belched gently. Adela waited. His next words came straight out of a B-movie. 'You've taken to travel like a duck to water now you're free. My birthday tomorrow, seventy-five but don't feel it. What d'you say to a party and making an announcement—'

'An announcement?' Adela sat up straight. Cruelly, she refused to help him. 'What announcement?'

Humphrey pulled out a large white handkerchief and wiped his moustache. He bent lower as if in preparation for a kiss. 'I'm pretty fit, my dear. Look, what I'm saying is why shouldn't we go round the world together? I know you're lonely.'

Stung, Adela said evenly, 'You once told Hugo and me that you liked pretty young things, Humphrey. I'm getting on for elderly – no, dammit, I *am* elderly. What can you be thinking of?'

'Marriage, that's what I'm thinking of, and you know it.' He straightened up and laughed with immense satisfaction. The sun flashed off his spectacles. 'Well, why not? You'd suit me all right, you don't look your age when you take trouble. I've always known it, that's why I've kept an eye on you all these years. Didn't always hit it off with dear old Hugo, even at Oxford. But we go back a long way, all of us.' He seemed not to notice her ungraceful scramble out of the long chair, the novel falling to the deck. His voice boomed on behind her. 'Done pretty well since the war. Shares in this shipping line. We can travel First Class all the way. Keep it in the family. Look, Adela, Hugo would be pleased to know you were taken care of—'

Not a B-movie. An Aldwych farce and a matinée at that. But all this should have been acted out in the moonlight, with an orchestra off playing softly – something like 'Moonlight Becomes You'. Humphrey never did anything right. Before he could move Adela was up and away. She was afraid she might burst into tears because she couldn't burst out laughing with Hugo. Her heart was beating to a suffocating rhythm and she reeled unsteadily past the companion way that led to an upper deck. Here she walked straight into Madame Arcati, who caught her arm in a steadying grip. Adela pulled back, alarmed. The woman's wide-brimmed red hat cast a deep shadow over half her face, so that the upper part was the colour of a rare steak above pale jowls. Nevertheless, Madame Arcati did not release her grip, walking her firmly to the rail.

'Take three deep breaths,' she said, and in encouragement put her hand on her own abdomen and took a powerful breath in through her mobile nostrils. Adela did as she was told, at least the woman's bulk protected her from Humphrey, should he walk this way. 'Tomorrow we go ashore to St Thomas and the Virgin Gorda, I believe,' Madame Arcati went on conversationally in her curiously orchestrated voice. 'I have heard that the Englishman who keeps the hotel plays cricket. The English will like that, of course.'

The phrase distanced her from things English. It was absurd, Adela reasoned light-headedly on her third deep breath, for this woman to lay claim to such an English name as Kindersley-Bowles.

'Where is your husband?' she asked, following her thought.

'In Alsace-Lorraine. He has a broken leg.' Madame Arcati gave a matter-of-fact nod. 'He is a poor thing, alas.'

To stop herself breaking into hysterical giggles, Adela gripped the rail tightly and looked down into the sea. How deep and shifting it was, half the height of a house below them: green and purple and streaked with turquoise. The heavy restless waters creamed round the bows as if the ship were a great white whale which the waves wished to taste and savour before devouring. Adela felt herself bending further over the rail, hypnotized by that powerful sea, held like Coleridge's mariner on a painted ship upon a painted ocean.

'I'm so sorry, please excuse me,' she said and broke from the restraining arm with a small grimacing smile, making unsteadily for her cabin, where she rang for a strong whisky and soda, no ice.

'The awful thing about you being dead, Hugo,' she said aloud quite fiercely, lighting a cigarette, 'is that you're not here to share a joke. Aldwych farce? We were too young for those, really. The Marx Brothers, more like. Yes, I can say that I have had a close encounter with Groucho, *sans* cigar. The Arcati is a dead ringer for that marvellous woman Groucho was always conning for a handout – I've forgotten her name – all innocent girlishness buried in middle-aged bulk, and buttressed by money. What the hell is her husband doing in Alsace-Lorraine with a broken leg?'

Nobody answered, and she sat on her bed and laughed until she cried.

Hugo had taken her to her first Marx Brothers movie and she had sat, stunned and smiling uncertainly, while he shook with laughter beside her. They were too bizarre, too destructive; their wisecracks came hot and fast. With a serious face, she had queried their sense of values, no respect for—

'Respect?' Hugo had exploded. 'Values? They're pulling values to pieces, that's the whole point! Life is a farce, darling. Remember dear old Thomas Love Peacock – we can be sure of nothing in this world except its nonsense, so we may as well laugh at it.'

He'd gone on about it on the bus home. Women resented comics because they were afraid of them. Women stood for order and decency. (In those days men could get away with remarks like that, she remembered.) That's why they hated W. C. Fields and the anarchy of custard-pie comedy – women didn't like to see men rebelling against momma's strictures about drink and lechery and—

'I've got the point,' she had interrupted coldly, stung to anger. She was not anxious to be lumped with middle-class morality; she wanted to leave twin sets and sensible shoes behind her. Hugo, as a young schoolmaster, had a tendency to lecture. So she had sneaked off to the cinema on her own and grown to love the absurdities and glorious fragmentation of so-called accepted values. It was a great release. In fact, she could do with the Marx Brothers now. Bring on the clowns. Yes, love was, after all, a shared anarchy.

'Damn it, Hugo! I miss you and it gets worse.' The whisky arrived and with it the steward brought a note, addressed to her in a large compelling hand.

'Do call in at my stateroom for a preprandial drinkie. I feel we have much to say to one another.'

The signature of Caterina K. B. spread confidently across the bottom of the page and somehow begged a red seal for an extra flourish.

She went to her dressing-table and pulled out her writing-pad. As she did so, the last line of her abandoned letter to Emma caught her eye. 'I feel there is something she yearns to tell me that I do not – but *not* – want to hear.' Too right. Her note in reply was brief.

'So sorry. So kind, but I intend to sleep through lunch. Terrible head. The sun.'

She rang for the steward, gave him the note and ordered another large whisky, this time with ice.

I'll have my preprandial drinkies all alone like all the classic drunks, she told herself. Then I can drown my sorrows and think about the past and fish up old guilts. How boring. Drinkie! She was right. There was the tiny playful girlie coming out of the statuesque madame. Why had the repellent Humphrey 'kept an eye on her' all these years? *If* he had. It was an affront to Hugo. She was no bolter. One peccadillo she had allowed herself, but he was not to know. Archie, that old devil, might have guessed, but of course had said nothing. And Rhys had looked so magnificent on a horse! Who could resist him? There was Hugo, pedalling along the lanes, head well down against the weather, pursuing a legend, a church, a lost village, a saint's well. Cycle clips over waterproof trousers, waterproof jacket ballooning out against the persistent Welsh wind that blew the soft rain straight in his face. Saddlebag buffeting the tin box on the carrier that contained his sandwiches, notebook, camera. All to feed his passion for Wales.

It had amused her that he learned the language, feeling it an obligation and a courtesy. Whereas the true-bred Welshman, arrogant and piratical, sat his horse by that heap of stones, the sun touching sparks of fire off his beard. All that nonsense about tonsils and the shell house as he looked from the child to her as she sat in the pony trap. Terror and desire at the impossibility of it, he being the local doctor watched out for wherever he rode. She had been restless that spring, ready for a challenge. But why go over it all again? It was like emptying suds down the sink. Down they went with a flurry and a shine and a last frothy gurgle. Done with.

Adela kicked off her shoes, lay back on the bed and

thought about her life, then drifted off to sleep. A knock on the door roused her from a dream in which she and Hugo circled each other, white birds in a brochure blue sky. Again the steward. This time with *Cheri* retrieved from the deck, a spray of orchids and a note from Humphrey: 'Think it over and don't forget my party tomorrow.'

She ordered tea; pictured Humphrey at his party, blowing merrily through his untidy moustache, thick lips parted over strong yellow teeth, raising his glass in salute to his own health and longevity. She shivered as if her flesh cringed from some intrusive intimacy, propped herself up on the pillows and clasped the book to her chest. She supposed she should put the orchid in water. She disliked orchids. In the days when she was young, girls pinned them to their corsage. Corsage! That was an anachronism to savour. How language changed, words losing meaning, others supplanting them. Like partnership for marriage. What a thin relationship that promised. 'Let me not to the partnership of true minds—' That would never scan. Emma's marriage had been neither, but she would survive. You were allowed one failure, surely?

When her tea came Adela felt better. The familiar motions, pouring it into a cup, drinking it, restored her and out of the blue came the realization that had it not been for her – her what? – misbehaviour, adventure, lapse from grace – her daughter would have had nowhere to go. Nothing to build on.

It was like playing solitaire, really; she always brought a travelling set along with her. You had to make the right moves or you were sunk. She had to admit as time went by she missed having a man at her side. Being without a man – constant companion, escort, lover – was to walk lopsided through the days, sleep in empty beds. But that did not mean that any man would fill the gap. No man could. Not for her, not now; Humphrey had cleared up this point. One was grateful for the clowns. Thanks to him she could complete her game of solitaire. The last shining marble had been taken out. The pitted ring was empty of players.

Some time later as the light faded Adela hung out a DO NOT DISTURB sign on the door and started her packing. She gave a great deal of thought to this, carefully wrapping shoes in tissue paper, sorting out her stockings; she had never liked tights. Carefully folding underwear, dresses, fitting them into her suitcase. She put aside an unworn pair of linen trousers, a pure silk blouse and skirt, a cashmere sweater (her latest extravagances). And, of course, the shawl Charlotte had given her for Christmas. Laid them in a cardboard box with her gold watch and a few pieces of jewellery. Sent out for paper and string and addressed the parcel to her daughter. On second thoughts she asked for a light supper to be sent in, with a bottle of claret.

She decided to keep on her pearls and wedding ring. Personal things that would be diminished if she left them behind. Her daughter's generation did not value pearls: she had kept this double string nourished by the warmth of her neck for many years in spite of Hugo's dislike of jewellery. But he had become accustomed to his wife's whim and at night registered the fact that the graceful movement of her hands at the back of her neck meant that she was unclasping her string of pearls. They had their own velvet-lined bed – she knew that Hugo would not want them to share his. Yet she always regretted the loosening of the clasp, her neck felt naked and cold without them.

It was said that real pearls (and these were real) improved by contact with the skin, which gave them warmth and lustre. Since Hugo's death she had scarcely taken them off. Perhaps now because she had been reading Colette, Adela wished they were larger and longer, like Lea's magnificent matched string so lusted after by her young lover. She recalled the sensuous Lea lying naked in bed in that pink room, the pearls lambent on the swell of her breasts. Sometimes Cheri would be allowed to unclasp them and wear them himself, striking attitudes in front of her pier-glass. Somehow they became the symbol of his utter desolation, the cause of his destruction. Love contains the seeds of death as well as of life, and how delicately, how heart-rendingly, Colette had shown this to be so.

Well, her modest string would go with her now.

Time perhaps to write a letter to Emma, as honest as she could make it. She owed it to her. It was far longer than she had intended and time was getting on. At last she put it into an envelope, addressed it. Locked her suitcase, sat on her bed and counted out six sleeping-pills, crunching them one by one, and, to disguise the taste, sipped at her third glass of claret. Together this would dull any last-minute fear.

'Full fathom five,' she quoted aloud to test her clarity of mind, 'thy father lies. Those are pearls that were his eyes.'

I can still draw a literary parallel, she thought proudly, but don't let's overdo it. She fastened a discarded, laddered pair of stockings round her left hand and wound them through the handle of her suitcase, securing the knot with a safety pin, which wasn't easy. The case was heavy, it should do the trick. Out of habit she glanced at her wrist to check the time, but of course her watch wasn't there. On her small bedside clock it said after midnight, most people would be in bed by now. A titter disturbed her – such a tinny word, such a tinny sound – had it escaped her stiff lips? Better get going or she'd look a right idiot, falling down like a drunk on a packed suitcase and having her stomach pumped out. There'd be no floating up or crying out in absurd panic – or worse, a coward's change of mind. In fact, she was filled with elation at taking another journey of her own volition – no package tour this. Moving on towards a new freedom, an undiscovered land. Detached and ready to let go; following Hugo, foiling old age.

She made her way, step by careful step, out of the cabin, past shut doors and up on to the deck where a light breeze gave her strength to reach the rail. Had she come to the right place? Was that the dark sea creaming and murmuring below? Would she go straight down, received and accepted, like her coin in the saint's well?

Neatly, as if rehearsed, she manoeuvred the heavy suitcase up beside her on to the rail, sat for a moment facing the deck, precariously balanced. Then she let go and brought her right hand up modestly over her knees to prevent her skirt from blowing up as she toppled backwards, flipping over like a frogman, but stylishly. As her head jerked back she saw the brilliant half moon; across its face drifted an inconsequential cloud in the form of a *commedia dell'arte* mask. For a second, light beamed through the eyeholes like a wink of complicity. Then was gone.

Emma was in her studio, sorting out sketches she had made on her early-morning walk. Despite the keen wind these February days were always full of a blue purity and sudden warmth that had encouraged her to take her sketch pad and set out for the lane that led to Glammon Lodge. In the ditches yellow celandine were showing and the hedges – well laid – sparked with green buds. There had been a smallholding off to the left where the farmer had in the old days supplied them with milk, and as a child she had come with her mother or father to collect it. There had been a haystack behind the hedge, she remembered. One January day, Mr Thomas had been cutting a wedge out of it to feed his animals. The rich smell had been like fruit cake.

No small farmer today could keep going like that, she supposed, no farmer would have a small haystack, thatched in the old way. She was right. The farmhouse was smartened up, a garage stood where the yard had been, and there was no sign of activity. Well, what had she expected? The sight made her falter, she wouldn't go as far as Glammon Lodge to see the changes there. Instead she climbed a stile and sat on it, to look long at the hills in the distance, at the river, and to listen to the scatter of curlews crying about the sky.

In the garden at Glammon Lodge there had been beech trees in the sweep of grass beside the drive and a great flood of snowdrops under the branch where the swing had been fixed. Her feet had brushed their delicate heads as she swung herself back and forth. Up and down. Snowdrops everywhere, frogspawn in the meander of the river beyond the kitchen garden. No, she couldn't go there. So she sat on a stile and drew from memory: a child on a swing, a haystack by a hedge. Dissatisfied, she had returned home. She had snowdrops there too and daffodils spiking up and wild garlic galore. But better, with the light as good as it was, to try to do some work. The proofs of her illustrations for the children's book had to be dealt with. Mark wanted ideas for the jacket; something to suggest fantasy and the magic of story-telling, but today she felt reluctant to pin herself down at her working table. This nervous restlessness, a sense of resentment at having to cast around for ideas was not unusual. Who was less free than a freelance illustrator?

Maybe coffee would help. Maybe she should clean these windows to let in even more light. As she moved towards them she heard a bicycle crunch to a stop on the gravel outside and knew the post had arrived. She envied Megan wheeling off after thrusting the letters through the letterbox. This was an allowable interruption and she started downstairs – it was time she heard from Charlotte again, time she came home. Those three months had stretched to four and she missed her. There was so much they could do together before she went off to Durham. But what if she hated it here? I'm not going to worry, she was telling herself when she came to an abrupt halt at the turn of the stairs. Long rods of sunlight spiked through the coloured glass panel set in the window above the small landing, laying lozenges of colour – red, green, yellow, blue – on the stairs and on her legs as she walked down. Why had she never noticed this before? She gazed through the window and there was the front garden cut up like a jester's suit, the chestnut tree multicoloured, the grass red. The image stayed in her mind, stored away.

Two letters on the mat, neither from India. One an official-looking envelope from the cruise company, one from her mother in a long white envelope. Taking them through to the kitchen, she put the kettle on to boil and slit them open with a breadknife.

She chose her mother's first. Two folded sheets. 'You'll be shocked, my darling. But do try to understand.' Straight in like that. No 'Dear Emma'.

Since your father died I know I've been on the go here and there. Who was it said that Dante was the first tourist, doing the circles of Hell? I've always wanted to travel, although I know that real travelling in the sense of discovery and freshness is long gone. No more Mary Kingsleys or Isabella Birds. Pushing out frontiers is not my line anyway. I've nothing to prove, but in the last couple of years I've satisfied my curiosity at least.

Emma made her coffee with powder from a jar, sat before it, her heart for some reason pounding.

I took this cruise because I wanted to visit St Thomas and the Virgin Gorda. They play cricket on one of these islands, which would have pleased your father. But there's this irritating old man who was at Oxford with him and sought me out. I'd no idea he was on board. As we walk around the deck he makes remarks about Hugo that are slantingly derogatory and then gives a short laugh and brushes up his moustache. I don't think you met him, although he surfaced from time to time over the years. Hugo was kind but never liked him. He's a widower – or divorced – I'm not sure which. Anyway, a survivor. The last person to share a raft with! I'm supposed to go to his 75th birthday party to drink his health. He—

Two lines here had been heavily scored through and however hard she tried to decipher them, holding the paper up to the light, she was unable to do so. The writing was becoming erratic, unlike her mother's neat and flowing hand.

I shall be coming up to 70 this year myself and I cannot celebrate other people's longevity – certainly not my own, certainly not Humphrey's – with Hugo gone. No-one amused me, cared for me, made excuses for me, maddened me as your father did. I can't really *talk* to anyone else. It's been the same since we first met. We *recognized* each other if that doesn't sound too bizarre. I see couples sitting opposite one another, quite dumb. So many marriages are wrung dry – we were lucky. We may not have done much, but what we did do, we did together. Hugo is the only man I want to care for and have beside me leaning on this rail under a ridiculous movie moon and Sidney Bechet's 'Petite Fleur' (they go in for nostalgia here, we're a 'mature' class of passenger) drifting through open doors and the clean dark sea islanding us.

Emma read on with growing disbelief. The writing was not disordered in itself, nor were the thoughts it expressed. There was still a control about the small neat hand, but the words tumbled hastily on to the page as if stored up for too long.

Just as I suppose I was conscious of my birth, so I want to be conscious of my death. After all, your father used to say that birth and death are bridges, closely linked. Last thoughts are important, he believed. I don't know his. Do we all rehearse our last words and, if so, are we allowed to speak them at curtain call? Morphine prevented your father doing so. I know I shouldn't take matters into my own hands – but at least I shan't be buried at a crossroads outside consecrated ground! I've made sure I'll go deep into this greedy dark ocean with no trouble to anyone. Can you understand that I believe that sometimes the dying is the healing? And I need to be healed of the sour stench of widowhood.

I've always hated funerals. And how I agree with the character in Marquez' wonderful novel that the dead should take their belongings with them. I've packed my suitcase and it will go down with me. Some things that will be of use to you are being sent on. Of course you'll have to clear my flat, that's unavoidable. Sorry about that, but everything can go unless you or Charlotte want anything. There's a fair bit of money. Certainly enough to help Charlotte through university. (Don't spoil her trip with this news.)

Oh Emma, I've done with small talk with other plucky widows, there are far too many of us: all redundant with blue-tinted hairdos and foam-rubber skin and crumbling hips. I hate the thought of being diminished by the years ahead. I know it sounds selfish, but I was spoilt by a thoroughly congenial marriage. Hugo has emptied the world for me.

I've tried, I really have. But it's goodbye, darling, now. And now that you've rediscovered your roots, you'll thrive. You'll be fine, strong on your own, unsapped by that cheerless marriage. You've got

Charlotte. You're a good painter – you have your father's dedication. You're in the Border country he loved – and he will be remembered by his books.

I could never have done this on land. At sea one simply exists outside society. An unnatural community if you like! Mothers normally die before their children and take too long about it. I won't say forgive me because you never will. It's too much to expect. Talk to Archie, there's more to him than people think. All my love, darling.

Mother. (I'm so glad we spent Christmas together.)

Emma went straight for the whisky bottle, poured half a glass and drank it neat. Then she opened the other letter. Miss Matty jumped up on to her lap, nudged her head hard against her wrist, waiting to be fondled. Automatically Emma's cold hand stroked the soft head, her fingers avoiding the tattered ear. She took out the other letter and read it through in a blur.

Dear Madam,

We very much regret to inform you that your mother, Mrs Adela Forden, disappeared overboard while the ship was anchored off the Virgin Gorda island. A thorough search revealed that her clothes and suitcase had gone from her cabin, but she left a parcel and a letter to be forwarded to you and this should reach you shortly. The purser is also sending an unfinished letter he found on the dressing-table. We can only surmise that your mother fell overboard. A half-empty bottle of sleeping-tablets was by her bed, so that if she inadvertently took more than her usual dose for insomnia and then went for a turn on deck, she might have been in a comatose state, stumbled and fallen. She kept to her cabin all day with a headache and had her meals sent in. Maybe a case of sunstroke – or was she a migraine sufferer? We pride ourselves in our safety precautions and certain areas of the ship are out of bounds to passengers. We cannot in these circumstances accept any liability to the Company, but we do extend to you our sincerest sympathy. We shall, of course, inform you if her body is recovered.

I suggest you telephone our Head Office if you have any further queries. You mother was greatly liked by all her fellow passengers who are shocked and saddened. A Mr Humphrey Barrington will be writing to you.

The captain had signed it. A flourishing hand, with relief in the final strokes; it had been a difficult letter to write, hedging his bets.

A kitten clawed its way up her leg to join its mother. Emma shook them both off and ran for the convenient lavatory the doctor had put in just off the hall for his patients, and was sick.

Talk to Archie? She could talk to no-one. All she could think of was that her mother, given to impulses and then never carrying them through – like her quilt-making project for the village, her enthusiasm for pottery – had thought out a plan and pursued it – yes, to the bitter end. Something had triggered off that determination. That it was an act of self-destruction made it so painful she could no longer stay in the house with its silence jelling around her. She walked unsteadily back into the kitchen, caught up the letter, took her car keys from the dish by the front door and went out to her car. She scarcely noticed Jess, who slipped in beside her.

She drove to Lake Vyrnwy, ten miles away along roads fairly empty of traffic. As a child she had been taken there to gaze down into the still waters that had drowned a village; far below, she had been told, lay the houses and little church which, as legend had it, kept its bell which swayed and peeled drunkenly at certain times of the year, sending up a strangled dissonance.

Generosity and understanding had no place yet.

Grief is selfish, a clergyman had told her after her father's death. You are grieving for yourself, not for the dead who are at peace. You must guard against self-pity. Too right I'm grieving for myself. Like my mother I'm selfish. OK. And now I suppose I'm grieving for her. But she was not. She was dry-eyed and choked up with rage. When parents die their children are in the front line and she was cut to the bone with fear. How could you do this to me? she thought furiously. At Christmas you spoke of a loss of identity. How d'you think *I* feel? Why do people walk away from me as if I were something on a market stall to be fingered and left, and no-one wants to buy? She got out of the car and for the first time noticed Jess running beside her, tail waving, head up as if to sniff this unaccustomed liberty. In a month the little bitch had grown sleeker, more confident; now her sharp barks of pleasure alerted Emma to the fact that she had no collar. She had been careful not to let her roam further than the garden, for fear of losing her. So when she sat down on the steep bank she called Jess over and held her close. Bereavement was more than a sense of loss: it was an unsought for, guilty freedom that made you aware of your inner chaos.

The sun flashed off the little amber-and-silver ring her mother had given her. Moving her hand along the dog's coat, stroking her from neck to tail, she looked at it, remembering its history. It had nothing to do with her, after all. It belonged to her parents. She eased it off her finger, held it high, then sent it spinning down towards the waters of the lake.

She sat on for a while with Jess at her feet and thought about her father. That was true grief, whatever that stupid man had said. Grief softened and made bearable by distance. He had died quietly, as befitted a gentle man, in his own time and out of pain, his thin wrist lying in her hand. She had taken off his watch, which ticked on for an hour, then stopped. The wristband was worn and pliable with his sweat. He had not been sorry to go, it was what he expected and he had no last words for her to carry away. Morphine had set him adrift on dark waters long before his pulse stilled. Emma was glad she had been there, alone by his bed, his hand in hers. Her mother had dozed off in the chair. That was a small, mean triumph to savour.

'Don't just stand there,' said Archie, uncurling his elegant legs from round the gate he was sitting on. 'I love doing nothing, but I hate being watched doing it. Actually I'm giving my new mauve stockings an airing. Prue won't have them in the house.'

'I don't blame her. And I'm not watching you, Archie. I'm looking for you.'

Emma had driven home, left Jess in the kitchen then walked up through the fields that encircled Talycoed. Looking, as she said, for Archie. She felt calm and dry of emotion and very tired. She seemed to have walked a long way, not thinking. This was going to spoil his day, the bit of it he liked to spend alone; all the same she held out the two letters to him.

'Em? Emma? What's all this?'

Looking sharply at her, he fished into his top pocket and put on his spectacles. She turned away as he started to read, heard a sharp intake of breath. After a while she turned to see that his face had fallen into an old man's confusion and grief, the letters loose in his hand. His blue eyes filmed over and he blew his nose, mopped his face.

'In that awful winter of '47 two farmers in the next valley shot their stock, then themselves. Couldn't keep going. Women don't do away with themselves, life anchors them.' He looked at the letter incredulously and said, 'Water's the kindest way. Glad she said come to me.' He put an arm round her shoulders, walked her away up through the fields. 'Something set her off.

Must have. She enjoyed being with us all, didn't she, at Christmas, and looking so lovely.'

Adela would have been pleased to hear that word.

It was Emma who would have to do the comforting, and the realization strengthened her. Maybe, as her mother had said, she was strong. He went on talking, as if to himself.

'So calm, that letter. So reasoned. She even makes jokes.'

Archie blew his nose again, coughed his voice back to something like normality.

'She wrote it for herself, not me,' said Emma neutrally.

'If she hadn't cared for you she wouldn't have sent it, my girl.' He tightened his arm round her shoulders, slowed his pace, hugging her to his side. He looked down at the top of her obstinate head with something like exasperation. 'That letter's so honest, so – raw. Respect her for it.'

Emma sighed, relaxed her body, moved away from his arm to walk apart. A small wind gusted past, ruffling her hair, blew silence around them. At last she spoke.

'She planned it, Archie, and carried it through – it's not like her.'

'She was one of those people' – Archie was slipping already into the past tense – 'who have an idea and their minds skip ahead of it. They've done it all in their imagination, so why go on? This time she did. Hugo used to say she was as unpredictable as the weather. Dear God, I can't believe it. I shall miss her.'

'I feel I let them both down, with that stupid marriage.'

'No-one could live up to theirs, Emma. Hugo would never set himself up as a role model. He never sought ¬ssurance from tyranny of any kind. Didn't you ever ¬im about it?'

¬wed out in those later years when I was

older. Never wanted to talk about Wales, although—'

Why had they switched to her father?

The silence between them lasted until they reached the edge of a spinney. The sunlight was hardening. With a sense of betrayal she said, 'Only once, when he was so ill, he gave my mother such an odd look. It was so resentful, almost savage. She didn't see it, but he said he felt he'd been torn up by the roots. She thought he was delirious. *Did* she make him leave Wales?'

'No. His decision. Came as a surprise to us all.'

'That baby she lost, then, maybe—'

'Yes, that's it,' said Archie quickly. 'He wanted to pull her out of a depression; she was quite ill for a time. Let's leave it there, my dear, and think of what we are going to do now.'

'Oh God, what are we going to *tell* people?'

He knew she meant Prudence. And Debby. The village would seethe with it. She quailed at the prospect. 'Do we have to tell the truth?'

He hunched up his shoulders, clapped his arms around his body as if to trap some warmth, defend some inner knowledge.

'I can't lie to Charlotte—'

'Of course not. She's on her way home, is she?'

'I don't really know—'

'The answer's in the captain's letter, Emma. Take it at face value. That's all you need to say to anyone else. If he can cover himself, so can you.'

'Can you keep a secret from Prue, then?'

Archie laughed. 'Oh yes. I'm a slippery customer, and secrets are safe with me.'

'What a splendid co-conspirator you are, Archie. I do love you.'

'Well, we're your family now if you'll have us. Off you go home and get some rest. I'll come over tomorrow. Not another word till then.'

But at the field gate on to the lane leading back to the village, she turned.

216

'I don't think my mother ever felt for me what I feel for Charlotte.'

'Possibly not. She had no need to. She had Hugo.'

Emma regarded him silently.

'Look, Emma, all your emotional energy and love is bound to flow somewhere. If it's blocked by a man you can't love, then it goes to your children.'

'Just like that?'

'Just like that. It's a simple pill to swallow.'

Emma laughed. 'Raging tragedies have been written about simple pills like that, Archie. Only very simple people swallow them.'

'Then be simple, for God's sake and your own, and get on with life.'

She was still thinking about this when she turned into her drive and found Ivor there, sitting against the front door. Her sober look was just as soberly returned, and he rose to his feet stiffly – as if he had been waiting a long time. There was something different about him, his ear-ring gone and the ear lobe crisp with dried blood.

'You look frozen. Come in and we'll have some tea.'

She would not ask what was wrong, for something had to be and she felt utterly incapable of extending a tendril of curiosity or care. In the kitchen he knelt down to be greeted by Jess, who had taken over the cats' basket. Uncomplainingly, they now slept in the Christmas box.

'I'll make the tea,' he said. 'You sit down. What's happened to you?'

At once, without hesitation Emma said, 'My mother's dead,' put a hand up to her cheek and, for the first time, wept.

For a long time, it seemed, Ivor sat rocking her gently in his arms. When she stopped crying he wiped her face with the nearest thing to hand, a clean teacloth he found on the table. She looked up, touched his ear, said, 'And what happened to you?'

'Had a run-in with Mervyn. Never mind about what, but he tore out my ear-ring. Said it was the wrong ear and I'd led him on. It was over girls, and—'

'Girls?'

'Look, Emma, I've never – well, you know. Don't know why, but—'

It could be comical, this clumsy confession, until she remembered his reaction to her joky remark when she was drawing him after the rat hunt. ('Think of going to bed with—')

'How old are you, Ivor?'

'Twenty, just. Sounds as if I'm – but I'm not that way, Emma. I like girls, but, well, they scare me. Never mind all that.' He tentatively brushed back her hair, put his lips to her cheek. 'I'm that sorry about your mam, she was lovely with Jess, wasn't she?'

Emma nodded, startled into gratitude by this feeling epitaph. In reciprocation then, there was something she needed to do, a risk to take. (Be simple, Archie had said, and get on with life.) So she stood up and took Ivor by the hand and led him upstairs, for the kindness and comfort that sex could bring.

In the weeks that followed two more letters arrived. Emma had come to dread the post. Still nothing from Charlotte. Her mother's unfinished, discarded letter sent on by the purser, almost against nature made her laugh. And another, both of which she showed Archie.

'She had everything to live for . . .' wrote Humphrey Barrington in his big confident hand.

I'm certain we would have been happy together. I had no idea she was a sick woman. She had more than a friend in me and in Mrs Kindersley-Bowles, who was concerned about her. This cruise has been quite spoiled for me, I am leaving the ship and flying back. If you would like me to call, just let me know. I send you my sincerest condolences, as an old friend of your father's and, of course, of your mother . . .

It went on, but Archie looked up and said, 'There's your trigger, Emma. Bloody man.'

The parcel Adela had packed so carefully arrived, but Emma put it aside. She couldn't face it yet. Up in her studio she found herself idly sketching on the back of an envelope. A woman peacefully drifting with the undersea current (as, in another element, parachutists floated in free fall), fishes nudging her shoeless legs, pulled further down and deeper by a suitcase, and a portly man vainly gesticulating from the rail of a ship . . . Then, seeing what she had done, crumpled the whole thing up, horrified at herself.

And yet. How did you cope with life unless you expressed it as well as you were able, in your own way? A writer wrote, a painter painted. Munch had his *Scream*. Bacon his Popes, Proust his *Recherche*, Scriabin his *Prometheus*: all therapy of the highest order.

She realized that her imagination was working on top of this shock, using it, making it manageable, and going to bed with Ivor played its part. For Emma, this physical act of intimacy had regained its initial simplicity. That's what it was, after all; simple, natural. A lovely mutual easement and pleasure. At its most basic, an extension of the talk and laughter, the shared tasks of the day. There was affection between them, not a rage of desire or even love. But Ivor was vulnerable as she had once been, so here was one man she could teach to be gentle with women. More than once, watching his young, peaceful face, caught perhaps in a ray of late sunlight on her bed in the old doctor's room, she wondered why God had made such a fuss about Adam and Eve. Hadn't He wanted his world populated? If not, then why such a convenient biological set-up? That, it seemed to her, was where the sullying of sexual mores had begun; flawed from its beginning.

She drew him naked in the bath, as she had once imagined him. He walked about the house with a new pride – naturally on the days Mrs Hughes didn't come – even sang as he dug the vegetable beds for planting or cut logs for her in the garden. One morning, he sat bare-chested on the stairs in the sun and called for Emma to come and see the coloured squares all over his body. He played with the reflected colours like a child, ducking in and out of the lozenges of light.

'Never saw that before,' he marvelled, and for once did not grumble when she ran for her sketch book. When he had gone home she added a paper hoop. She had her jester, multicoloured, holding up a hoop; her jacket illustration with all the characters of the stories flying through it.

When you burst through the hoop, Mother, did you break out of life like a clown leaping through? Was it amazingly different, the other side of it, dark into light? As she worked, she had the image of some divine jester juggling with men and women, up with them and over. Each had a turn in the air before they fell away, spiralling down to rest in that dexterous hand.

Ivor would move on, must do. But she would stay – for nowhere people bred nowhere children. Sending down the tap root her parents had failed to do, making a home for Charlotte and herself and maybe Charlotte's children. Home was where your school reports were still in a box in the attic with your first certificate of music, birthday cards laboriously printed with crayons, broken toys, board games with half the counters missing. A shell house.

Then Charlotte called from Bangkok. They were flying home. They argued about where to meet. Not Heathrow. Dirk can put me on a train – what's the

220